WORST DATE EVER

J. S. COOPER

Copyright © 2021 by J. S. Cooper

All rights reserved.

No part of this book may be reproduced in any form or by any electronic or mechanical means, including information storage and retrieval systems, without written permission from the author, except for the use of brief quotations in a book review.

Editing by Sarah Barbour.

Cover Photo by Wander Aguiar.

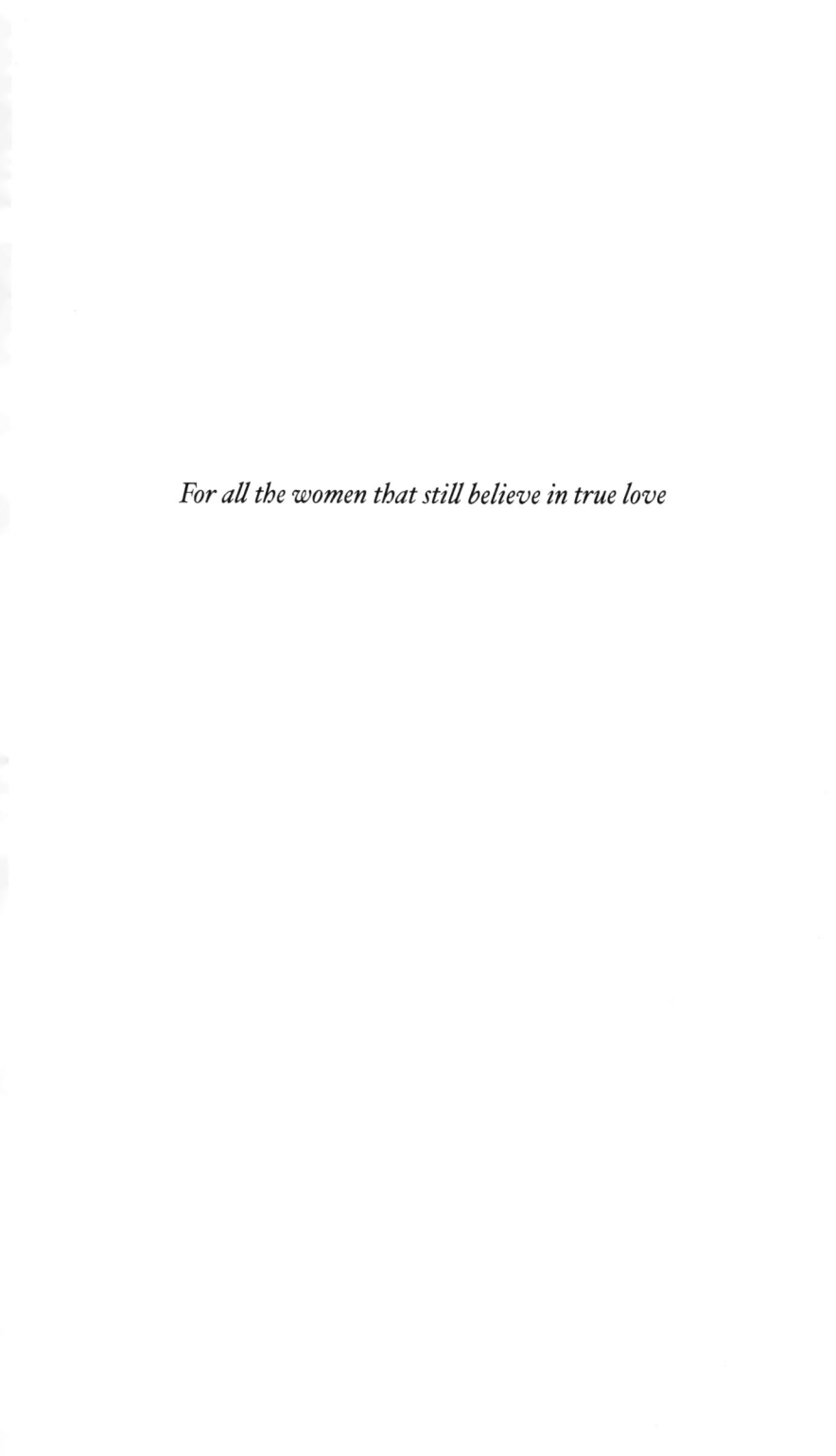

For all the women that still believe in true love

About This Book

"Go on a date," she said. "You'll love it," she said.

She was wrong.

It had been one year, two months, and seventeen days since my last date when my best friend Abby decided to sign me up for a dating app. She guaranteed that she could get me the best date of my life within one week. I didn't really want to do it, but I figured what did I have to lose?

Turns out that I had:

1. $500
    2. My dignity
    3. My patience and

4. My innocence to lose

Okay, so I didn't really have my innocence to lose, but believe you me, Jack Morrison was my worst date ever. And I've been on a lot of bad dates. Trust me when I say that that was the longest ten hours and 33 minutes of my life. I never wanted to see or speak to him again.

But it turns out you don't always get what you want in life because Jack showed up the very next day at a family gathering I was attending as a fake plus one. As you can imagine, that was a real pickle. Jack wanted to know why I went on a date with him when I'm dating someone else. But he can't know the whole complicated truth of the matter. I'm in a fake relationship, and now I'm being blackmailed by the worst date ever.

Prologue

※

"Are you one of those women that doesn't need a man?" The smug, entitled look on his face made me want to slap him.

"Are you one of those men that doesn't know how to give an orgasm?" I retorted. I hated the fact that I could see that I'd amused him.

"Oh, I've given plenty of orgasms." He smirked. "Is that your problem?"

"What?" *Ignore the urge to wipe that smile off of his face, Isabella*, I lectured myself as I studied his handsome face. He seemed like the sort of jerk that would get off on me putting my hands on him.

"Are you acting like Miss Havisham because you've never been pleasured properly before?"

"Are you acting like Austin Powers because you're an ... idiot." I finished weakly.

"That's the best come-back you have?" This time he did laugh, running his long fingers through his golden blonde hair. I hated the fact that this man was so handsome. It should have been illegal to be that handsome—and that much of an ass.

"Anything more complicated would have gone over your head." I resisted the urge to stick my tongue out at him.

"Well, isn't this just the best first date ever?" He grabbed his beer and took a large chug. "I bet I can guess why you're single."

"I bet I can guess why you are too," I drawled slowly and let my eyes drift downwards then back up to his eyes. "Pity." I gave him my most dazzling smile and sat back feeling proud of myself.

I should have known it wouldn't last very long.

Chapter One

✦

Bank Account Balance: $1678.39
Days Since My Last Date: 425 days
Current Weight: 175 lbs

QUOTE OF THE DAY: "Today is the tomorrow you worried about yesterday"
—Dale Carnegie

"WHO NEEDS men when we have food?"

I surveyed the feast in front of me. The dining room table looked like a smorgasbord of fatty foods. There were three opened pizza boxes, a basket of fries, a plate full of chicken wings, and a side of spaghetti and meatballs. The smell of brownies baking in the oven filled the air with a sense of comfort, and I smiled in happiness.

"I feel like I'm in heaven right now." One of my best friends, Emma, grabbed another slice of pizza and took a huge bite. "This is a real feast."

"Well, we have to enjoy our last night of freedom." I giggled as I rubbed my stomach. "Starting tomorrow, we have to cut out all carbs."

"It's going to be torture." Chloe, another best friend, helped herself to a meatball and sprinkled parmesan cheese on top of it. "I'm not sure how I'm going to survive."

"It was your idea." Abby stood next to the wall with a glass of wine in her hand and savored a long sip as if it were her last. "I don't know why we agreed to do low carb for the next 28 days," she groaned. "Yes, I want to lose twenty pounds, but at what cost to my sanity?"

"Let's not worry about it until tomorrow." I was just happy to be enjoying the evening with my four best friends and roommates. At twenty-eight, we should have all had our own apartments, but living in New York was expensive, and so we rented a three-bedroom with a large closet and split the rent. Chloe got the closet, so she paid the least amount of rent, but she also made the least amount of money out of all of us, so she didn't mind.

In fact, none of us minded living together. Our apartment was pretty bomb. We were in Little Italy, which was literally down the street from Chinatown, and our place was gorgeous, even though we only had one bathroom—which was beyond hard with four women, but we made it work. We'd all been best friends we'd been roommates our freshman year at Columbia University, and we were used to sharing small spaces.

"Oh, Isabella, a package came for you. I put it on your dresser." Abby's eyes lit up. "It was heavy. What did you get?"

"Just some new watercolor paints and a new ceramic palette." I grinned. "I finally treated myself to some Schmincke paints and some nice squirrel hair brushes."

"That means nothing to me." Abby took another sip of wine. "I thought it was a dildo or something."

"What?"

"Well, it's been over a year since you've gotten any action," she pointed out with a sly smile.

I just rolled my eyes. "Don't remind me. I feel like I'm probably a virgin again." I shook my head. "I'm all dusty and cobwebby down there."

"We all are." Chloe sighed as she grabbed a breadstick. "What I wouldn't give for a piece of dick."

"Chloe!" Emma giggled.

"So I have an absolutely brilliant idea!" Abby looked around the table at all of us, a gleam in her eyes. For some reason, I felt like I was sitting at a table at the United Nations. Her expression was far too intense for my liking.

I'd known Abby since we were 18. That was 10 years. She'd never had a good idea. Well, that wasn't fair. She'd had some ideas that were good, but that was a very rare thing, especially when she got excited like this.

"What's your idea?" Chloe said, munching on another breadstick.

"Yeah, come on. Tell us," I prompted. "What's the idea, Abby?"

"Do you really want to hear it, Isabella?" she said with a grin.

"Yes. That's why I asked."

"Okay, so you know how we all hate online dating apps?"

"Yeah, can't stand them," Emma agreed. "Like, literally can't stand them."

"I hate them. Kill me now," said Chloe.

"Yeah, I agree with both of them. They suck."

"Swiping is like the devil's game. It is soul-sucking. But I have a brilliant idea about how we can combat dating apps to make them work for us," Abby said.

"Um, okay? What's the idea?"

"Well, what if we each create a profile for another person, and we select the dates for each other?"

"What do you mean?" I could already feel that I didn't like this idea.

"I mean, what if we create profiles for each other and swipe for each other? That way, we're not so invested in the conversations or the men we do or don't interact with."

"I don't know. You might swipe on guys I don't like and—"

"But that's the whole point!" Abby sounded exasperated. "We're all too picky. How are we four beautiful young women with everything going for us still single? We have college degrees from an Ivy League university. We all have jobs. Granted, we don't make a lot of money, but we still have jobs. We're intelligent. We're beautiful. And yet, none of us have men, and none of us have any prospects either. We're too picky."

"I definitely think you're too picky, Abby," Chloe said with a laugh.

"And you're picky, too," Abby said, pointing at Emma.

"I guess it's true," I admitted.

The last time I'd been on a dating app, I hadn't connected with many men, probably because I left-swiped a lot more than I right-swiped. But so many of them seemed dull and boring or unattractive or not funny or immature. I mean, there was a long list of reasons why I swiped left, but maybe, just maybe, I had missed an opportunity with a great guy because I was being too picky?

"Okay, well, tell me more."

"Yay, yay, yay!" Abby squealed. "Does that mean that we're going to do it?"

"I didn't say I'm in yet," I interrupted her quickly. "I just said, 'I want you to tell me more,' and if I like the idea, *then* maybe I'll be in on it."

"I agree," Emma nodded, "Tell us more."

"Chloe, are you in?"

"I was in as soon as you said you're going to help us get a date."

"Yep. Okay, so it's just Isabella I really have to convince," Abby laughed. "Well, here's the thing—we'll each choose a name at random. For example, perhaps I'll get Isabella." She nodded at me. "I'll choose photos of you, of course, and create a profile for you. And then I'll swipe for you, and then I'll get a date for you. And that's what all of us will do. And maybe, since we know each other really well, we'll know the sort of guys each other should be dating. Sometimes, you need someone else to find the dates for you. That's why people go to matchmakers, guys."

"I guess ..." I chewed on my lower lip. I still wasn't convinced, but what could it really hurt, right? "Okay, so we're going to set up one date, or we're going to set up multiple dates?"

"I think we should just set up one date to start," Emma said. "That way, we'll see if we like the choices that we're making, and if it's a bust, then we don't do it anymore. I mean, what can it hurt? We've all chosen plenty of crappy dates for ourselves, so what's one more bad date?"

"I guess that's true. But do we get to veto photos that you might choose or—"

"Nope," Abby said quickly. "We have no input in the profiles we make for each other."

"I don't know if I like that," I said, shaking my head, "What if you choose something really fugly or me in a bikini or—"

"We all have to trust each other," Abby said, "No one can tell anyone else what to do."

"Can we at least see the profiles?"

"Nope," she said quickly, "because if we see the profiles and we don't like something, then we're going to be nitpicking and la-di-da-di-da, and you know that just is not going to work."

"Hmm ... I don't know about this."

"Come on, Isabella. It'll be fun. Come on. You don't want to become a nun, do you? Or do you," she narrowed her eyes, "is this your way of telling us that you're going to join the convent or something, Maria?"

"Maria?" Was she really mocking me with a joke about a character from one of my favorite movies?

"You know, like from the *Sound of Music*? Maria von Trapp?"

"Oh my gosh, you're such an idiot." I shook my head, "Of course, I'm not trying to become a nun. And of course, I do want to get laid, and of course, I want a boyfriend and I want to have fun and I want to go on dates, but ..."

"But you just haven't met the right guy, right?"

"Yeah, I haven't met the right guy. Fine," I agreed with a sigh. "Let's do it. I'm in."

"Yay. Awesome! Everyone, hands in the middle of the table."

"My hand's dirty," Chloe complained.

"Well, wipe it off then."

Chloe wiped her hands off, and we all put our right hands in the middle of the table on top of each other.

"One for all and all for one. Let's get the best dates possible, girls," Abby said with a squeal. "Yay, I'm so excited! Let me get some shots of vodka so we can all celebrate."

"Should we be taking those shots of vodka now?"

I was a little confused, "I mean, none of us have a date yet, let alone a good one. Shouldn't we save that for afterward?"

"Nope, we celebrate now, and we celebrate afterward. And then if anyone meets their husband from this, you owe the person $1,000."

"What?" Emma screeched. "I don't think so! I don't have $1,000 to give."

"If you find your husband, he can pay the $1,000. How's that?"

"Well, if he's rich enough to pay $1,000, who am I to say no?" she giggled.

"You do realize that $1,000 is not that much money, right?" Abby said, shaking her head.

"It might not be much money to you, but it's a lot of money to me."

"It's a lot of money to all of us," I laughed. "None of us are going to be millionaires anytime soon."

"Speak for yourself," Abby sniffed. "You never know. Maybe I will."

"Uh-huh. Sure thing, sister," I started laughing, "Go and get those shots before I change my mind."

"Okay," she jumped up. I sat back and grabbed another breadstick wondering what I had just agreed to. It was either going to be the best decision of my life or the absolute worst.

Chapter Two

Bank Account Balance: $1650.32
Days Since My Last Date: 427 days
Current Weight: 178 lbs

QUOTE OF THE DAY: "The future belongs to those who believe in the beauty of their dreams." – Eleanor Roosevelt

"IT SHOULD NOT BE this hard to find a decent man to date." I looked at Abby over the tuna tartare on the table in front of us and repressed a groan. I like tuna tartare ... but not really. It was one of those upscale, fancy dishes that Abby loved to order that I went along with because I didn't want to look like a total pleb. I was more of a mozzarella sticks and onion rings appetizer sort of girl, but you didn't come to a fancy restaurant like this and order mozzarella sticks.

I didn't even think they had mozzarella sticks on the menu. And even if I wanted to order mozzarella sticks, I couldn't because we were on a diet, which already sucked.

"Girl, I'm telling you. I can help you find the man of your dreams." She grinned at me. "Let me help you."

"Abby, why should I believe you can help me find the man of my dreams when *you* haven't been able to find the man of your dreams?"

"Well, you know that saying," she said as she grabbed a wonton cracker, dipped it into the tuna tartare, and took a bite.

"No. What saying?"

"We all have the keys to each other's problems."

"Mm, I don't know about that. I mean, why couldn't you apply the same skills that you think you have on yourself?"

"Because, oh my gosh, really? Bella, you know I want you to be happy."

"I know you want me to be happy. I want me to be happy as well. I want you to be happy. I want everyone to be happy. I—"

"Enough, Bella." She rolled her eyes. "Fine, if you

don't want me to help you find true love and happiness now that you're thirty—"

"I'm twenty-eight, Abby."

"I know," She grinned. "*Almost* thirty and still single. I want true love and happiness, too. This is not where we saw ourselves being at this age, is it?"

"I mean, I don't know. I'm kind of happy being young, fabulous, and single. Aren't you?"

"Yeah. But on Friday nights, it would be nice to be young, fabulous, and in a relationship." She giggled. "I'd like to get laid again. Do you know how horny I am?"

"Oh, my gosh! Keep your voice down." I glared at her and glanced at the table to the right. I could tell that the two men that were sitting there were eavesdropping because one of them was grinning at his friend in a way that told me he thought our conversation was absolutely hilarious. He was probably thinking to himself how lucky he was that he wasn't on a date with one of us crazy women. Who went to a fancy restaurant on a Friday night and bitched about being single loudly while eating tuna tartare? I mean, give me mozzarella sticks and a steak any time of the week. I didn't have to be in an expensive restaurant bitching about my horrible love life.

"Look, I've got an idea," Abby interrupted my thoughts.

"Hm, another idea?" I raised an eyebrow. "What are you, related to Einstein now? Every time you have an idea, it works out so badly for me."

"Fine, I'm not going to tell you."

"Tell me."

"No, not if you're going to act like that."

"Act like what?"

"You know how you're acting, Isabella."

"No, I don't, Abigail."

"Well, let's wait to meet up with the girls later, and you can make up your mind then."

"First you need to tell me what your idea is." I took a sip of water. "I'm not going to have them there trying to convince me before I even know what your idea is."

"Bella, listen to me, just let me go on the app and go on one date. And if you don't like it at all, you never have to go on another one." Abby batted her big eyes at me. "I promise it will make you happy."

"Really? You think a date from a dating app is going to make me happy?" I raised an eyebrow at her. "You really don't think it takes much to make me happy, do you?"

"What?" She laughed, "you just need to meet some nice guys."

"Nice guys do not exist—"

"Yes, they do."

"You didn't let me finish my sentence. I was going to say nice guys do not exist on dating apps. There may be some out there in the world, but they're not on dating apps."

"I promise you'll meet a great one."

"How can you promise I'll meet a great one? Do you have some sort of connection to the love gods that I don't know about? And if you do, why haven't you used this connection to hook me up before?"

"Oh, Belle Belle," she laughed, "you're silly."

"No, I'm not silly. I'm just speaking like a woman who has gone on many dates in her life with many assholes and losers. I do not need to go on another one."

"But that's your problem. You just automatically assume that every guy is going to suck. Every guy doesn't suck."

"I never said every guy sucks. I just said that the guys I go on dates with suck."

"Okay, but that's why we're following my first brilliant idea."

"Hmmm," I said suspiciously.

"What you're doing isn't working for you," she shrugged, "and I'm your best friend. I know you better than anyone. I can ensure that you go on a date with a really awesome guy."

"I don't know about this, Abby."

"Please, Bella, *please*?" She pouted. "You agreed the other night."

"I was high on carbs." I sighed. "I just don't know. It doesn't really seem like a good idea."

"Just one date. It's not like I'm asking you to go on 10 billion dates, just one. And wouldn't it be nice for you to go on a really cool date before your trip this weekend? Where are you going again, Connecticut?"

"Yeah, I'm going to Greenwich." I rolled my eyes, "And how are you going to get me a date before then? I leave on Friday, and today is Monday."

"Well, let's see. If I can get you a date for Thursday night, will you go on it?" Her eyes gleamed.

"I'm not really liking the look in your eyes."

"Trust Me. Would I ever do anything—"

I put my hand up, and I stopped her. "There are many things that you would do that would greatly annoy me."

"What? That's not even what I was going to say." She made a mock-innocent face.

"Fine," I said, "You can sign up for the dating app. But I'll choose the photos, and I—"

"Nope," she shook her head. "I'm going to do everything. You just have to show up for the date."

"Well, am I even going to know anything about the guy before I show up for the date? And do you really think you're going to get me a date by Thursday? I find it very unlikely. Guys in New York City, they do not go on last-minute dates, at least not the ones that I know."

"It's not last minute," she shook her head. "Today's Monday, and the date will be on Thursday."

"So you're going to get me a date by Thursday." I paused, "Wait, are you going to talk to him? Because if you talk to him, he's going to think I'm lying because it wasn't me and—"

"Stop, Bella. I promise you that I've got it all covered."

Famous last words. I should've known not to trust Abby. I should have known this was an awful idea, but I was game for anything and always had been all of my life. And that's probably why I always found myself in the most ridiculous situations.

Chapter Three

※

Bank Account Balance: $1500
Days Since My Last Date: 430 days
Current Weight: 175 lbs

QUOTE OF THE DAY: "When things do not go your way, remember that every challenge—every adversity—contains within it seeds of opportunity and growth."
— Roy T. Bennett

HAVE you ever seen someone and instantly known they were going to equal trouble? I mean, I agree with the saying "Don't judge a book by its cover," but sometimes you need to listen to your gut. At least if you're smart, you will. There are some men that you know need to be taken down a notch or two as soon as you see that cocky smile cross their face. There is a confidence that handsome sexy men have. It's attractive because they are attractive. But when you really think about it, it's downright annoying because they have all the power.

I knew as soon as I saw Jack Morrison that I should walk out of the restaurant. The way his hazel-green eyes looked me up and down before settling on my eyes, the way he cooly flipped his slightly too long dirty blond hair away from his forehead, the way his jeans fit snugly on his muscular body, they were all signals to me that this man was going to be trouble. I knew I shouldn't have trusted Abby. She had kept her word and gotten me a date for Thursday night, but as I stared at his cocky face, I wasn't sure if I actually wanted to carry through with it.

"Isabella?" His voice was deep and husky with a slight twang that made me wonder where he was from. He had on a crisp white shirt and dark slacks. His olive tan contrasted with the white of his shirt, and I wondered if he was that golden color all over his body.

"Yes, Jack?" There was a slight snip to my voice because he was ten minutes late. I hated it when men were late for dates.

"The one and only." He tilted his head to the side and flashed his perfectly even white teeth. Of course, he'd have a perfect smile. Why wouldn't he? He tilted his head slightly as he studied me. "I thought you were going to be a blonde."

"Okay, and?" I couldn't believe that he hadn't apologized for making me wait. How rude!

"And nothing, I just thought you were going to be blonde. Like um, Pamela Anderson?" He looked like he was waiting for something.

"So you're disappointed?" My jaw was slightly slack now. Was this asshole kidding? I had spent two hours getting ready for this date and he was already trying to insult me.

"I didn't say that." He blinked. "You could always dye your hair." His lips twitched as he studied my face. "Don't kill me." He held his hands up and chuckled. "It was a joke."

"It wasn't very funny."

"You're much hotter than Pamela Anderson." He flashed a little smile as he said it. As much as I already hated him, I was a little flattered.

"Uhm thanks, I guess," I said with a flip of my long chestnut brown hair.

"Shall we grab a seat?" He gestured towards the tables.

I should have just said no and left then. Everything in my body was screaming at me to get out of there, go home, order a pizza, and veg out in front of the TV, but of course I was a dumbass. Why would I listen to the voice of reason inside my head? Instead, I listened to the devil whispering to me that he was the hottest guy I'd ever seen in my life. And I didn't care if he was late and slightly rude—I wanted to flirt with a hot guy.

"I don't see why not." I shrugged as I looked around the restaurant. I was hungry—*really* hungry. The low-carb diet I'd been on with my friends was not helping me much. I hadn't lost any weight, and my stomach was grumbling morning, noon, and night. I knew that meant that I should be eating more, but the prospect of eating more grilled chicken and broccoli was hard to face.

"So, is that a yes?"

I felt his palm on the back of my shoulders, and I turned to look at him with a raised eyebrow. "I don't think you know me well enough to be touching me yet."

"Yet, huh?" He grinned as he dropped his hand.

"Well, I don't know that you'll *ever* know me well enough to be touching me."

"Let's see what you have to say by the end of the night." He winked.

"Hmm. I don't think I'll be saying anything by the end of the night."

I should have left the restaurant then and there. But there was something I enjoyed about his sexy banter. It had been too long since I'd been in a situation where I could flirt, where someone found me attractive, where I even felt a little turned on, which was crazy because I didn't even know the guy. And he was already kind of annoying. But there was something about his charisma and charm.

And hey, who can ignore his good looks? Tall, built, sparkling green eyes, the sort of dirty blonde hair that reminded me of hot surfers. Yeah, he could get it. Well, he could have gotten it when I was younger. Now I was a little more choosy, or at least I pretended to be.

"Let's have a seat."

"Do we know where we're sitting?"

"I know where we're sitting." He took my hand, and I looked at him again. He dropped it quickly. "Sorry. Too soon?"

"Yeah," I nodded. "This is a first date."

"I know," he laughed. "I guess I just feel like I know you after our conversations online."

"Yeah, but you don't."

Trust me, you really don't know me. We've had zero conver-

sations online. I was really wishing now that I had demanded that Abby let me see the messages that they had exchanged. I had no idea if she'd been flirty with him, if she'd been a tease, or what she told him about me.

This hadn't been the best thought-out plan, but Abby's plans rarely were.

"So, how would you like this table?" he said. We'd made our way to the back of the restaurant to a cozy little corner. There were three candles on the table and a vase of roses.

"Is this normal?" I glanced around at the other tables—there were no candles, no roses.

"If you go on a date with me," he said as he pulled out my chair. "Would the lady like to sit?"

"Would the lady like to what?"

"I'm pulling out your chair and being a gentleman."

"Um, thank you." I slid into the seat, very surprised when he pushed it in for me.

"I take it you've not been on many dates with many gentlemen?"

"I guess not." I shook my head. "I'm happy if they open the door for me, let alone pull my chair back for me. Thank you."

"Wow. I got a thank you. Dare I say you're impressed?" He sat down across from me.

"Um, does it kind of detract from the gentleman

act if you want kudos for it," I pointed out with a smile.

"I don't know. You really think?"

"I don't know." I grabbed the menu and opened it quickly. I was really hungry.

"So, what do you think you're going get to eat?" he asked.

"Oh, I'm not sure." My stomach growled as I studied the delicious items on the menu. This was going to be a hard one because there were so many things that I wanted and so many things that I shouldn't have. "Maybe I'll get a salad, uh, grilled chicken salad." It even sounded boring.

"Oh," he looked at me in surprise, "A grilled chicken salad, huh? You're going to come to a steak restaurant known for its English specials and get a salad?"

"What's an English special? I didn't know the English were known for their steaks."

"Well, you can get a prime rib with au jus gravy and roast potatoes, and Yorkshire pudding and some vegetables."

"Oh, like a Sunday roast?"

"Yep," he nodded. "And trust me, it'll be the best steak you've ever had in your life. Also the best Yorkshire put in I've ever had in the States."

"You know, I've never had Yorkshire pudding," I

admitted. "I've always heard about it and read about it, but I've never had it."

"Oh?" He looked surprised. "You've never been to England?" He looked at me over his menu.

"No, I've never been to England. I'd love to go, though. It's on my top five list of places to visit. I absolutely love Jane Austin and Shakespeare and Dickens and, well, I'm a bit of an Anglophile."

"You're a bit of a what?" he said, leaning forward.

"I'm a bit of an Anglophile. Like, I absolutely love the British. I love the royal family, I love Prince William, I love Prince Harry, I follow all the drama ..." I paused. "Maybe this isn't something I should be admitting out loud, but you know what I mean. I just like royalty and ..." I bit on my lower lip. "Sorry, I'm talking a lot, aren't I?"

"No. It's nice to finally meet you in person and hear what you're interested in."

"Yeah. I studied Art History, and—"

"I didn't know that," he shook his head. "Interesting. That's not what I would have guessed."

"Oh," I raised an eyebrow. "Why?"

"I mean, because of your love of sports and all."

"My love of ...?" I said. "Oh, yeah. Yeah. I love sports. Football, basketball, baseball, golf, swimming, you name it, I love it. I'm so sporty, and I love watching it on TV and I like going to games."

I just went with it. Obviously, Abby had lied and said I love sports, and well, I didn't want to give it up too soon, so who cared if I pretended I liked sports? Lots of women pretend that they liked sports.

"Oh, so you're into football, huh?"

"Oh, yeah, super into football."

"Who is your favorite football team?" He leaned forward slightly as if he were really interested in my answer.

"Um, well, you know I live in New York."

"Yeah?"

"So, I love the New York Knicks, of course."

"The New York *Knicks*?" He raised an eyebrow. "That's your favorite football team? The Knicks?"

"Um, well, no, I, I ..." I stumbled over my words. "I was just joking. I actually love the New England Patriots because I love Tom Brady," I said, remembering something my dad had once mentioned about Tom Brady and the New England Patriots. They were definitely a football team. I hoped.

"But they're not in New York." He frowned slightly.

"Yeah. I mean, I live in New York, so of course, like I love New York teams, but my absolute favorite is the Patriots because they're an awesome football team, right?"

"Yeah ..." he nodded slowly, "and you know Brady is not with the Patriots?"

"He's not?" Was this something I was going to have to tell my dad? Had he gotten it wrong?

"I mean, he used to be with the Patriots, but he just won the Super Bowl for the Tampa Bay Buccaneers this year. You knew that, right?"

"Well, of course. I mean, I wanted to go to Tampa Bay and be at the Super Bowl, but I didn't have money for the ticket because I am an artist." I knew I needed to shut up because I was obviously sounding like an idiot. "But anyway, tell me more about you and what you're interested in."

"I love sports as well. I really love football."

"You do?" I squirmed in my seat. I didn't want to talk about football anymore. "What about art? Are you into art?"

"Um, a little bit. So, you're an artist?"

"Yeah. I love art. I live art."

"So, what do you do? Are you a painter, a sculptor?"

"I'm so glad that you know there are different types of art. Most people just think it's drawing or something. But no, I'm a painter. Mainly watercolor. I used to do oil painting, but it just got too expensive and too messy. So now I do custom watercolor paintings, and I teach classes. One day I'm hoping to have my own little gallery and teach my own classes, you know?"

"Sounds admirable. Would I have seen any of your work anywhere?"

"Oh no, I'm not Andy Warhol or Monet or van Gogh or anything. I'm not famous. Maybe one day. Though I don't know that I'm good enough to be famous, but ..." I paused. "Sorry. Sometimes I mumble."

"Are you nervous?"

"No, I'm not nervous. Are you?"

"No. You're very different from what I thought, but I guess we all have different sides to us, don't we?"

"Yeah, I guess so."

I had no idea what he was talking about. What different sides did I have to me? I was pretty much an open book as far as I was concerned. I loved art, I loved my friends, I loved food, I loved coffee shops, and I loved having a good time. What else was there? Well, there was one thing, but that wasn't anything I was going to discuss with him. He did not need to know my personal goings on.

"So, have you decided what you want to eat?" he asked me, changing the subject.

"I figure I'll get what you recommend, the steak and roast potatoes and Yorkshire pudding."

To hell with the diet. It wasn't going that well anyway. Maybe I'd start again next week or next month. I knew that Abby, Chloe, and Emma would be upset, but for all I knew, they cheated as well. Low carb was hard. I was craving potatoes, and I was dying to try Yorkshire pudding. I mean, when was I ever going to have an opportunity like this again. For the prices this restaurant was charging, it was probably really good. And if I was getting a free meal, I was going to get something I wanted, not a grilled chicken salad.

"Okay. So, let me get the waiter. Would you like to share a bottle of wine as well?"

"Of course, why not? All in, right?"

"Sorry, what?" he said.

"Oh, nothing," I said quickly, blushing. Had I just said "all in" out loud? Shit. That was meant to be something I said to myself.

"So, what would you like?"

"Let's get a bottle of red wine."

"Okay. Any wine that you're interested in in particular?"

"I don't know, maybe a Cabernet Sauvignon, or a Merlot, if you prefer?"

"I was thinking of a Pinot Noir, but I don't mind a Cab."

Okay, great, let's do a Cab, it's my favorite."

"Okay. Learning something new about you already."

"Yeah, I guess that's what the night will be, full of surprises," I said with a grin.

"I guess it will. I think tonight it's going to be a very good night, Isabella."

"Well, I sure hope so." I paused. "Even though I'm not Pamela Anderson," I laughed.

"Hey, I never said I was *into* Pamela Anderson, did I? Maybe, just maybe, I prefer brunettes."

"Well, maybe, just maybe, I prefer brunettes as well," I said smugly. His eyes lit up, and he shook his head and chuckled.

"Touché." He ran a hand through his very attractive blonde hair. "Maybe I'll have to change your mind."

"Maybe you will, but maybe you won't," I said, loving the flirtation. I sat back and smiled to myself. Maybe tonight would be a good night after all.

Chapter Four

Bank Account Balance: $1500
Days Since My Last Date: 430 days
Current Weight: 175 lbs

QUOTE OF THE DAY: "Nothing is impossible, the word itself says 'I'm possible'! -Audrey Hepburn

I WAS FEELING QUITE happy about the date. Happy that I had stayed, and happy that I was getting to know Jack. I was even starting to think Abby had actually had a good idea for once. I didn't know I was going to tell her that, but it was fair to say that I was feeling pleased and enjoying myself. Initially, Jack had annoyed me, but he wasn't so bad.

Of course, you should never count your chickens before they hatch because inevitably something is going to go wrong.

"So, Isabella," asked Jack, "Were you named after Isabella Rossellini?"

"Was I named after who?"

"Isabella Rossellini."

"Oh, you mean the model?"

"Yeah, the model."

"No," I answered with a light chuckle.

"Oh, okay. Who were you named after then?"

"I don't know," I shrugged. "Who were you named after, Jack? Jack and the Beanstalk?" I giggled, but I could tell from the look on his face he didn't think it was as funny as I did.

"No, I wasn't named after Jack and the Beanstalk. Were you named after Miss Piggy?"

"Excuse me?" My jaw dropped. "What is that supposed to mean?"

"It was a joke."

"That wasn't a very funny joke." I stared at him through narrowed eyes. "I really hope you're not going to try and become a comedian in your lifetime because I don't think that it's going to go well."

"Well, I really hope that you're not going to become a manager for any comedians in your lifetime because with that sort of support I don't think someone will ever go far."

"What's that supposed to mean?"

"It means that you're a dream killer."

"I'm a dream killer? Excuse me?"

"Or should I say you're a dream crusher?"

"I'll crush something, and it's not your dreams." I took another sip of wine.

"Oh, yeah? Is that your way of coming on to me?" He laughed. I felt his hand touch my knee under the table.

"Get your hand off of me!" I glared at him. "I didn't say you could touch me."

"But I thought we were having a good time."

"This is the first date. And if you think this is having a good time, I'd hate to see your idea of a bad date."

"I didn't know you were so interested in any other dates of mine." He raised an eyebrow. "Kind of weird, isn't it?"

"What's kind of weird?"

"The fact that you're on a date with me and you're talking about my other dates. Or is that your way of trying to figure out how many other dates I go on?"

"Dude, I don't care how many other dates you go on. I don't even care if you have another date tonight.

Like, you're lucky I'm even here." I shook my head. "Maybe I should actually just go."

"What?" He looked annoyed. "Why would you leave? I thought we were having a good time. Plus you ordered your steak, and it's expensive."

"Okay, so I've got to stay because the meal's expensive? What, do I have to sleep with you as well?"

"I didn't say that. I don't understand where your attitude is coming from. I'm sorry that I touched your shoulder and I'm sorry that I touched your knee. I thought we were having a moment. I thought we were flirting, which many adults do. But hey, if we're not, then—"

"Fine. Sorry. It's been a long time since I've been on a date and maybe I just don't know how to act anymore." I didn't really think that was the case, but I was trying to be polite.

"So, Isabella?"

"Yes, Jack? Why do you keep saying my name?"

"Maybe I like your name." He sighed. "You're a difficult woman to be on a date with."

"I'm difficult?" I thought back to our conversation thus far. Okay, maybe I was being a little difficult. But he had rankled me from the very first moment we'd laid eyes on each other, and I was finding it hard to get back on track.

"Sorry. Shall we start over?"

"Sure."

"Should we walk back to the front of the restaurant?" He grinned.

"What?"

"You wanted to start over, right?"

"Yeah, but ..."

"So let's go to the front of the restaurant and pretend we're meeting for the first time.

"But we're already seated and we've already ordered our meals, and—"

"Hey. It will take two minutes. Let's do it."

"I guess." I felt like an idiot, but as he stood up, I stood up as well. We walked back to the front of the restaurant. Several other diners stared at us, and our waiter gave us an odd glance.

"Okay, you go outside."

"What?" I looked at him.

"Go outside. Pretend you're walking in for the first time, and I'll stand here."

"Huh. This is weird."

"It's fine. Trust me. It will be good for us."

"Okay," I said, as I walked outside. I grabbed my phone from my handbag and texted Abby, "I am going kill you when I get home. This date is an absolute bust and weird, and—" I quickly put my phone back in the handbag. I couldn't afford to spend more time texting Abby. I took a couple of deep breaths and walked back into the restaurant. I looked around and saw Jack standing in the corner. He beamed as soon as we made eye contact and walked over to me. He held his hand out.

"Hi. You must be Isabella. You're gorgeous. I'm your date, Jack."

I stared at him for a few seconds and tried not to laugh. This was a very different greeting. I took his hand and shook it.

"Hi, Jack. Yes, I'm Isabella. It's so nice to meet you."

"You're even more beautiful than your photos suggested."

"Um, okay. Thank you."

"Your hair looks like it could be in magazines for shampoo advertisements. Your lashes are so long and luscious that if I didn't know better, I'd think you were a spokeswoman for Maybelline—"

"Oh my gosh, dude. You're really pouring it on strong."

"What?" He winked at me. "I wanted to make a good first impression—well, okay," he laughed. "A good second first impression."

"Fine. Shall we make our way to the table?"

"Why of course," he said. He looked at my hand and then stepped back. "I will not take your hand because this is our first date and we don't know each other well enough for me to touch you."

"Okay. Thank you." Even though he was trying to be nice, a part of me wondered if he was teasing me and being deliberately obnoxious on purpose. Like did he really have to throw in that comment? We walked back to our table, and he looked at my chair and then at me.

"Now I couldn't quite tell if you enjoyed me pulling the chair out for you before, or not."

"I did," I nodded.

"Okay." He pulled the chair out for me again, and I sat and he pushed it in. He then walked around to the side of the table and sat down. "You know what, Isabella?

"What, Jack?" I picked up my glass of wine and took another long sip. I could tell this was going to be a long night.

"I think that you could be the new star of *Baywatch*. Forget Pamela Anderson."

I groaned and held my hands up. "Are you kidding me? This is not any better. In fact, that might be worse. I think that—"

"What?" He held his glass of wine up, his eyes sparkling. "Are you just telling me that I'm a bad first date?"

"I don't want to say that to your face, but—"

"Would you say it behind my back?"

"Yeah," I laughed. "I'm going to tell my best friend who—" I nearly said, *arranged this date*, but stopped myself right time. "Who encouraged me to go on a date." I took another long sip of wine. "I'm hungry. I hope our meal is here soon."

"Yeah, you do look like you enjoy a good meal."

"Excuse me? Did you just call me fat?"

"No, I didn't mean it like that! I just meant to say that you were studying the menu for so long that I could tell that you're the sort of person that likes to eat." He made a face. "Okay. Even I know I put my foot in it this time. Please, forgive me."

"What? You're asking me for forgiveness? I'm shocked."

"Why?"

"Because you don't seem like the sort of guy that would be asking for forgiveness."

"Oh, really? So you can tell the sort of guy I am?"

"Um, obviously, probably, not really, but ..."

"But what?"

"I don't know. Maybe we should change the subject. Talk about something else?"

"So what would you like to talk about?"

"Um, what do you do for fun?"

"What do I do for fun? We had an entire conversation about it just yesterday."

"Really?" I sighed. "I'm trying to make conversation here and you're making it really hard."

"*I'm* making it hard? I'm a little offended that you can't remember anything about me. Or are you just talking to that many guys?"

"That's really none of your business. I'm sure I'm not the only woman you've been talking to."

"True. So maybe this will jog your memory. I'm really into movies."

"Okay, then?"

"Remember my favorite filmmaker is Roberto Rossellini?"

"Um, not really. But I guess that's why you were curious about my name," I said, finally understanding.

"Yeah," he nodded, "I'm not sure if you know, seeing as you're into art at all, but Roberto Rossellini was actually one of the creators of neo-realism. And I think he's one of the most influential directors of all time."

"Hm, I actually didn't know that. What are some of his movies? Is there one that you would recommend?"

"You've never seen *any* of Roberto Rossellini's movies?" He looked shocked.

"I can't say that I have, but if there's one that you recommend—"

"There are many that I recommend. *Germany*,

Year Zero, or *Europe 51*, *Rome, Open City*. Well, he wrote those. Are you wanting to know the movies that he wrote or the movies that he directed?"

"I mean ... I don't really know."

"Have you seen *Garibaldi*?"

"No."

"Oh, it's amazing. I'm a bit of a history buff as well, and Garibaldi is about how Italy's national hero, Giuseppe Garibaldi—" He paused, "I'm not sure if you've heard of him?"

"Vaguely. Maybe I took a class in college," I shrugged. "Not really."

"Well, the movie is about how Garibaldi left a military campaign known as Expedition of the Thousand in 1860 and conquered Sicily and Naples. It's amazing. I just think that—" he paused, "Sorry. I told you I'm a movie buff and a bit of a film nerd. I don't want to bore you."

"It's not boring. That sounds cool. Maybe I'll see if it's on Netflix."

"I doubt it's on Netflix." He looked a bit pained. "But maybe. What's your favorite movie?"

"I don't know if I want to admit it."

"No, tell me."

"*Eternal Sunshine of the Spotless Mind*."

"Oh," he chuckled, "of course."

"What's that mean, of course?"

"Well, when I meet women, their favorite movie is usually either *The Notebook* or *Eternal Sunshine of the Spotless Mind*. And if they're trying to impress me, they say *The Godfather*."

"Okay. So you're saying that I'm a cliche?"

"No. What's your second favorite movie?"

"Well, now I just know you're going to judge me."

"No, tell me."

"It's *The Sound of Music*."

"Really? *The Sound of Music*?"

"Yeah. Why are you so surprised?"

"I don't know. You didn't look like a woman that would be into *The Sound of Music*."

"I love musicals. I love that movie. I've been watching it since I was a little kid. I watch it every Christmas. It's really sentimental to me, you know?"

"So does that mean that you want to be a nun someday?"

"Oh, hell no." I started laughing and shook my head. "Couldn't be a nun."

"Oh, and why is that?" His voice lowered.

"I think we both know why that is."

"No. Why don't you care to enlighten me?"

"Because," I paused, "I like—"

"Yeah?"

He leaned forward and I knew he wanted me to talk about sex because he was a typical man. And even though I did want to talk about sex and even though I did want to flirt with him, I didn't want to give him what he wanted. So I took another sip of my wine and I said, "I like ..."

"Yeah?"

"... indulging in chocolates," I said with a small smile.

"What?" He sat back in his chair. "What are you talking about? What has that got to do with being a nun?"

"Well, nuns aren't meant to do anything in excess. And sometimes I feel like I eat chocolates in excess, you know?"

He groaned. "Oh my gosh, Isabella. You really are one of a kind, aren't you?"

"I like to think so," I said, pleased that I'd gotten under his skin for just one moment.

Chapter Five

⁂

Bank Account Balance: $1200.39
Days Since My Last Date: 0days
Current Weight: 173 lbs

QUOTE OF THE DAY: "To be yourself in a world that is constantly trying to make you something else is the greatest accomplishment." - Ralph Waldo Emerson

"SO YOU'RE QUITE the comedian yourself, aren't you?" Jack said, a smirk on his face.

"No, I never said I was a comedian. Why would you say that?"

"Chocolate?" he raised an eyebrow. "Really? Chocolate?"

"What did you think I was talking about?" I said innocently.

"We both know that you know what I thought you were talking about." His voice was deep and husky.

I swallowed hard. Of course, I knew he was talking about sex, and of course, a part of me was talking about sex, but I didn't want to be that sort of girl, at least not right away.

"You're so different than you were when I was talking to you online," he frowned slightly, looking puzzled.

"Oh, how so?"

"You're a little bit more mischievous, not so direct." He was thoughtful for a second. "I don't know. Maybe you're using humor to deflect your insecurities."

"What insecurities?" I said, far too quickly.

"I don't know. I don't know you well enough to know what they are. Unlike *you*," he smiled, "I don't just assume I know someone based upon a first meeting."

"I didn't assume anything about you. It's not my fault if you took what I said seriously or—"

"I'm not a psychiatrist or a psychologist, but normally when women are this bitchy on a first date, it means one of three things."

"Excuse me, are you calling me a bitch?"

"No, that's not what I'm saying, but you are being combative. Do you not agree with me?"

"Uh, I don't know. What about me is being combative?"

And then I stopped myself because of course, I *was* being combative, and I didn't want to be. He was right. I did have a guard up, and not all of it was due to him. A lot was due to my ex, who'd been an asshole and who'd totally broken my heart. He cheated on me, and then he gaslighted me to make me feel like it was my fault, and for a couple of months I'd really thought it had been. But thank God for my best friends. They'd made me see the truth. They helped me realize that him cheating on me had nothing to do with me and everything to do with him being the biggest douchebag that he was.

"I can see I've got you thinking." Jack smiled. "I like that."

"What? You like that I think, or are you like that—"

"Oh, my gosh. Isabella, really? Sorry."

I gave him a little smile. "So let's not talk about me. Let's talk more about you."

"You keep saying that. You love to deflect."

"Yeah, and?"

"I don't know. It's just interesting."

"Well, I am interesting, or did you think I was not going to be interesting?"

"Let's just say you're a little bit more interesting than I thought," he nodded. "I don't know that ..." he paused. "Well, it doesn't matter."

"It doesn't matter what?"

"I don't know. This is kind of an interesting first date, if you know what I mean."

"No, I don't know what you mean."

"I mean, it's not great, is it?"

"Excuse me. Are you saying I'm a bad first date?"

"Um, honey, let's just say this is not the best first date I've ever been on."

"Oh, really? You've been on better dates than with me?"

"Yeah, definitely. In fact, I would even go as far as to say that almost all of the dates I've been on in my life have been better than this."

"Wow, how rude!"

"What? I thought you women like honest men."

"You're not being honest. You're being—"

"What, I'm a pig because I told you you're a bad first date?"

"You know what? *You're* a bad first date."

"It's funny, though, don't you think?"

"What's funny?"

"It's funny how you haven't left, even though you think I'm such a horrible guy."

"I'm here for the meal."

"Oh, so you're one of those girls, are you?"

"One of what girls?"

"You're one of those girls that goes on dates to get free dinners."

"Oh hell, no. I'm not one of those women. How dare you?" I glared at him, daggers shooting from my eyes.

"I *dare* because to me it doesn't even seem like you wanted to come on this date. You're acting like you're here against your will. You seem surly and—"

"Surly? Are you kidding me? You did not just use *surly* to describe me, did you?"

"I mean, I could also say 'sexy,' but I feel like you would pull my hair out if I said that."

That took me aback a little. "What ... what made you think that?"

"Okay, you're sexy, and that's the only reason why *I'm* still sitting at this table. How do you like that?"

My jaw dropped. I didn't know what to say. I mean, I couldn't tell him off for what he just said, because then he'd be right. But the only reason he was still here was because I was sexy? Did he mean that my personality was bad and it was my looks that had him here?

That was the first time anyone had ever said anything like that to me. I normally assumed my personality was much better than my looks. Not that I was ugly, but I was no Cindy Crawford or Elle Macpherson or Claudia Schiffer or Kendall Jenner—and I hated Kendall Jenner, but she had a nice body, nothing like mine. I would need to go on a million more diets and lose a million more pounds and work out a million more hours before I was even half close to looking like Kendall Jenner.

" ... Thanks?"

Chapter Six

"Thanks?" Jack raised an eyebrow. "Are you one of those women that doesn't need a man?" The smug entitled look on his face made me want to slap him.

"Are you one of those men that doesn't know how to give an orgasm?" I snapped back. I hated how amused he looked.

"Oh, I've given plenty of orgasms." He smirked. "Is that your problem?"

"What?" *Ignore the urge to wipe that smile off of his face, Isabella*, I lectured myself internally as I stared at his handsome face. He seemed like the sort of jerk who'd get off on me putting my hands on him.

"Are you acting like Miss Havisham because you've never been pleasured properly before?"

"Are you acting like Austin Powers because you're an ... idiot?" I finished weakly.

"That's the best come-back you have?" This time he did start laughing, running his long fingers through his golden blonde hair. I hated the fact that this man was so handsome. It should be illegal to be that handsome—and that much of an ass.

"Anything more complicated would have gone over your head." I resisted the urge to stick my tongue out at him.

"Well, isn't this just the best first date ever?" He grabbed his beer and took a large chug. "I bet I can guess why you're single."

"I bet I can guess why you are too." I let my eyes drift downwards and back up to his eyes. "Pity." I gave him my most dazzling smile and sat back, feeling proud of myself.

I should have known it wouldn't last very long.

"You're very mouthy for someone who was begging me to go out tonight."

"Excuse me? *Begging* you?"

"Or giving me an ultimatum, anyway."

"Say what?" What had Abby done? Was I going to have to commit homicide? I was too pretty to go to jail for murdering my best friend.

"'I have to meet you right away ...'" He raised his

voice in a high-pitched falsetto. "'I don't want anyone else to get you before I meet you.'"

I pressed my lips together. It was official. I was going to have to kill Abby. What the hell had she been thinking? She'd made me out to be a desperado. And just because I hadn't had sex or a boyfriend in well over a year didn't mean I was desperate. "I was ... joking."

"You were joking? Riiight." Jack nodded his head as if he didn't believe me at all. "And were you also joking about the fact that you ..." He paused. "I guess we'll see."

"What?" I leaned forward. "What did I say?" What else had Abby told him?

"You can't even remember? What, do you have amnesia or something?"

"No, I don't have amnesia," I snapped at him. "You know, for someone who's supposed to be trying to impress me, you're not doing such a hot job."

"I could say the same thing, girlie."

"Don't call me girlie."

"Sorry. I could say the same thing, *woman*." He shrugged. "Oh, thank God."

"What?" I said, and then I saw the waiter was approaching us with our meals. Oh, well. I guess that meant it was too late for me to leave, but I was going to enjoy the heck out of this prime rib and roast potatoes, and then I was going to get out of here.

"Waiter?" I said as he put our plates down.

"Yes ma'am?"

"Can you bring us another bottle of wine, please?" I smiled and then looked over at Jack. I wasn't even going to ask his permission. "In fact, why not bring two? I think we're going to need them."

"Two, ma'am? At the same time?" He looked at me with a hesitant expression, and then he looked over at Jack.

"I'm not sure why you're looking at him, but yes, I said two bottles. Thank you."

"And you can go ahead and bring me a beer as well," Jack said with a smooth drawl. I could hear a hint of amusement in his voice, and I looked at him through narrowed eyes. Did he think this was funny?

"Yes sir, sure. I will be right back. Same wine, ma'am?"

"Yes, please."

"And sir, what beer would you like?"

"Why don't you surprise me?" Jack sat back. "Actually, bring me your beer with your highest alcoholic content."

"Okay, sir. I will check with the bartender."

"Thank you," he said.

"Enjoy your meals."

"I'm sure we will." I sat back and waited for Jack to say something, but instead, he picked up his wineglass and held it towards me.

"Bon appétit." He raised his glass.

I grabbed my wineglass and clinked his. "Bon appétit."

I couldn't believe we were acting as if everything were fine when we had just been arguing seconds before. This was the weirdest first date ever. In fact, I would go so far as to say the worst first date ever. In fact, the worst date I'd ever been on in my life.

It wasn't all his fault. I knew that I had a bit of an attitude, and he was right: I hadn't really wanted to come on this date. But his opening comments had been off-putting, and so far, the rest of the date wasn't going swimmingly. If not for the fact that I was hungry, annoyed, and just couldn't care less, I would've left a long time ago.

But Abby was going to get it from me, though I wasn't sure I was even going to have time to talk to her unless she was up when I got home. I was supposed to go out of town the next day. I was going to a family retreat with my gay BFF, Lucas, and I was going to need all my energy for that one. But I would think about that later.

"So, Isabella?"

"Yes, Jack?" I cut into my prime rib and took a

bite, almost moaning out loud. It was sumptuous. The best steak I'd ever had in my life. I cut into the roast potato and dipped it into the gravy, and I thought I was going to have an orgasm then and there. Potatoes had never tasted so good, and these were some sort of herb roasted potatoes. They were salty and garlicky, and I could taste a hint of rosemary. Oh, my gosh. I thought I had died and gone to heaven. But then I blinked and saw Jack sitting there in front of me.

"So, who are your favorite artists?" he asked me with a small smile. "Remember, we're starting over? We can't just have a horrible date for the entire time, can we?"

"I mean, we started over, and it already sucking again."

"Wow, I've never been told that I suck as a first date."

"Well, I'm an honest sort of woman, so I tell you how it is."

"Oh, well." He chuckled. "I do appreciate honesty in a woman."

"Well, that's good."

"You know the sort of women I don't like?"

"No, who?"

"Gold diggers."

I tried not to roll my eyes. I didn't want to be

judgmental, but Jack didn't really look like he had much gold to be digging. His watch looked cheaper than mine. The leather strap was worn and cracked. His shirt looked like it came from Walmart, and that was being nice. Not that there was anything wrong with Walmart, but a distinguished businessman didn't buy shirts at Walmart. I couldn't remember what his shoes or his trousers looked like, but ... I shrugged. And his haircut? It looked like he hadn't had his hair cut in a long time, or maybe he was going to one of those stores where you paid $10 a cut.

Not that I was judging him for it. I was a broke-ass myself, but let's be real. I wanted to start laughing. I loved how men always started talking about gold diggers as if they had two pots to piss in. It was always the poorest guys that were worried about gold diggers. *Don't worry, I'm not after your $100, bro.*

I kept my mouth shut, though.

"What's so funny?" he asked.

"What? I'm not laughing."

"But you have a smirk on your face."

"No, I don't. Don't worry, though, I'm not a gold digger by any means, and I certainly wouldn't be digging for gold with someone like you."

"Someone like me?"

I had no idea why he looked impressed, but I shrugged. "Why are you giving me that expression?"

"I'm curious what you mean by 'someone like me.'"

"I mean someone who is so absolutely, ridiculously, obnoxiously annoying."

"I'm ridiculously, obnoxiously annoying, am I?" He chuckled some more, and then picked up his glass of wine again. "Okay. And you consider yourself a prize?"

"Yeah. I'm a trophy. I'm like *the* trophy."

"So you consider yourself a trophy-wife sort of person?"

"I didn't say that." I shook my head vehemently. "I would never be a trophy wife!"

"Yep, I can see that."

"What's that supposed to mean?"

"I mean you don't seem to have the temperament to be a trophy wife."

"Excuse me?"

"I mean most trophy wives are beautiful. And yes, you're beautiful," he added quickly. "But your personality? Meh."

"My personality is meh?"

"Would you prefer me to lie and say your personality is winning?"

"Whatever. I think my personality *is* winning, actually, and I've never had any guys complain, so there."

"And that's why you're still single. Because you're beautiful and you have a winning personality."

"Well, you're no prize yourself, mister. I mean, you're handsome, but your personality sucks."

"So you do think I'm handsome?" He grinned like he'd just won the first prize at the Kentucky Derby.

"Why do you look like the Cheshire Cat right now?"

"Are you saying that I have a wide smile? Are you saying I have perfect white teeth? Are you just saying that I look like a cat? A purple cat, in fact?"

"Well obviously you don't look like a purple cat, but—" I stopped myself. "Ugh, I don't know why we're going back and forth like this. We don't even know each other. You'd think we were long-lost enemies from high school or something."

"I know, right? Did you have a lot of them?"

"Did I have a lot of what?"

"Enemies in high school."

"No, why?"

"You sure? You just seem like you'd be the sort of woman that did."

"And you wonder why I think you're an obnoxious asshole."

"Yeah, but you obviously think I'm hot, or you wouldn't be here."

"That's not true. Maybe I was just hungry."

"So if I was fugly, you'd still be here?"

I shot him a glare. He was correct, of course. If he'd been truly ugly, I would've left the moment I saw him. "I mean, I don't know about that. I just ..."

"You just what? Let's be honest with each other. You think I'm hot. I think you're hot. Obviously, our personalities don't mesh. I don't really know what all that crap you were talking about online was, but obviously, you have some sort of alter ego. Maybe you're one of those girls who likes to flirt online, but in person you're shy. I don't know." He shrugged. "But obviously we're both here for different reasons."

"And what would that reason be?" I stared at him. I couldn't believe what he was saying, but I was intrigued.

"Because we probably both want to get to know each other just a little bit better." He winked.

"Excuse me?"

"You think I forgot what you said?"

"What did I say?"

He lowered his voice. "You think I forgot that you told me how horny you are?"

"I *what*?"

Oh, I was definitely going to kill Abby. I didn't care if I went to jail for life. I didn't care if I got the death penalty. She was dead. How dare she tell the man I hadn't had sex in ages!

His mouth curled in disdain. "What, were you drunk the night you told me? Regretting it?"

"I just think that my personal life is my business, and, uh ..."

"And what? So you're not interested in getting to know me carnally?"

"You did not just say that."

"What if I did? You didn't answer my question. Are you deflecting again? Am I making you uncomfortable? Or am I making you just even hornier right now talking about it?" He leaned forward. "Are your panties wet, Isabella?"

"Oh no, you did *not* just ask me if my panties are wet." I grabbed my glass of wine and drained it. He poured some more into the glass. "That is not the sort of thing you ask someone on a first date."

"I think we've established that this is a crappy first date and there's unlikely to be a second one," he said. "So I think I'm okay asking whatever I want, don't you?"

I just stared at him, flabbergasted. I had no idea how to answer that because he was correct. There was definitely not going to be a second date. I couldn't stand him. I literally couldn't stand him. The smug look on his face was infuriating, but I couldn't lie to myself. He was very attractive, and he was right. My panties were wet. I was somehow turned on by this absolute ridiculousness, and I couldn't lie to myself. "So what are you suggesting?" I said softly, leaning forward.

"Well, what would you like me to suggest?"

"I wouldn't like you to suggest anything." I shook my head. "It's not like ..."

"Come back to my place tonight," he whispered.

"What? Are you joking?"

"Come back to my place, just tonight. We do whatever you want to do, nothing more. Shit, you can slap me if you want to. I know you'd like that."

"Huh?" What was he talking about?

"I'm open to whatever you want to do, but it's just one night. We never have to see each other again. We don't have to exchange phone numbers. I bet we can both get out our frustrations on each other tonight."

"So you want me to go to your apartment to bang? Really? Is that what you're saying to me?"

"Well, I didn't quite say it in those words, and I don't think I'd be so crude, but yes. I would like to bang you, Isabella not-Rosselini."

I was in two minds. Part of me wanted to get up and leave, but something in me wanted to stay. I wanted to fuck the shit out of this man and not care about it. I didn't feel self-conscious with him at all. Maybe it was because I knew I was never going to see him again. Maybe it was because I didn't want anything from him and didn't feel the need to make a good impression.

"Fine," I agreed. "After the meal, we'll go back to your place, and we'll do whatever I want to do. And maybe I'll bang you, and maybe I won't."

"Fine." He sat back, triumph in his eyes.

I had a feeling that I'd just lost something very important. But as I picked up my wine glass and took another sip, and then looked down at my delicious plate of food, I decided I didn't care. I was going to enjoy tonight for what it was.

Maybe that had been my problem my whole life. Maybe I had been looking for too much too soon. But with this guy, I wasn't looking for anything but to get off, and I had a feeling he'd do a good job of it.

Chapter Seven

I licked the spoon from my chocolate fondant and ice cream and sat back feeling happy and content. I was full on carbs and loving life. Tomorrow, of course, I was going to hate myself because all my hard work had gone down the drain for this one meal, but I didn't care. There was something about eating bad food that made me really, really happy, and if that meant I was going to be overweight for the rest of my life and never look like a skinny model, then so be it. It was a price I was willing to pay.

Jack watched me finish my dessert, a strange look on his face. "Enjoy it?" he said.

"Yup, it was absolutely delicious. I'm surprised you didn't want a dessert as well."

"I didn't need it. So, is there anything else you'd

like? Maybe an after-dessert liqueur? I mean, you've got to get your money's worth, right?"

"Excuse me?" What was he implying? "I don't know what you think you're saying about me, or why I'm on this date, but I'll have you know that I am not a gold digger. Not that you look like you have much gold to dig. In fact, *I* am paying for this meal." The words were out of my mouth before I knew what I was saying.

Please say no, please turn me down, please beg to pay!

"Wow, a modern woman. I like it." He grinned at me. "Thank you."

"Thank you ...?" I repeated. Oh, God, why, why, why, *why* did I let my pride get the better of me?

"It's not often that a woman offers to pay, and I don't want to disrespect you in any way by insisting that I pay." He smiled. "Don't worry, I'll make it up to you in the bedroom."

"Thanks," I said weakly. Shit, now I regretted having gotten an expensive meal and all those bottles of wine and the dessert. Ugh, and the side salad, and he'd gotten a beer as well, or was it two—or three? Oh no, what had I done? I barely had any money in my bank account and my credit card was close to maxed out. Trust me to put my mouth in it.

"So, Isabella, I have a secret for you."

"You have a secret for me?"

"Well, maybe I should say I have a surprise for you."

"Oh yeah, what's that?" *Please say you were just joking. Of course, you're not going to let me pay. You're a perfect gentleman, and you want to prove that to me, even though you've been an asshole for most of the evening.*

"You'll see when we get back to my place."

"What makes you think I'm going back to your place? Maybe you're coming to my place."

"Well, does that matter?" He grinned. "There are things I can do to you, Isabella," he said in a sultry voice. "The things I'm going to do to you, I'm going to make you cum all night."

I didn't know quite how to respond to that. "Umm, what did you just say?"

"I think you heard me." He winked. "I'm ready to get out of here aren't you?"

"Umm, kinda." Oh, shit what was I doing? This was my last opportunity to say no.

"Are you going to—" He paused. "Actually, I want it to be a secret surprise."

"You want what to be a secret surprise?"

"You know." He winked again.

I had no idea what he was talking about. I also knew that I wanted to take him down a couple of pegs. Yeah, I wanted to go back to his place, and yeah, I wanted to have some fun. But I didn't want him to think that he was getting one over on me. I paid for the dinner, and I'm giving it all up to him, and he's an asshole?

Oh no, no, no, no, no matter how horny I was, I wasn't going to let it go down like that.

I smiled to myself. Maybe I'd let him go down on me and get me off and then I just leave and leave him with blue balls. That would serve him right.

The waiter brought the bill over and left it on the table. Jack pushed it towards me. And I glared at him.

"Something wrong?" he said, softly looking at me with wide innocent eyes that showed me that he wasn't a good actor. He knew that I didn't want to pay for this bill, and yet he was still going to let me. Asshole.

"No, not at all." I opened the bill and groaned under my breath. $532.

Oh my gosh, the things I could have bought for $532. I was going to have to sell a lot of artwork to make up for this. I was going to have to do a really good job this weekend with Lucas and his family because I needed something in my financial situation to change, and to change soon. I pulled out my credit card and was about to place it into the receipt wallet when I realized that I didn't even know if I had $532

—plus tip, which Jack had not even offered to pay—on my card.

I slipped my card back into my wallet and pulled out my debit card. Oh, man, my heart sank at the thought of my hard-earned $532 going to pay for this meal. Yeah, it was delicious, and yeah, just ten minutes ago, I'd been thinking about how I thought I'd died and gone to Heaven. But now I realized I was alive and I felt very much like I was going to Hell. I slipped my debit card in and waited for the waiter to come back and pick it up.

"Thank you for the meal, Isabella. I really appreciate it."

"You're welcome, Jack," I said, and then, because I didn't know and I was genuinely curious, I said, "What's your last name, by the way, Jack?"

"Morrison," he said without even thinking about it. "I'm Jack Morrison." He stared into my eyes as if that should mean something to me, but it didn't.

"Any relation to Jim Morrison?" I said vaguely thinking, maybe he was a grandson.

"No," he shook his head. "No one in my family is musically inclined. Okay, and what's your last name, Isabella not-Rossellini?"

"You don't have to call me Isabella not-Rossellini. My last name is Wilder."

"Oh, like Jack Wilder?

"Yeah," I laughed. "I hadn't thought about that."

"Interesting. Isabella Wilder." My name rolled off his tongue as if it was poetry. "I like it. So does your last name describe how you are in life?"

"Um, what do you mean?"

"Are you a wild person? Are you wild in bed? Are you passionate? Ferocious?"

"Well ..." I gave him a sly smile and nodded as the waiter took the credit card wallet from the table. I lowered my eyelashes a couple of times and then smiled and licked my lips. "Actually, the name does mean something."

"Oh," he says staring at my lips. I had him just where I wanted him.

"Yeah. It means that I'm the wildest girl you've ever gone on a date with. In fact, I'm probably wilder than any girl or woman you've ever been with. So get ready, big boy, because I am about to rock your world."

He swallowed hard. "I like the sound of that."

I could tell that he was loving what I was saying. I could also tell that he wasn't quite sure if I was being serious or not. I twirled a strand of loose hair then ran my finger down between the valley of my breasts and bit on my lower lip as I stared him directly in the eye.

"I'm the sort of woman that likes to give as much

as I get. If you know what I mean." I slipped a finger into my mouth and sucked. "And if you give me what I'm looking for, I think tonight just might be the best night of your life." From the look on his face, I could tell he was buying what I was selling, hook, line, and sinker.

I almost started laughing.

Chapter Eight

꽃

My heart was thumping in my chest as we walked out of the restaurant. I wasn't even thinking about the astronomical bill I just paid. All I could think about was going back to Jack's house. I was going back to have a one-night stand. I have never had a one-night stand before in my life. I'd never hooked up with someone that I just met either, especially not on an online dating app, especially not when I hadn't even been the one to have the conversation with him in the first place, and especially seeing as I had no idea what Abby had been talking to him and saying.

But the way my body felt, I didn't care.

He took my hand as we stood outside the restaurant and waited for a cab. "I assume this is okay now," he said.

I didn't bother responding. What sort of idiot would I be to complain about him holding my hand when I was about to feel his fingers in much more intimate places? I blushed just thinking about it.

"You may hold my hand," I said softly, and he squeezed it. I felt him run a finger up my palm and then up to my wrist. He stared at my lips for a second, and I thought he was going to ask me if he could kiss me. But Jack Morrison was no gentleman.

He didn't ask for permission. He took what he wanted.

His lips pressed into mine, soft and succulent. He kissed me passionately, and I felt his hand in my hair, playing, pulling, teasing. I gasped as he slipped his tongue, warm and salty, into my mouth.

I ran my hand up to the back of his neck and tugged gently on his hair. He gasped as my other hand slipped down to grab his ass. He hadn't been expecting that. He thought I was just a shy little woman with a big mouth, but oh, I was oh so much more than that.

Just because I had never had a one-night stand didn't mean I wasn't sexual. It didn't mean that I didn't have fantasies, and it didn't mean that I didn't want to touch him. I wanted to touch and tease and feel every part of him. I just didn't care how he felt about it. I didn't care what was going to happen in the morning, because we both knew what was going to happen.

This wasn't going to lead to a relationship. He wasn't the man of my dreams. He was an asshole—but he was a hot asshole. He was an asshole who was going to make me come all night long. And then I would leave, grinning as he begged me to stay for more. That was my hope, anyway. I wanted to turn him on so badly that he would beg me to stay, and yet I would still just walk out his door, not caring.

He deserved it. I mean, he had left me with a $532 bill, which had come out to $600 once I put the tip. I'd only been going to leave a $50 tip, but he'd raised an eyebrow and I'd had to change the number. I mean, I knew people in the service industry didn't get paid much, but I didn't get paid much either. And it killed me when I had to write that $68 tip. I knew Jack thought I should pay even more than that, but I just couldn't go over $600. I just couldn't, not when my bank account was as meager as it was. But I couldn't think about that now.

Jack pulled away and broke off the kiss as a taxi stopped. "We need to get back to my place stat," he growled and pulled me into the backseat. "We're going to Madison," he told the cab driver. I missed the cross street because I was too focused on his right hand which was now on my leg, running up my thigh, slipping inside of my dress. Oh, shit. He wasn't going to do something here in the cab, was he?

The cab sped off, and I gasped as I felt Jack's fingers stroked between my thighs all the way up to my panties.

"Too bad," he murmured.

"What?" I trembled as he kissed the side of my face, and then I felt him whispering and blowing into my ear at the same time.

"I was hoping you had no panties on."

He winked at me before kissing me again. His hand caressed my breast, squeezing it through the flimsy material, and I shivered slightly. I reached down and grabbed the front of his pants. I could feel that he was hard, and from what I could tell, very thick.

A part of me wanted to unzip him right there, bob my head down, and make him come in the cab. I could give a good blow job, and I knew it. But he had to earn it. He wasn't my boyfriend. I wasn't just going to give him a good blow job in the back of a cab for nothing.

And then he pulled away from me, and I felt bereft. I wanted his touch. I wanted him near me. "We're nearly there," he said. "I don't want you ..."

"You don't want me to what?" I said, missing the end of the sentence.

"I don't want you to come in the cab." He winked. "I want to see your face properly the first time I make you come."

"The *first* time, huh?"

"Oh yeah," he grinned. "I'm a master orgasm giver. You'll come many times tonight."

"We shall see," I said. "I certainly hope so."

"Yeah? I have a feeling that you'll be doing more than hoping," he laughed.

"Hm. Okay, then." I squeezed his cock, and he groaned as I slipped my fingers down between his legs.

"What are you doing, Isabella?"

"What do you think?" I unzipped his pants and reached my hand in. He groaned again as my fingers came into contact with his warm flesh. I could feel it hardening between my fingers, and I licked my lips. I pretended like I was going to bob down between his legs, and his eyes narrowed as I instead rested my head on his shoulder.

"You're a tease, huh?" He shook his head and grabbed my hand and pulled it out of his pants. "I don't like teases."

"Well, who doesn't like a good tease?" I said.

"Me," he groaned. "You're something else, Isabella Wilder."

"Yeah? Well, I think you're something else as well, Jack."

"You can't remember my last name, can you?" he said with a grin.

"Of course I can," I said, flustered because he was right. I couldn't remember his last name.

"You can't remember my last name." He burst out laughing now, and it completely broke the intimate sexual tension that existed between us. I slipped my hand out of his jeans, and he zipped himself up quickly. Our eyes met in the back of the cab as it sped down Fifth Avenue.

The lights from the street shone in the car as I stared into his eyes. They were a beautiful golden green, a color I'd never seen before. I reminded myself that he was just a handsome face. Just an obnoxious, arrogant man I'd met at random.

Still, there was something about him. I felt a spark that I'd never felt with anyone else before in my life. But I shook it off. Maybe it was just the alcohol. We'd shared two and a half bottles of wine, after all.

"Tonight's going to be a good night, I think," he whispered.

"Yeah, we'll see," I said. "I mean, it's still the worst date ever, but perhaps it can get a little bit better."

"Perhaps." He leaned forward and kissed me again. His lips this time were in no way soft. They were demanding. His tongue slipped into my mouth, and I sucked on it. I ran my fingers into his hair, and I pulled on his hair as he reached his hand behind the nape of my neck, and he tugged my hair in return, moaning slightly as he bit down on my lower lip. And then he pulled away.

"Don't tease me anymore tonight, Isabella, because you know what happens to naughty girls, don't you?"

Chapter Nine

We stopped outside of Jack's building I looked around myself in awe as we walked into the foyer. A man at the front desk greeted us with a smile.

"Good evening, Mr. Morrison. How are you tonight?"

"Great, Charles. Thank you." He nodded. "My guest and I will just be going up."

"Okay. Have a good evening, sir."

The doorman gave me a polite nod. I smiled back as we walked back to some elevators. "This is nice," I said, taking in the Carrara marble floors. It was clearly expensive. Jack just smiled. When the elevator arrived, we stepped in and I noticed that he pressed the button for the top floor.

I looked at him in surprise. Did he really live here

or was this some sort of elaborate joke? But then, why would the doorman be in on his joke? Unless the doorman was his friend and this was his way of trying to impress women. Yeah, maybe that was it. It had to be it.

Right?

"What are you thinking about?" Jack studied my face as I stood there playing with my fingers. I was starting to feel nervous. I was in over my head. What had seemed like a great idea in the restaurant suddenly seemed foolish and wanton. "Come here," he said.

As if I were hypnotized, I took a couple of steps towards him. He grabbed me by the waist and pulled me towards him. I could feel his hardness against my stomach as he leaned down and kissed my forehead and then my cheeks and then finally my lips. "Not having second thoughts, are you?"

"Maybe." I looked up at him through lowered lashes. My heart was racing. I could feel it all over my body.

"If you want to leave, you can. I'm not going to hold you here against your will."

"Did I say that you were?"

"Ah, Ms. Combative Isabella is back."

"I'm not combative."

"Yeah. You are, just a little bit." He shrugged. "I don't mind. I kind of like it."

"You kind of like it?"

"I think it means good things for the bedroom."

"Oh?"

"Yeah. I can see you being crazy in bed. Can see you scratching my back, like a cat." He groaned. "I'm not going to say anything else. I don't want to get myself too turned on."

"Oh, are you turned on?"

"You can feel it. You know that I am. What about you? Are you turned on?"

"Maybe," I said with a smile.

In response, his hand slipped down to my ass and gave it a firm squeeze. I moaned slightly as I pressed my body into his. I leaned up and kissed him on the lips. This time, it was my turn to chew on his lower lip and tug a little bit. I wanted this. Maybe a small part of me was nervous, but most of me was horny and ready, and I wanted him badly.

He moaned as he lifted the back of my dress up his hands slipping inside my lace panties. I gasped as his fingers caressed my naked ass.

"So ...?" he whispered.

"So," I breathed, wondering what he was going to do next. I didn't have to wait long because then I felt him moving his hand toward the front, slipping it down between my legs and touching my wetness. His fingers gently rubbed my clit and he groaned as he felt how wet I was already.

"Oh, shit. You want me so badly, don't you?"

"Maybe, maybe not."

"Maybe not nothing," he groaned and kissed me hard. I moaned against his lips as his fingers teased me. This was fucking hot. I'd never made out in an elevator before, and I'd certainly never had someone play with me in an elevator, but there was a first time for everything, and I liked it.

He lifted me up, and instinctively, I wrapped my legs around his waist. He leaned back into the back wall of the elevator, grunting as I wrapped my hands around his neck, and pulled his face into mine so that I could kiss him harder. "Oh, fuck. I would fuck you right now if I could," he said.

"Oh, yeah?" I mumbled against his lips, wishing that he would. I groaned when I heard the ding of the elevator, and he let me slip back to the floor.

"We're nearly at my apartment. I guess we'll have to do it next time."

"Yeah, next time," I said, even though we both knew there was not going to be a next time.

He grabbed my hand and pulled me out of the elevator. I gasped as we walked into a huge apartment with wall-to-ceiling windows. I stared all around me.

I could see the New York skyline from a distance. "Oh my gosh, is that the Chrysler building?" I walked over to the window. He laughed as he came up behind me.

"Yep."

"Wow, this view ... I don't know what to say."

"Surprise."

"Is this the penthouse?"

"Yep," he nodded.

"But anyone can get here. They just have to press the button. There's not even a—"

"No one else can get here." He shook his head. "That's my private elevator."

"But it goes to all floors."

"Because I have access to every floor," he explained. "No one has access to this floor except for me."

"Oh, wow." I stared at him through narrowed eyes. So he was rich. Really rich. "And you let me pay for dinner?" I poked him in the arm. "Really?"

"What? You offered."

"But you're rich, I'm not."

"So why did you offer if you didn't want to pay?"

"Because you were calling me a gold digger!"

"Does it make a difference that I make more money than you?" He looked into my eyes. "Are you saying that you *are* a gold digger?"

"No, but you could at least have offered to pay the tip."

"I could have." He grinned. "But I didn't."

"You're an asshole, you know that, right?"

"I think we already figured that one out," he said, "or at least you did."

"Whatever." I shook my head.

"Why? What do you want to do to me? Am I a bad boy?"

"You're a really bad boy."

"Are you going to cook me some dessert now?"

"What? What are you talking about?"

"The kitchen is that way." He grabbed my hand and pulled me to the side of the apartment where we came to a large, open-plan kitchen with a huge white island in the middle.

"Wow. This is beautiful."

"Everything you need is in the cupboards," he said, "You can find it."

I blinked at him. "Find what?"

"Aren't you going to make me a dessert?"

"Uh, why would I be making you dessert?"

"Isn't that what you wanted?" He looked at me through narrowed eyes.

"What are you talking about?"

"I thought you said you love to come back to a

guy's place and make them dessert before the *real* dessert."

"Um, okay ..."

Obviously, this was some bullshit that Abby had come up with. Maybe I'd take the death penalty twice because she had really talked a lot of nonsense.

Jack and I stared at each other for a moment. "So ... I guess you're not going to make me dessert," he observed.

"I'm not enough?" I said softly as I walked over to him.

He gazed at me through narrowed eyes. "Maybe. Why? What have you got to show me?"

"Oh, I have everything to show you, big boy." And then I did a move that I'd only seen in movies. I pulled up my dress and let it drop on the floor so that I was just standing there in my bra, panties, and heels. His jaw dropped and he whistled as he looked over my body.

"Okay. I have to admit, I didn't see that one coming." He swallowed hard. "You are so fucking hot, but I guess you already knew that."

I smiled. "Now it's your turn."

"My turn?" He grinned. "What do you want me to take off first?"

"Hmm, let me think," I said, as I walked over to him

and press my finger on his lips. I grabbed him by the collar of his shirt and pull him down to kiss me. I kissed him hard and then reached down and squeezed his cock. He groaned as my fingers left it. "Come with me."

I led him to his massive living room and pushed him down on the couch. "You know something I've always wanted to do?"

"No." He shook his head. "What?"

"Do you have any music?"

"Music?" He looked confused.

"Like a stereo, an iPad, Spotify. Something I can play some music on?"

"Yeah. Why?"

"You'll see," I said. "Where do I access it?"

"Hey, Google," he said, and I laughed.

"Fine. Okay. And do you have any mood lighting in this fancy penthouse of yours?"

"Of course," he said. He pressed something on the wall and all the lights in the apartment went out. It wasn't dark, though. Because of the city lights, we were surrounded by lights from every other building in New York City.

"This is good."

"What are you going to do?"

"You'll see," I laughed. And then I thought for a minute. "Hey, Google, play Drake."

"Playing Drake," Google responded.

Before I could count to ten, Drake's latest hit was playing. I started swaying my body back and forth to the beat of the music, almost but not quite touching Jack. He reached up to grab my waist and I pushed his hands away. "No, no touching. They don't allow touching here."

"They don't allow touching, where?" He looked confused and looked around. "This is my apartment."

"Shh," I said, putting my finger against his mouth. "No talking. Izzy doesn't like it when you talk." I leaned closer and brushed my breasts back and forth against his nose and lips.

"Izzy, huh?" He grinned. "Well, where are we, Izzy?"

"We're at the strip club. The most exclusive strip club on the Upper West Side. No," I changed my mind, "actually, the Upper East Side."

"Oh, I see. And you're a stripper?"

"I'm an exotic dancer. The best you've ever seen."

"Well, you're the best something I've ever seen." He nodded, his eyes lighting up, and I laughed. He was an asshole, but I was glad he was going along with it.

This was actually a fantasy of mine. I don't know why, but I'd always wanted to be a stripper for one night at an exclusive strip club and seduce the hottest man there and have him begging for more. And this was real life. I was never going to go to a strip club to be a private dancer. And I certainly wasn't going to fuck some stranger in a strip club, but hey, I could live out my fantasy here and no one would judge.

Jack wouldn't judge me. He didn't know me. And even if he did, I didn't care because tonight was just about me and him fucking our brains out and having the time of our lives and living out my fantasy. I've known as soon as we'd walked in and I'd seen his amazing penthouse. This felt like something out of a fucking amazing movie. More amazing than a movie, but I wasn't going to think about it too hard.

"So, Izzy, can I—?"

"Shh," I ordered. I put on a Russian accent. "Izzy doesn't like it when you interrupt." He laughed. I think he realized that I didn't really know what I was doing, I was just having fun.

"Well, Izzy," he said, with a French accent, "please let me know how much the dance will cost."

"You'll see afterwards. It will be worth all the money you've got."

"All the money I've got, huh? Well, then, that's going to be one really good dance."

"It's going to be the best dance of your life." And then I straddled him. I moved my hips back and forth and closed my eyes as I sang along to the music. I could feel him growing harder and harder beneath me. And I loved it. I started flicking my hair back and forth and running it across his face.

I felt his hands on my waist and opened my eyes. "Naughty boy. Customers cannot touch."

"What if I throw in another hundred?" he said, his eyes veiled.

"Hmm, I don't know."

"Fuck, Izzy. You're fucking sexy as hell."

"Am I?" I stood up and turned around, moving my hips back and forth so that my butt was in his face, gyrating, but not touching anything. He groaned and I laughed as I turned my head around to look at him.

And then he slapped me on the ass. I should've stopped him, but it felt dirty. It felt sexy. And then he slapped me again, not hard, just teasing. I groaned as I felt his fingers slip between my legs and he rubbed me through my panties. "Naughty boy," I turned around and dropped onto my knees, looking up at him between his legs.

"I am a naughty boy, aren't I, Izzy? Are you going to punish me?" he said, looking down at me.

I nodded my head without speaking. And I reached up and I grabbed his belt and pulled it out of his pants. I quickly unbuckled his pants and unzipped him and started pulling them down. I groaned out loud as I saw his hard cock through his tight black boxers. I licked my lips and he grinned.

He started undoing his shirt and I let him. If he wanted to help me, who was I to say no? He threw his shirt onto the ground and then I quickly undid his shoes. He slipped them off and then I pulled his pants off.

Now he was sitting in only his boxers. His chest was magnificent. He was strong and muscular and tan. I leaned forward and kissed him in the navel and then licked my tongue across his washboard abs. I felt his hands in my hair and moaned as he tugged. I pushed him back and then kissed my way down his stomach towards his cock. I placed my mouth on his cock through the material and he groaned as I sucked the tip. I then pulled his boxers off and his cock sprang free. He was ginormous, probably the biggest guy I'd ever seen in person. I licked my lips again and he laughed.

"Like what you see?"

"Maybe." I *loved* what I saw. I got up straddled him again, allowing the length of his cock to sit between my legs so that as I rubbed back and forth, I could feel the tip of him rubbing against my clit.

"Oh, shit," he said, grabbing my hips.

"Oh, yeah."

He undid my bra. I let him unclasp it and it fell to the ground. He moaned as I reached and grabbed his head and pulled it down into my breasts and rubbed my nipples across his face then took one in his mouth. I moaned as he tugged and teased me. This was so fucking hot. I could feel my panties were drenched as I felt his hardness between my legs. His fingers ran down my back up and down, up and down lightly tracing the curve of my spine as I increased my tempo on top of him.

Without warning, I jumped up and turned around so that I was straddling him with my back against his chest. I grabbed his hands and placed them on my breast so that his fingers were teasing both of my nipples. I moaned as he pulled and tugged on them and kissed my neck. I wasn't going to last much longer, and I didn't think he would last much longer, either. I stood up and pulled my panties off, loving the look in his eyes as I stood there naked in front of him. And then I sat down on his lap and I pulled my legs up so that my calves were hanging over his shoulders on either side.

And then I started dancing. Moving my hips back and forth so that my pussy was mere inches from his lips, know that he could smell my wetness. He groaned for a few seconds. And then before I knew what was happening, his tongue was licking my clit and he was holding me on his lap. His mouth was buried into my pussy and I started moaning as he sucked on my clit and his tongue entered me. This wasn't exactly how I planned it to go, but I wasn't going to complain. The feel of his warm tongue licking and teasing me was pure joy. It was fucking amazing. So amazing that I was on the verge of an orgasm within a minute. He obviously knew what was happening because he then pulled away and shook his head laughing.

"Sorry, I forgot. I'm not meant to touch, Ms. Izzy."

I moaned as I moved my leg and sat back down on top of him, placing his cock between my legs. And I started rubbing back and forth on him, my breasts bouncing against his chest as he held my hips. I leaned forward and I kissed him. I could feel the tip of him close to my entrance. It was too fast, too soon, but I had no desire to stop it.

"Fuck." Jack pulled me off him and jumped up. "Come." He grabbed my hand and he pulled me towards his bedroom. "I don't have any protection out here."

I followed him to his bedroom. He had a king-size bed and a view that was unlike anything I'd ever seen before. He grinned as he came up behind me and ran his fingers down my spine and down the crack of my ass.

"I take back what he said," he said softly in my ear.

"Oh, what was that?" My entire body was ready to be taken by this gorgeous hunk of a man.

"This isn't the worst date ever," he growled as he pulled me towards him. "This is the best fucking date I've ever been on in my life."

And then he pulled me down onto the bed with him.

For once, I agreed with him. This was the best fucking date ever.

Chapter Ten

Jack kissed me on the lips and ran his fingers down the side of my body. I trembled as he stared down at me.

"You're nothing like I thought you would be, you know?" he said, as he kissed me once more.

"Oh, yeah?" I said, running my hands down the side of his muscular body, shivering at the warmth. How was it that he was so perfect? How was it that he had a body that looked like it was sculpted by one of the great sculptors? He was even better than Michaelangelo's *David*.

"You're fucking sexier than I ever thought you would be." He kissed the side of my neck. "I want you to touch yourself," he whispered softly in my ear.

My eyes flew to his. "What?"

"Touch yourself for me. We played out your fantasy. Now play out mine."

He took my hand and placed it between my legs. That obviously wasn't an unfamiliar place to me, but it was an unfamiliar feeling touching myself in front of someone. I've never done that before, but I had fantasized about what it would be like. I closed my eyes. I was horny, and I could feel myself becoming hornier as I played with myself. I didn't feel ashamed or nervous, and when I heard him gasping, my eyes flew open. He reached down and grabbed my hand, moving my fingers up and down on my own clit.

"Where the fuck is your condom?" I said, all thoughts of leaving him with blue balls gone. I needed to get fucked by this man. I needed to feel him inside of me. Nothing would feel better.

"Someone's a little anxious, aren't they?" he chuckled as he reached over to his side table and opened the drawer. He pulled out a bunch of condoms, ripped one open, and slid it down on his hard cock. "So, Izzy, what position would you like to start with?"

"Shut up." I pulled him down on top of me, wrapping my legs around his waist. He kissed my lips, and I ran my fingers through his hair, pulling hard and moaning as his tongue entered my mouth.

We kissed and rolled around on the bed, and then

I felt the tip of his cock at my entrance. I moaned as he slid into me slowly. It hurt slightly, and I gasped. He paused and pulled out, shock in his eyes.

"Are you a virgin?" he asked.

"No," I laughed, shaking my head. "I told you it's been a while."

He stared at me for a few seconds, and I could tell he was trying to figure out whether or not I was telling him the truth.

"Look, it's been over a year. I guess I'm a born-again virgin. And it's not going to hurt for long. Please." I reached up and pulled him down, and he groaned as I bit his lip and ran my fingers down the back of his ass. I felt the tip of his cock at my opening again, and he reached down and rubbed my clit. He could feel how wet I was. I moaned as I spread my legs for him, and he grunted as he pushed inside me a little bit at a time, until he was fully inside of me, stretching me out, and it felt like heaven.

"Oh, my God, you feel so good," I gasped. Then he started thrusting, and my breasts bounced against his chest as he hit all the right spots.

"Oh, yes. Please, please, please! Jack, fuck me harder. Fuck me harder!" I screamed. That seemed to turn him on even more. Pulling my legs over his shoulders, he fucked me deep and hard, like I'd never been fucked before in my life. His eyes stared down into mine, and when I went to close them, he shook his head.

"I want to see your face. I want to see your eyes as I make you come," he whispered then leaned down and sucked on my nipple. Then he reached down and started playing with my clit as he fucked me, and that was all it took. I screamed as he pounded into me, his balls slapping against my underside, and then I came fast and hard, my body shimmying and shaking underneath him. He stilled for a few seconds and then slammed into me one, two, three times, and I felt his body shuddering as he came as well.

He collapsed on top of me, kissing me on the side of my face before slipping out of me.

He pulled the condom off of his still hard cock and placed it on the side of the bed. I laughed, reaching over to stroke the side of his face. I'd never expected to be here naked, fucking some strange guy on a first date, but it felt good. It felt amazing.

"What are you thinking about, Izzy?" he panted.

"I don't know," I said. "What are you thinking about, Jack?"

"I'm thinking about how I'd like to take you in the kitchen and fuck you over the kitchen counter." He laughed. "Give me ten minutes."

"Oh, really?" I said. "Do you really think I'm going to allow you to do that?"

"I bet I could talk you into it." He reached over and sucked my nipple. "This is fucking hot. You know that, right?"

"I know that. I'm hot and you're not," I laughed.

He snorted with amusement. "You don't think I'm hot?"

"Okay, maybe a little bit."

"Yeah, that's what I thought. You couldn't find anyone hotter than me, I'm sure."

"Excuse me?" I blinked at him. "Are you joking? You don't think I could find anyone hotter than you?"

"Maybe. Maybe not." He shook his head. "So now that you're here, what do you think you want?"

"What do you mean what do I think I want?"

"I mean, now that you're here in my penthouse, you've got me to fuck you, what else do you want?"

"What do you mean what else do I want?"

"You've obviously been playing games with me this entire night, Isabella, and you probably thought by sleeping with me, you were going to hook me or something? But the charade is over."

"The what?" I blinked at him. What the hell was he talking about?

"I said, the charade is over."

"What charade?"

"You don't know who I am?" He looked at me with an expression that I couldn't quite read.

I just shook my head. "Ah, you're Jack Morrison?"

"Yeah, I'm *the* Jack Morrison."

"Okay ...?"

"And now you've got me."

"Well, for one night."

"What's your game plan?"

"What do you mean, what's my game plan?"

"Are you going to try and take photos of us? Are you going to sell it to the tabloids? Are you—"

"I don't even know what you're talking about." I sighed. "What is your problem?"

"I think you know," he said, as he reached down and ran his fingers along the valley of my breasts. "All of a sudden, you pop up on a dating app, beg me for a date on Thursday night, tell me how much you love football, tell me how much you want to fuck me on my kitchen counter because you haven't had sex in a while, tell me that you want to make dessert for me. And then we meet, and you're playing these games. You pretend you don't know who I am, you pretend you don't know much about football. All of a sudden, you forget every single conversation we've had. And then just because you decide to come back and fuck me, none of it adds up. So I want to know what your endgame is."

"I cannot believe I wasted my money on you or fucked you." I jumped up out of the bed and glared at him. "You know what? This *was* the worst date ever. You sucked. You absolutely sucked. You know what? I got mine, and I'm gone." I grabbed the sheet and pulled it off of the bed to cover myself, but it wouldn't come. He started laughing, as I hobbled into the living room so that I could grab my clothes.

"Where are you going now, Izzy?"

"I'm leaving. It's done. This date is over."

"What? Here we go again." I could hear the skepticism in his voice. "Really?"

"Really, what? You're an asshole."

"I'm an asshole?"

"Yeah, you are."

"Really?" He stared at me, glaring at me in the living room. "I'm the asshole."

"Yeah, you are."

I grabbed my bra and panties and then looked around the floor for my dress and picked it up. He grabbed my arm and pulled me to him. I could see his eyes searching my face as if he didn't quite understand what was going on. I reached up and touched his chest because I couldn't stop myself. Then, I leaned up and kissed him on the lips.

"You know what, Jack, it's been real, it's been fun, but it hasn't been real fun. Bye." I pushed him away.

I quickly pulled on my dress, stuffed my bra and panties into my bag, and hurried to the door where we'd come through the elevator. I looked around for a button, but I couldn't find it. I was standing there, pissed off, annoyed, and now embarrassed because I didn't know how to get out.

I turned and looked at him. "Can you get the elevator for me, please?"

He studied me for a few seconds and shrugged. "If you really want to leave."

"I do. I think this date is done." I averted my eyes from his. I was fuming. Literally fuming. I was pissed with him, I was pissed with myself, and I was pissed with Abby. I knew this had been a bad idea from the very beginning and of course, I'd been right.

He walked over and pushed a button I hadn't seen. Ten seconds later, there was a beep. I walked into the elevator and glared at him. He stared back, his expression inscrutable. I didn't know what he was thinking, and I didn't care. I just wanted to go home, scream at Abby, and forget that this date ever happened.

Chapter Eleven

※

Bank Account Balance: $700
Days Since My Last Date: hours
Current Weight: Most probably 180

QUOTE OF THE DAY: "The greater the obstacle, the more glory in overcoming it." -Moliere

I WALKED into the apartment still angry as hell. It was four o'clock in the morning. I knew everyone was asleep, but I didn't care. I went straight to Abby's room and I didn't even knock on the door. Instead, I opened it and turned on the lights. She sat up, groggy and confused.

"What's going on?"

"I am pissed as hell at you, Abby!" I said, raising my voice and slamming her door behind me. I felt bad for Emma and Chloe. I didn't want to wake them up, but at this point, I didn't care.

"Isabella, why are you mad at me? What have I done?"

"Dude, what the hell did you say to this guy?"

"To what guy?" She yawned. "Do we have to have this conversation now? I was in the middle of a really great sleep. I was actually dreaming that Henry Cavill was taking me on a date, and—"

"I do not care what Henry Cavill was doing. That dude, Jack Morrison, was an asshole. The biggest asshole I've ever met in my life. And—"

"Oh yeah, the date. I forgot it was last night." She looked nervous. "So it wasn't good?"

"No, it was absolutely awful!"

"And yet you're getting back now?" She looked at the Apple watch on her wrist. "It's nearly time to wake up, and you're just now getting back? But it was a bad date? I don't understand."

"I knew as soon as I met him that he was a jerk. You know he made a comment to me about Pamela Anderson?"

"Oh?" She blinked sleepily. "Really?

"Yeah. He was like, "Oh, why aren't you blonde? Or some bullshit like that."

"Oh, really?" She looked away. "And what else? I mean, you obviously stayed."

"Yeah, I stayed and—" I sat down on the bed. "I actually hooked up with him."

That woke her up. "You hooked up with him?" she gasped as she sat up. "As in you made out with him, or more?"

"Girl, I am a born-again virgin no longer."

"Oh my gosh, you slut. You slept with him?"

"Do not call me a slut, Abby. We are not there again yet."

"Oops, sorry. I'm just a little bit confused. How'd you go from hating him, to sleeping with him, to now hating him again?"

"Because he's an asshole. Everything he says is mean and arrogant and oh, I'm just so pissed off! I knew this was a bad idea."

"Was the sex bad?"

"No, the sex was amazing, like totally amazing! Like toes curling, orgasmic, wonderful." I sighed not even knowing what to say. I leaned back on her bed. "Oh, Abby. Why?"

"I don't understand. So the sex was good, but then it went bad?"

"Yeah. Then it went bad. He really thinks he's all that."

"Oh no, really?"

"Yeah. He was going on like I was some sort of gold digger. Like he was some sort of famous hotshot, just because he lives in a penthouse. And then he was acting like I was playing a game of like, not knowing who he was. Like, who the hell is Jack Morrison?"

"Jack Morrison." Her eyes widened. "Oh ... I thought he looked familiar."

"So you know who he is?"

"No." She shook her head quickly. "Not at all."

"Well, yeah, he was acting like he was some big deal, but he's not a famous actor because I'd never seen him in any movies. He is not a famous director because I've never heard his name before in my life. I thought maybe he's related to Jim Morrison, but that was obviously a no. Maybe he's big on Wall Street. Who knows? And then he was going on about football. Like I care about football, whatever."

"Oh, he mentioned football?" She toyed with her hair.

"Yeah. Why?"

"Oh, just interesting. And what did you say when he mentioned football?"

"He was like, "Oh, do you love football?" And I was like, "Yeah, whatever. I love it." And then he asked me who my favorite team was. And I said the New York Knicks."

"The New York Knicks?" She laughed. "You know that's a basketball team, right?"

"Oh shit. I had a feeling it sounded familiar, but not that familiar." I shrugged. "Whatever, we soon changed the subject."

"Oh, I'm so sorry that you didn't have a good time." She paused. "Well, that you had a good time in the bedroom, but not really." She shook her head. "I'm still half asleep, so I'm not really sure how you're feeling about the date. But whatever I did that was bad, I'm sorry. Can I please get a little bit more sleep? I have to wake up early."

"Fine." I jumped up, "But I'm letting you know that if you've ever tried to set me up on a date again, or have any sort of ideas with regards to dating, please leave me out of it. I'm not interested. Okay?"

"Okay." She nodded, "Fine. Night, night, Isabella."

"Night, Abby." I stomped out of her room down the hallway to mine and sat on the edge of my bed thinking. He had been cute, and he'd been amazing in bed. And I guess I'd had no plans on seeing him again anyway. So I didn't have to stress it too much. But he'd been such a jerk. I wish I'd been able to take him down a couple of notches. Maybe I should have withheld sex. Ugh, or maybe I should have told him that the sex was bad. Oh, well it was too late now. There was nothing that I could do about it. I was never going to see him again.

I also had to be up early. I was meeting my best friend, Lucas, for a late breakfast and then we were going to go to Connecticut. But he had to tell me about his family first. I really didn't want to go to Connecticut, but Lucas had made me an offer that I couldn't refuse. I needed to shower and sleep and put this all behind me because the day was about to start and I had to be on top of my game. Lucas had so much information to give me for the weekend, and if I got it wrong, then it was going to screw both of us.

And the last thing I needed was something else going wrong in my life.

Chapter Twelve

❧

Bank Account Balance: Too little to care
Days Since My Last Date: Don't want to think about it
Current Weight: 700 lbs

QUOTE OF THE DAY: "Jack Morrison is the absolute worst date ever in the history of the world." - Isabella

"OH, ISABELLA DARLING, THERE YOU ARE." Lucas hurried up to me, a cup of coffee in his hand, and I gave him a quick hug.

"Hey, Lucas. Sorry, I'm running late," I yawned. "Late night."

"No worries, doll." He grinned and gave me the

coffee. "I had a feeling that you might be a little bit late."

"Oh, don't say that. I hate to disappoint you. I don't want to be the sort of person that's known for being late."

"No, it's not because you're always late. Don't worry."

"Then how did you know I was going to be late today?"

"Because I texted you three times and you didn't respond."

"Oh!" My hand flew to my mouth. "I'm so sorry. I didn't even check my phone. It's just been a crazy morning."

"Yeah, so are you going to tell me about it or not?"

I laughed and shook my head. "I don't think we have time. We need to get ready for this weekend, right?"

"Yeah, we do." He made a face and grimaced. "I really hope we can pull this off."

"You *do* think we can, right?" The doubt in his expression worried me. If he didn't think we could, we definitely couldn't.

"Well, I think so." He shrugged. "I mean, I don't think that my grandparents or my parents are going to want to spend too much time with us, and I think it's very unlikely that anyone's going to be questioning us about much. So as long as we know the basics, we should be good."

"Okay. Well, I mean, I do know the basics. We've been best friends for years."

"Yeah, but we've got to convince people that we're in love, not just best friends." He made a face. "And that's going to be hard for me."

"Well, thanks, Lucas," I gave him a playful punch on the shoulder. "It's going to be kind of hard for me too."

"Don't lie, Isabella." He shook his head. "I know you had a crush on me when you first met me."

"That is not true."

"Ah, yes, it is. You've told me before."

"I thought you were cute. I did not have a crush on you."

"Yeah, same difference."

"It's not the same difference. And anyway, as soon as I realized you were gay, I was just like, whatever."

"Uh huh." He started laughing. "But let's remember, no one in my family knows, and they *cannot* know, or I will not get this inheritance."

"So, tell me exactly what your parents know." I sighed, "Are you sure you want to go ahead with this lie?"

He nodded. "Yeah, I do. I need this money. I really want to open this coffee shop, and I'm not going to get the money for it unless I show that I'm in a meaningful relationship that looks like it's going to lead to marriage and kids. My grandparents are old-fashioned like that." He rolled his eyes.

"So, okay, we're going to go to Greenwich, right?"

"Yep. Greenwich, Connecticut, the land of old money."

"And we're going to spend time with your entire family?"

"Yep. It's a huge family reunion." He sighed. "Which I absolutely hate. I cannot stand my family."

"Oh, don't say that, Lucas."

"What? I mean, it's true. My cousin's a dick, my parents are full of it, and my grandparents are bigots."

"Your grandparents aren't bigots. You don't know that, anyway."

"Um, I'm pretty sure that they would not be happy with the fact that I'm a homosexual. So what would you call that?"

"It's 2021, who's not cool with that?"

"I mean, I'm sure they'd say it was fine for *other* people's kids and grandkids, but not for me." He waved one hand dramatically. "How am I going to carry on the family name and who am I going to leave my money to when I die? These are all things that my grandparents think about. These are all things that wealthy families think about." He sighed. "Completely ridiculous, but it is what it is."

"I'm sorry. That's horrible. It sucks that you have to hide who you are."

"I mean, I don't really see them that much. And hey, I don't mind hiding who I am to family members that I rarely see if it means inheriting millions of dollars," he shrugged. "Does that make me sound cold?"

"Kinda does," I admitted. "But hey. My stomach growled. "So are we going to get breakfast?"

"Yeah, we can get breakfast. What do you want to get? Like quinoa bowls or something?"

"What?"

"I mean, you're on your low carb diet, right? So I don't want to make you get pancakes or French toast or—"

"Ugh, I want pancakes and French toast so badly. You don't even know. Come on, let's get them."

"But, Isabella, you told me not to let you eat badly."

"Ah, fuck it. I already ate bad yesterday. I had steak and roasted potatoes and Yorkshire pudding and—"

"Oooh, that sounds divine. But where did you have that? Because I know you bitches weren't cooking that at home."

"No ... I kind of went on a date."

"Ooh, a date! With who, you naughty girl? Tell me more."

"Trust me, there's not much to tell. It wasn't that good. The guy was an asshole."

"Umm, that good, huh?"

"That good. What about you? Have you been dating anyone recently?"

"No, I've been trying to get my business plan together," he sighed. "Which sucks because I really, really need a boyfriend, but it can wait until after I have my business."

"Okay, so what's the plan for this weekend?"

"Okay, so we're going to go this evening. I figured we'll take the train."

"Okay."

"And there will be a car waiting at the train station to take us to my grandparent's house."

"Okay, nice. And are we staying in the same room?"

"Unlikely." He shook his head. "My grandparents are old-fashioned, remember? They do not allow boyfriends and girlfriends to sleep in the same bedroom. They don't even allow engaged couples to sleep in the same bedroom. You have to be married to sleep in the same bedroom." He rolled his eyes. "Like come on, is this the 1800s?"

"Their house, their rules. I guess you have to respect them, right?"

"Uh huh. So our goal is really just to impress on them that we're very much in love and that we're planning on getting married soon."

"Okay."

"And that you want to have loads and loads of kids."

"Okay, well that sounds easy enough."

"Yeah, and then I will ask my granddad to give me part of my inheritance early so I can start my business."

"How much is a part?"

"I figure a couple of million."

"A couple of *million*? You think your granddad's going to give you a couple of million dollars to open a puppy cafe?"

"Well, I'm not going to tell him it's a puppy cafe. It's a coffee shop and it will also focus on art, which is where you come along."

"Yeah, I guess so. So you're going to tell him that part of the space is going to be used for me to host my art classes and sell my art as well?"

"Yep. Puppies, coffee, and art. What more could you want?"

"So you *are* going to tell him about the puppies?"

"I mean, I don't know. I mentioned the cat cafe I

went to once, and they didn't seem impressed. If I feel like they're warming to the idea, I might throw in a couple of puppies because my grandmother loves dogs. But if I don't think they're going to love the idea, then I won't."

"Did you even find out if it's going to be okay for there to be puppies at the coffee shop? Isn't that like a health code violation or something?"

"I don't know." He shrugged. "I'll worry about that later. I mean, a cool coffee shop with lots of art sounds pretty cool and Bohemian even without the puppies, right?"

"Yeah, it does. It sounds really cool. Oh my gosh, it would be absolutely amazing, Lucas. I wouldn't have to work and work and work at all these different community colleges, teaching these classes for a couple hundred dollars a week. It would just be so cool if I could just be based out of your coffee shop. I really wish I had a rich family so I could contribute too."

"Girl, don't worry about it. It's not your fault that you come from middle-class people," he said. "Oh my gosh, I sound like a total snob, don't I? Don't blame me, blame it on my upbringing. My parents are snobs. I mean, I'm lucky that I came out as cool as I did, having the parents and grandparents that I did."

"Oh my God, Lucas, you're so crazy."

"What? You know you love me."

"I do."

"So have you been back to Columbia recently?"

"No," I shook my head. "You?"

"Yeah. I like to go and hang out on campus, feel like I'm a young stud again."

"You're such a goof."

"What? Those were the best days of my life. I loved going to university, and if I cared enough, I would try and get into grad school. But I don't."

"Lucas, you're crazy."

"I know. You just told me that. So did you get a new wardrobe?" He looked me up and down.

"What do you mean, did I get a new wardrobe? No, I didn't get a new wardrobe."

"Oh, well, then we need to go shopping because this is not going to impress my parents."

"Umm, I don't have money to buy any new clothes," I pointed out.

"What? You don't have a credit card?"

"I do have a credit card but it's almost maxed out."

"Oh my. We'll use my credit card."

"No, Lucas, we can't use your credit card. That's just not cool. It's—"

"Look, you're doing this to help me, and I need

you to have some new clothes. And we can return them if it doesn't work out."

"Are you sure?"

"Yeah, I'm sure. You need to look like a sexy biatch, babe."

"Umm, okay. You got to let me know just how flirtatious we're meant to be in front of your parents and family. Kissing? Hugging? Holding hands?"

He shuddered, "Oh, I don't know if I can kiss you. I think that would give it away."

"Well, thank you."

"What can I say? I like the D."

"Eww, Lucas, really?"

"I know, I know, too much information."

"Yeah, way too much information. Please don't.

"What? What? You've been to gay clubs with me, you know what happens."

"I do, and I don't want to think about it. I don't want to think about anyone's sex life, but my own."

"Totally understood," he nodded. "So, breakfast, shopping, twelve o'clock train? Would that work for you?"

"Yep. That works for me."

"Awesome. This is going to be so fan-TAH-stic," he sang.

"Lucas?"

"Yes, Isabelly?"

"You know, you're not going to be able to sing like that once we get to your parents' house?"

"Oh, trust me." He straightened his shoulders and put on a gruff voice. "I can be as masculine as every other straight dude out there." He nodded, "I just model myself after my cousin."

"One particular cousin or all of them?"

"One particular cousin," he nodded. "He's as alpha and as heterosexual as they come. Trust me, if I want to play a straight man, I just do exactly what he does."

"Okay, then. Well, hopefully, it goes well."

"It will," he said, "because you're gorgeous, honey. And when my family sees you, they are going to love you, and they are going to be throwing money at us to open this business. Hey, I just thought of something."

"What?"

"Can you bring some of your watercolor papers and maybe some of your artwork?"

"I can. Why?"

"Because I think it'd be really cool if you did some watercolors at my grandparents' house and show everyone how talented you are."

"Oh, Lucas, you're so sweet. That's such a nice thing for you to say."

"I mean, you *are* really talented, so I mean it, but I think if you also paint something for my grandmother, she'll be impressed and she'll love it. Trust me, they have millions of dollars, and they have Picassos and Monets, shit, I even think that they have a Frida Kahlo in there, but if she gets something painted by the artist at her house, she'll love it. Trust me, I know my Nana. She loves me."

"She loves you yet she wouldn't like it if you were gay?" I said gently.

He sighed and shook his head. "I don't know. It's not really something I want to find out. Not until I have my money. After I have my money and I have the coffee shop, then maybe I'll tell them." He looked down at the ground for a few seconds. I could tell that he wasn't as upbeat and happy about the situation as he was pretending to be.

I rubbed his shoulder then took his hand. "Hey, Lucas?"

"Yeah?" he looked up at me, his blue eyes shining.

"I'm here for you, you know. If you do want to tell them or you don't. Whatever you need, I'm here for you."

"Thanks, Isabella," he said softly. "Everyone should have a friend like you."

"I know," I said with a smile. "That's why breakfast is on you. I'm broke right now."

"Of course, use me for my money."

I giggled. "Lucas, you don't have much money

either, remember? That's why we're going to your grandparent's house this weekend and pretending we're a couple."

He started laughing as well. "So true. But hey, if anyone can fake it, we can." We headed down the street towards a breakfast place.

I looked at him as we walked and thought to myself how perfect he would have been for me if he were only straight and interested in dating someone like me—then I wouldn't have to go on dates with douchebags like Jack Morrison. I could just be in a happy, healthy relationship with someone who got me and appreciated my art. Was that really too much to ask for? I didn't think so.

Instead, I was going to play Lucas's fake girlfriend to his bigoted rich family, and hopefully, at the end of it, he'd have his coffee shop and I'd have my art studio, and I'd be able to sell my art. It would be beautiful. I didn't like lying to his family, but the end goal was something I believed in. It would be an amazing opportunity for both of us. I knew I wasn't a great actress, but I was going to do my best to play my role.

Chapter Thirteen

※※※

"Wow ..." I whispered in the back of the limo.

"What?" Lucas asked.

"I know you said you were rich, but I didn't realize your family was *this* rich." I looked up in awe at the house in front of us. It wasn't even a house. It was a mansion. A huge stone mansion that looked like it belonged in the English countryside.

"What, I didn't tell you that my grandparents had an indoor pool, an outdoor pool, private beach, English gardens, and much more?" He laughed. "Oh yeah, and we're right on the water, and they have two boats."

"Wow." I pulled my gaze away from the house to look at Lucas. "This is crazy."

"And we're going to have a room that gives us a water view. Well, you'll have a room that gives you a water view, and I'll have a room that gives me a water view. My parents have 16 bedrooms at their house, but my grandparents have 18."

"Wow."

"And yeah, this is on nine acres of land."

"Oh, you're enjoying this now, aren't you?"

"I didn't even tell you about the wine cellar and the grotto and the six fireplaces."

"Lucas, this is incredible. I didn't realize that your family was so wealthy."

"I mean, that was kind of the point of us coming here. What did you think I meant when I said I wanted part of inheritance now? Did you think that my family was only worth a couple of million?"

"I don't know, but this is just above and beyond anything I've ever imagined someone wealthy being like. I mean, I watched *The Real Housewives of New York* and even they don't live in places like this."

"Uh, they don't have money like my family has money," he said. "But wait until you meet them. They're just as douchey as some of the people on that crappy show."

"Don't call it crappy. You love that show."

"I know," he laughed, "but I have to pretend."

"Yeah. I guess so." The limo stopped and we got out of the car. I stood in front of the house in awe. I just had no words. It was breathtaking.

"So yeah, this is a custom-built, stone, Georgian house with 340 feet of private Long Island Sound shoreline."

"You sound like a realtor." I glanced at him and cracked a smile.

"I know. My family would love it if I went into real estate."

"They want you to be a realtor?"

"Well, no, not a realtor, real estate. I did tell you that my family is in the real estate market, right?"

"No, I don't really know what your family does."

"Oh, shoot. I thought I had told you everything." He bit his lower lip. "Oh well, doesn't matter. At least they'll think that you're into me for me and not just what my family does."

"So your family's in real estate?"

"Let's just say that we have a commercial and residential real estate empire." He laughed. "As well as investing in many other companies. My grandfather inherited the company from his grandfather, so we've had a lot of money for a long time."

"Oh wow. And your grandfather still runs the company?"

"No, my dad and my cousin do.

"Your dad and your cousin. Oh, interesting."

"Yeah. It's a long story, but essentially my dad had an older brother who passed away and he passed on his shares of the company to my cousin—"

"What's your cousin's name? Shouldn't I know that?"

"His name's John."

"Okay. So John has the majority of the shares?"

"No, but John is much better at business than my dad," he laughed, "and so John basically runs the companies. He's everyone's favorite. You would think my dad would hate him, but my dad loves him because my dad gets to spend the money, hang out at the office, and not do much work. John is basically the head of the family. My grandparents love him and my parents love him."

"Do you not have any other cousins?"

"I do. But they're all women," he laughed, "that's why it's so important to my grandparents that I get married."

"So John isn't married?"

"Oh, goodness, no, John's a playboy. I don't see him getting married for a long time."

"But isn't that unfair that your grandparents want you to get married but they don't want him to get married?"

"Oh, they know he'll get married one day, but right now they're happy that he's making billions and billions of dollars for the company."

"I see."

"I know, it's weird. Lifestyles of the rich and famous, hey?"

"Yeah. It's totally outside of my world purview. I remember when my dad got a wage increase to $80,000 a year and we felt like millionaires."

"$80,000 a year." Lucas chuckled. "That's nothing. I could spend that in a week."

"Seriously, Lucas? Yeah, you could spend it in a week, but my family was very happy to live off of it for a year."

"I know. I know. I sound completely and utterly pretentious, don't I? It's being here. It makes me a snob. I'm not really one. You know that."

"It's okay. We're just from two different worlds."

"Yeah. But I don't want to be one of those people that's not in touch with the people. I can't be if I'm going to own a coffee shop."

"I know that," I nodded. "So we're going to go in and meet them?" I was slightly surprised that no one had come outside to greet us. But I guess we were family and not really friends.

"Oh, yeah. I'm not sure who's here yet. We may be the first. I wanted to get here before my parents and my cousins got here."

"Okay. So it's your cousin John and who else?"

"I have another uncle who had three daughters."

"Okay."

"So they'll probably all be here."

"And that uncle is not involved in the family business?"

"Oh god, no. He's an actor." He shuddered. "And not even a good one at that."

"Would I have seen him in anything?"

"Did you ever see a movie called *Dawn of the Dead Poolboy?*"

"Do you mean *Dawn of the Dead?*"

"No," he laughed, "I mean, *Dawn of the Dead Poolboy*. Don't ask. It was an 'indie movie.'" He did finger quotes. "And I don't think anyone saw it except for the family because he made us."

"Well ... at least you're supportive of each other."

"We had to be supportive of him because he used $5 million of my grandparents' money to make the movie."

"Oh wow. And it made no money?"

"Actually, it made *less* than no money because he spent $6 million on that piece of crap. He overpaid a bunch of Z list reality stars." He rolled his eyes. "It was a joke."

"Yikes."

"But he's fine. My grandma loves him because he's very handsome and his daughters are pretty smart."

"Are they part of the family business?"

"Nah. But I'll tell you more about that later. We should go inside. I can see my grandmother peeking out of the window."

"You can? Which window?"

"I'm not going to tell you because I know you'll look."

"Hey, I won't."

"I know you too well, Isabella. I've known you long enough to know that you do everything I tell you not to do."

"Fine," I laughed. I smiled at him, "How do I look?"

"Beautiful, my dear, absolutely beautiful." And then he gave me a quick kiss on the lips.

"What was that for?"

"Remember, my grandma is looking." He grabbed my hand and squeezed it. "We have a role to play, my dear. If we want to open this coffee-slash-art shop, we have to play it to the hills. We have to be Oscar-winners here."

"Okay, let's do this."

"We got it. I have faith in you, Isabella."

"I hope so." I swallowed hard as we walked towards the front of the building because I didn't have that much faith in myself.

Chapter Fourteen

As we walked towards the front door, it sprang open and a butler and housekeeper in traditional uniforms stepped outside.

"Pick your jaw up, Isabella." Lucas laughed. "My grandparents are extra."

"They have a *butler*?" I stared at him, shaking my head. "I had no idea you were so rich." I looked at him incredulously. "How did I have no idea?"

"Because our friendship is built on love and mutual respect. Not money." He paused and squeezed my hand. "You don't know how grateful I am to have a friend like you, Bella." He was serious now. "I'm so lucky. And thankful you're here with me. You're an amazing friend for helping me."

"Well, I'm not selfless," I grinned at him. "I'm also eager for you to open this coffee shop so that I can have a base for my artwork." I sighed wistfully. "That would be absolutely amazing."

"Hi, Anna. Hi David." Lucas stopped at the front door and beamed at the butler and housekeeper. They still had very strict expressions on their faces, but I could see that Anna's eyes were glittering. They were staying professional, but it was obvious to me that they loved Lucas.

"Hello, master." David and bowed.

Lucas laughed at the look on my face. "David, knock it off." He turned to me. "David never bows at me. He's only being like that because you're with me."

"I see you've brought a girlfriend, Mr. Lucas," David said once again, in his proper English accent.

"Yep. This is my girlfriend. My beautiful, wonderful Isabella."

"Hi, nice to meet you." I smiled at David and could tell looking me over. Anna, too. They weren't smiling at me at all. It made me nervous. Uh oh. Did they think I was a gold digger? Did they think I was here for his money?

"Nice to meet you, miss," he nodded. "Your grandparents are in the study, Lucas. I think you should go through now."

"Okay. We're going to face the old king and queen already, are we?" Lucas shuddered and then started laughing as he saw the expression on my face. "Oh, don't worry, Isabella. They don't bite."

"Why do you have an English accent all of a sudden?"

"Oh, didn't I tell you that Edith is from England?"

"Who's Edith?"

"Oh, my grandmother. She's English. I thought I told you that. Oops." He looked at me and just shrugged. "Oh, well."

"Uhm. I feel I should have known this," I whispered in his ear, hoping that David and Anna weren't paying too close attention to us. "If I didn't even know your grandma's English, how are they going to believe that we're actually dating and together?"

"It'll be fine. Of course, they'll believe us," he whispered back. "Who knows everything about their partner's grandparents?"

"Me. I know everything about my partner's grandparents. When you like someone, you know everything about them. And if they don't tell you, you stalk them. Trust me. I've done a lot of stalking in my life."

"Oh, really? What sort of stalking?"

"Facebook stalking, Google stalking. Shit. I could work for the CIA or FBI if I had to. I know how to get the information I need about a guy I like."

"So, are you telling me that you didn't like me, Isabella? You didn't like me enough to stalk me?"

"Well, you're my friend."

"Shh," he said quickly and looked around. "The walls have ears, my dear. The walls have ears."

"What?"

"Let's just make sure that whatever we have to say about our little plan," he gave me a look, "is said outside of the house. Preferably when we go to the village."

"What is going on? What are you talking about?"

"Oh, look. Here's the study." He gave me a meaningful stare.

What had I let myself in for here?

We walked into the study and I gasped audibly. His grandparents were going to know I was so out of my realm in this house. I could see pieces of art that I'd only read about in art history books.

"Oh my gosh. Is that a Jackson Pollock? And an Edward Hopper? Oh my gosh, Edward Hopper! I love him. He's my—" I turned to the side and realized that we had an audience. "Hi." I gave them a little wave. Lucas' grandparents sat on the couch looking me over.

"Edith. How are you, my love?" Lucas gave his grandmother a broad smile.

"It's Nana, you cheeky boy. You know that," Edith said as she stood up. "Lucas, so good to see you."

"So great to see you too, Nana," he laughed. "And Pap."

The older man next to Edith smiled at him. "Lucas. So, you brought your girlfriend with you."

"Yes, I did. This is the beautiful, wonderful Isabella."

"Hello." I followed behind Lucas and walked over to his grandparents. "Nice to meet you, Mr. And Mrs. ..." I paused, as I realized I didn't know their last name. Oh shit. How could I not know their last name?

"Isabella, don't be so formal. Call them Nana and Papa," Lucas said.

"Uhm. I don't really think that's appropriate, Lucas. They're not my Nana and Papa."

"But one day they will be. Won't they, my love?" He turned to his grandparents. "I wanted you to be the first ones to know. Isabella and I are going to get married."

I glanced sideways at him. What was he doing? He had already put a spotlight on me. We hadn't said anything about being engaged. We had just said that we pretended to be dating.

"Nana, Papa, this is Isabella. Please be nice. I don't want you scaring her up. And Isabella, this is my Nana, my Papa, Edward and Edith Windsor."

"Windsor?" I frowned at Lucas. "But that's not your last name."

"I know," Lucas rolled his eyes. "None of us have their last name."

"What?"

"Yeah, it's complicated, but Papa thought it would be better for his sons to take their wives' last names."

His grandfather looked old-fashioned and distinguished. I was frankly very surprised. I've never heard of anyone wanting to ensure that a family of sons took their wives' last names. "But I thought you wanted to continue the family line …?" I said, not really understanding.

"I do."

Edward stood up and he and Edith walked over to me. Edward held his hand out. "Nice to meet you, Isabella. I'm glad that Lucas has finally brought you to meet us. I understand that you're to be engaged soon?"

"Well, I don't know about that. We're very happy in our relationship, but we wouldn't want to rush anything now, would we, dear?" I shot daggers at Lucas with my eyes. He just grinned back at me.

"And I know you must be wondering why I don't want my family name passed on," Edward continue. "Not that I don't love it, but much like the Kennedys, the family name seems to be cursed." He shrugged.

"And I wanted a generation to live without the name, so none of my grandchildren actually have my name, which is a pity."

"It is a pity, but they obviously still love you, dear," Edith said. "Oh, Lucas?

Guess who else is coming early."

"I don't know. Who?"

"John."

"Oh, great." Lucas rolled his eyes and stared at me. "That's my cousin that I was telling you about, the one that runs the family business."

"I see. You sound excited to have your grandsons around," I said to Edith.

"Oh, yes, both of them are such bright brilliant boys. Of course, Lucas didn't want to work for the family business, but ..." She sighed. "It's a good thing we have John. He's absolutely fantastic. Even if he was ..." She paused and then looked over at her husband.

"Well, he had other ideas at first. He was into sports," Edward said shaking his head, "Which is fine in college, but you didn't play sports as a professional. At least not football."

"Oh, he was a soccer player?" I asked.

"Oh no, that's a ruffian sport." He shook his head. "American football."

"Which is still rough, dear," Edith said.

"Yes, but it's American. Unlike soccer." He smiled at his wife mischievously. And then he looked at me. "Oh, don't mind me, dear. It's just a little joke between my wife and me. She grew up with soccer, which of course in England they call football. And I grew up with American football. And when we first met years and years ago, we had a conversation about how we both liked football, but we were talking about two very different sports. And you know, she's a little bit of a snob and preferred soccer. And I guess I'm just a Yankee who loves American football. But our oldest grandson, John, whom you'll meet later, was professional for a bit. One of the best in the league." Despite saying he disapproved of his grandson playing professionally, I thought I could hear the pride in his voice. "Do you know much about football?" he asked me.

"No, I know absolutely nothing about football." I laughed, "Which is funny because actually someone was asking me about that the other day."

"Who was that?" Lucas asked.

"I was ..." I suddenly remembered who I was standing in front of and what I was doing here. I'd nearly just ruined everything. Imagine if I'd said, "Oh, I was on a blind date and this guy asked me if I knew anything about football and I lied and pretended I did." Our cover would have been blown.

"Oh, just one of Abby's friends. I'll tell you later," I said quickly. I looked at Edith and Edward and smiled at them. "Abby's one of my best friends and my roommates. She is really funny and she has a lot of different ideas and friends." I knew I was babbling. "I have two other roommates as well, Chloe and Emma. We all went to college together."

"Oh, yes?" Edith smiled though I could tell she had no idea what I was talking about.

"Yeah, we went to Columbia. Well, that's where I met Lucas."

"So you two have been dating since college?" Edward looked at me with a curious expression on his face. "That's been quite a while, and we're now just meeting you."

"Oh no, well, we were friends first, Papa. And then we became lovers," Lucas replied.

I glared at him. If he wanted his grandparents to think he was straight, he needed to stop acting so dramatically and flamboyantly. My gaydar would have been going off like crazy if he'd said that in front of me, but maybe they were old so they didn't realize.

"Oh, I do think that friends first is such a beautiful thing," Edith said with a polite smile. "So, we'll have Anna show you to your rooms." She looked at me and took my hand. "I'm sure Lucas told you, but we are rather old-fashioned. Even though we try to be hip with you youngsters, but I do believe that you shouldn't share the same bedroom. It's just untoward, you know. It's not the done thing." She gave me a sweet smile.

She had the most beautiful green eyes I'd ever seen. She must have been a beauty when she was younger. Not that she wasn't beautiful now, she was, but she must have been absolutely stunning. I then looked over at Edward. He was a handsome man as well. They must have been the most handsome couple in their friend group. I looked over at Lucas and grinned.

"Well, I know Lucas will miss me, but I'm fine with having my own room. You do have a very beautiful house. I was admiring as we got out of the car and walked up."

"Oh, Lucas will have to show you around. We have tennis courts and pools."

"And yes, I already told her that we're on the water and we have boats, Nana. Oh, and we have a bowling alley," Lucas added. "You love bowling, don't you, Isabella?"

"I do love bowling, and I can't believe you have a bowling alley!" I could tell that I was sounding far too excited and impressed. "Sorry." I smiled at Edith self-consciously. "I guess you're used to living in such a magnificent house, but I'm from a totally different income bracket." I wanted to groan out loud. Why had I brought up money? I was just so out of my league.

"Oh, my dear, don't worry. We do know that we are in an elite bracket." Edith patted my hand again. "But enjoy. Our home is your home. And we're just so glad to meet you. And then later this weekend, Edward and Lucas will talk about the business plan."

"Oh, that would be absolutely fantastic, Papa," Lucas nodded enthusiastically. "You know, it would be such a help to get some of my inheritance early."

"And *you* know I'd much rather you go into the family business," Edward said dryly. "John is doing a fantastic job, of course. But there's just so much to oversee, and I do wish that more of my family would be involved."

"Yes. But you know I'm not interested in real estate and mergers and all that boring stuff," Lucas groaned.

"I know. I know," Edward sighed. "But fine. Anna!" he called out. The housekeeper hurried into the room.

"Yes, Mr. Windsor? Did you call?"

"Yes. I think that it would be very nice for you to show Lucas to his room and then also show Ms. Isabella," he nodded graciously at me, "to her room.

Then we shall meet in an hour for some afternoon drinks?"

"Sounds good to me," I agreed happily.

"Yes, sir. Of course, sir." Anna walked over to me. "Ma'am, I will show you to your room now, if you don't mind?"

"Of course," I said following behind her. "Well, it was nice meeting you, Edith and Edward. I mean, Mr. and Mrs. Windsor."

"Edith and Edward is fine, dear," Edith assured me.

"I'll see you later, Lucas."

"Will do. I'm going to just show Nana some photos on my phone and then we'll meet up later?"

"Sounds good," I said.

Anna led me down a long hallway and I could see her looking me over. "So, you and Mr. Lucas have been dating for a long time?" she asked me.

I was surprised because I didn't think that the help were meant to ask questions, but what did I know? No one I knew had a housekeeper or a butler or lived in a mansion. Everything I knew about how servants were meant to act was from watching *Downton Abbey,* and that was set years and years ago. Maybe times had changed for servants.

"Oh yes, we're terribly in love," I said quickly,

wondering if she was trying to get more information to pass back to Edith and Edward.

"Oh, terribly in love, eh?" She looked at me. "Hmm, I see."

I wanted to ask her what that meant. What did she see? But she didn't ask me any more questions. Then we came to another corridor and walked down it, and I was starting to think I was going to get lost in this house. But thankfully, she stopped at the second door and opened it. I walked inside and gasped. The size of the room was bigger than my apartment back in New York City. It was humongous and it was so bright and airy. It was beautiful.

"Wow. This is amazing."

"I'm glad you like it. This is one of our guest suites." She nodded. "You have an en suite bathroom, of course. Full shower, full bathtub. There's the TV, the remote control's on the side. If there's anything you need, just let me know." She stood at the doorway while I walked around the room. I wondered if she was waiting for a tip.

"Oh, I don't have any cash on me." I chewed on my lower lip. How could I have not gotten cash? "I'm so sorry."

"Cash?" She blinked and then she looked like she was repressing a smile. "Don't worry, ma'am. We don't take tips. No. Is there anything else I can do for you?"

"No, I'm good. Thank you."

"Well, welcome, ma'am." She looked at me for a few more seconds as if she were studying me and then she smiled. "I hope you enjoy your stay here."

"Thank you. I'm sure that I will."

"When you hear the bell, come back down to the drawing room and there will be refreshments. Is there anything in particular you would like for an afternoon snack, ma'am?"

"No, I'm okay. Anything that's available, I'll be happy for. Thank you."

"Oh, you're welcome."

And with that, she was gone. I walked over to the bed and sat down. I was completely out of my element, and I wasn't at all confident I'd be able to get through this weekend successfully. I had already nearly messed up so many times, and Lucas wasn't making it easy. I really, really hoped that he wasn't planning some stupid over-the-top proposal or something because I wasn't sure if I'd be able to keep it together. His grandparents seemed like lovely people, not the sort of people that I would expect to be bigoted towards gay people. I guess appearances could be deceiving, though. I sighed and pulled out my phone just so that I could text Abby. I saw that she had sent me a text message and I opened it up.

"Hey, girl. So sorry that your date didn't go as

planned. Please forgive me if you think I gave him false expectations or hope. I didn't mean to do that. I just really wanted you to have a good time. Call me when you get there. Love you."

I smiled as I read her message. I knew she felt bad, but it wasn't her fault. She hadn't made me sleep with him, and she hadn't made Jack the asshole that he was. He was an asshole all by himself. I lay back on the bed and closed my eyes thinking about that night with him. He was an asshole, but he'd been an amazing lover. It would have been nice to make love one more time with him, to just be absolutely crazy. It'd been a fun night. I mean, yeah, he'd been obnoxious, but the banter had been fun. It had made me feel alive. It made me feel things that I hadn't felt in years.

I miss being in a relationship. I miss being with someone. I missed flirting and touching and kissing and ... Oh, well, it didn't make any sense to think about him right now. I was never going to see him again. That part of my life was over as soon as it had begun.

I needed to concentrate on this weekend because if we were successful and Lucas got the money, it could change my life. Things would start to look up for me. I wanted my own art gallery and I wanted to be able to teach my own art classes in my own space.

And it was within reach now, and that was so exciting. So very, very exciting.

I would get through this weekend and I would do the best job that I could. I would make everyone believe that I was in love with Lucas and that we were a couple that would last forever. I would do that for him, and more selfishly, I would do it for me.

* * *

"I'll just have some lemonade. Thank you." I smiled at Anna as she handed me a glass and took a seat next to Edith on the couch where she had indicated I should sit.

"So, Isabella, what is it you do for a living?" she asked me. Lucas was standing on the other side of the room with his grandfather discussing who knows what.

"I am an artist," I said looking around the room. "I see that you have some fantastic pieces of art."

"Oh, yes. You mentioned you recognized the Pollock and that you like Edward Hopper, eh?"

"Yes. 'Room By The Sea' is one of my very favorites."

"Oh, indeed." She nodded. "Very nice. Very nice. So what sort of paintings do you do? Oil paintings? Are you in a gallery? Are you in the MoMA?"

"Oh, nothing that fancy," I shook my head. "I mainly dabble in watercolors and teach classes here and there. Teach kids and sell pieces at art fairs and stuff like that. Nothing big, though. Maybe one day if I'm lucky. Though I'm not as talented as many of these brilliant artists."

"Oh, you shouldn't put yourself down, dear. I'm sure you're very talented. Lucas was telling us about you, I remember now."

"Oh?" I was surprised. "Really? When?"

"Oh, maybe ..." She paused. "It was a few months ago or I don't know, maybe it was Christmas. My mind, you know, a little bit befuddled and hazy sometimes." She shook her head. "I'm getting a little bit older. Don't tell anyone, though," she said with a small smile.

"Oh, of course not. I didn't know Lucas had told you about me before."

"Oh, he didn't tell us you were dating. He was just talking about you, but I should have known then. I mean, he was going on and on about how talented you were and how you were teaching him something called the wet-on-wet technique." She shrugged. "Is that something that you're familiar with?"

"Oh, yes." I laughed. "I remember now. I took Lucas to Central Park and we were painting, and I was teaching him the wet-on-wet because he likes more abstracts, loose art, and he wasn't getting the hang of it, but it was a good time. I didn't know he'd told you about that."

"Yes, dear. He talks about you often." She smiled. "And his eyes always light up. I should have known then that you were something."

"Oh, well, you know ..." I bit my lower lip. I hated lying to her. She was such a sweet old lady, and I just felt horrible. Just then, the doorbell rang and her eyes lit up.

"Oh, that must be my other grandson, John. I'm so happy that he's here. Excuse me, if you don't mind." She stood up. "I'm going to go and welcome him. Not that I want Lucas to be jealous or anything, but I haven't seen John in such a long time. He's been taking care of the family business and has been doing a wonderful job. He really is the best grandson one could ever hope for. Not that Lucas isn't of course," she added, "but he's a different sort of grandson, you know?"

"Oh, I know." I laughed. "Trust me and sure, go ahead. I'm sure John will be happy to see you."

"Oh, I hope so." She hurried towards the door. "Edward, you stay here with Lucas. I'm going to go and greet John and bring him through to the drawing room. Okay?"

"Okay, dear." Edward nodded and I walked over

to join him and Lucas. Lucas saw my face and started laughing.

"Oh, yes. Everyone knows that John is Edith's favorite, but it's okay, because I know she loves me too."

"We don't have favorites. You know that Lucas," Edward shook his head.

"Come on, Papa. I know that John's your favorite too. When he was in the NFL, all you could do was boast to all your friends that you had a grandson that was a starting quarterback."

"Yes, but we've been proud of your achievements as well, dear. When you were trying to make it on Broadway, we came to several plays."

"You were in a play on Broadway?" I looked at Lucas surprised. "I didn't know that."

"No, I was trying to make it on Broadway," Lucas laughed. "I was in two plays off, off, off, off, off-Broadway." He laughed.

"Well, I don't want to say I'm glad you stopped, but I was happy when you told me that you weren't pursuing that career path any longer." Edward turned to me. "So, you're an artist, dear?"

"Yes, I am."

"You'll have to show me some of your work before I give this money to Lucas. I understand you're going into business together?"

"Oh, well, I mean, we're not really going into business together. It will be Lucas's business, and I'll just be working there."

"Yes, but if you were to be married, it will be both of you guys' businesses, won't it?"

"Yeah. Well, I mean ..." I didn't know what to say. I chewed on my lower lip and shot a glance at Lucas. Why, oh, why was I in this situation? I could hear Edith talking to someone along the corridor and I was thankful that she was going to be back with whoever this John was.

"John, come in. I want you to meet Lucas's girlfriend, Isabella."

"I'm looking forward to meeting her," a familiar voice replied.

I turned around, horrified to see Jack Morrison standing there.

His eyes narrowed as he stared at me. "Well, hello there, Isabella not-Rossellini."

Fuck, fuck, fuck, fuck, fuck! This was not good at all. I darted a look at Lucas. He looked confused.

"What's going on?" He came to my side and placed his hand on my shoulders. "Isabella, this is my cousin, John."

"Hi, John." I forced a smile onto my face. "Nice to meet you."

"My friends call me Jack," he replied, "I wish my

family would. Everyone else aside from them calls me Jack."

"I see." So he hadn't been lying about his name.

"And you're here with Lucas? Hmm." He stared me up and down and then looked at his cousin. "And you guys are dating?"

"Yes. We're dating. We're very much in love," Lucas glared at his older cousin.

"And how long have you guys been dating and in love?" Jack asked, a weird expression on his face.

"Months," Lucas said, "Years, really. I can't even remember how long it's been, but it's fantastic."

"It's fantastic, is it? Hm." Jack looked at me. "So you're in love with my cousin, are you?"

"Yes. Very much," I said my voice cracking. *Please do not bring up the fact that I had sex with you last night, please!*

"Interesting." Jack eyed me and I could tell that he wanted to say something else, but he didn't. "Papa, so good to see you."

"And you too, my boy. You've been making me so much money. I love it."

"Well, I'm glad to hear that." They hugged quickly. And then Jack stepped back. "I think I'm going to need something strong. You've got any gin?"

"Of course. Come with me. I'll fix you a glass,"

Edward said, and I watched them walk to the side of the room.

Lucas came closer to me and whispered, "Do you know Jack?"

"What?" I said blinking, trying to be innocent.

"That was a really weird interaction. Do you know him?"

"Um ..." I nodded imperceptibly looking over at Edith. She just seemed to be standing there. I wasn't sure she was listening to our conversation or she was just staring at her other grandson dotingly.

"Why didn't you tell me that you knew him?"

"I didn't know he was your cousin."

"When did you meet him?"

"Last night."

"What? How?"

"Remember the date I told you about?"

"Oh my God, not the guy you had the one-night stand with?"

I nodded. "Yep."

"Ugh, I should have known my cousin was the obnoxious asshole that you banged." He looked around the room and then pulled me to the far side. "What are we going to do?"

"What do you mean?"

"What if he tells my Nana and my granddad? Then it's over, it's done."

"Yeah. I mean, this is not really the best situation for us to be in."

"You're going to have to tell him to keep quiet."

"But he's going to know that we're not together."

"No, he doesn't have to know that we're not together." He shook his head.

"He doesn't have to know we're not together?" I raised an eyebrow. "I just slept with the guy. He'll know."

"Dude, lots of people are in relationships where people cheat."

"No," I shook my head. "There's no way I'm going to let him think—"

"Isabella." And he glared at me.

"What?" I was annoyed.

"You're going to have to figure this out before he says something to them." He groaned.

"Oh, this *sucks*." I bit back a series of curse words. "I thought I was never going to see him again. And now he's here, and I have to spend the whole weekend with him—"

"*Please* don't have a meltdown. Please, please, please." Lucas groaned.

"Oh, I knew this was a bad idea."

"Why did you go have to go and choose *this* week to go and finally get laid!" he hissed.

"It's been years, that's why!"

Edith, Edward, and Jack glanced over at us and I lowered my voice. "Anyway, let's talk about this later. Remember you told me that the walls have ears?"

"Ears, eyes, and everything in between," he said.

"We're screwed. You know that, right? We're screwed. There's going to be no cafe. There's going to be no art studio. There's—"

"It'll be okay. Let's see what we can do, okay?" I squeezed his hand.

Jack strolled back over to us. "So Lucas, I didn't know you had a girlfriend." He said the word girlfriend in such a weird way that I had a feeling that Jack knew that Lucas was not interested in dating girls. I mean, he was self-aware enough to know the world that we lived in. I didn't think he was that oblivious to his cousin's sexual orientation.

"Yes, she's my girlfriend. Okay? We were on a break recently," Lucas said quickly, "because we weren't sure that we wanted to be together. But we decided this morning that we really wanted to be together because she realized there's no one better out there than me."

"Really?" Jack's lips curled up and he stared at me. "So this morning you realized that Lucas was the best that you could do?" I could tell that he wanted to laugh.

"What's that supposed to mean?" I glared at him.

"I don't know," he shrugged, "but a lot of things make sense now."

"What makes sense?"

"I don't know." He coughed. "Gold digger."

"Excuse me? What?" I looked over at Lucas who was busy looking at his phone. "Did you just call me a gold digger? Lucas, your cousin just called me a—"

"Hey, I got to go. I'll be right back." Lucas was typing something into his phone as he quickly left the room.

"What the hell?" I was absolutely going to kill Lucas. How could he just leave me here in this awful situation?

"So, we meet again," Jack said softly leaning in close towards my ear. "You left so quickly the other night. I didn't think I'd see you again."

"I was hoping I'd never see you again."

"Really? You don't replay that night over and over in your head? You're not tempted to touch yourself every time you think of it?" he said softly.

"Shh!" I glanced furtively around the room. "You cannot be saying this here."

"Why not?" he laughed, "because you're dating my cousin?" He rolled his eyes. "Really? Did you need a rich man that badly?"

"How dare you?" I glared at him.

"How dare I what? You want me to believe that you're in love with my gay cousin?"

"So you know?"

"Of course I know. Probably the only people who don't know are Nana and Papa. And I'm sure they know as well, they're just in denial. Lucas doesn't really think he has everyone in the family fooled, does he?" And then he shook his head. "Of course, he does. He's completely oblivious. He always did think he was a much better actor than he was. So why the charade?"

"You can't tell anyone."

"I'm not going to tell anyone. Why the charade?"

"Because Lucas wants to start a business, and he can only get some of his inheritance if it looks like he's going to be getting married and having kids soon."

"So you're going to marry my cousin so that he can get part of his inheritance early?" He raised an eyebrow. "Wow. I thought you had higher standards than that."

"What's that supposed to mean? You don't even know—" I stopped myself. "You know what? Whatever."

"Whatever indeed, huh? I guess you don't want to be honest about anything, do you, Isabella Wilder?"

"Why are you saying my name like that?"

"Hm. Why do you think?"

"I don't know."

"Maybe it's because you're in my bed not twenty-four hours ago, and now you're here at my family home trying to pull a con on my grandparents so that you can get millions of dollars and who knows what you're going to do with them. In fact, who knows what you would have tried to do to me the other night if I hadn't been smart enough to catch onto your game."

"You know what? You are as big as a jackass as I thought. Maybe you're even more of a jackass than I thought." I shook my head. "If I wasn't here in front of your grandparents, I would slap you."

"You would love that, wouldn't you?"

"What?"

"Is that one of your fantasies, Isabella? Slapping me?"

"No, of course not," I blushed. "I mean, I don't know." The idea was kind of a turn-on.

"You know what I'd like to do to you right now?" he said.

"What?"

"I'd like to put you over my lap and spank you. You need a really good spanking, Isabella Wilder. And then, once I spanked you, I'd fuck you."

"How dare you?" I couldn't believe what he was

saying. And why did his voice seem so loud? What would Edith and Edward think if they knew I'd been with both of their grandsons...well, I'd only been with one, but they didn't know that.

"How dare I what? I fucked you already. Why would it be such a surprise that I'd want to fuck you again?"

He laughed, and before I could respond, he walked away from me.

Chapter Fifteen

I had to resist the urge to run after Jack and tell him to hold on.

He was a football player? No wonder he'd been quizzing me about my love of football. He'd obviously known I was lying through my teeth. No wonder he'd mentioned his name so many times, like I should have known him. Maybe he thought I was pretending not to know him because I was a gold digger.

I pulled out my phone and quickly put his name into Google. His photo and Wikipedia page came up immediately. He was a big deal. A handsome, rich, big deal. And he knew I was a liar. I knew that he knew, but I wasn't going to admit it.

Lucas walked over to me and raised an eyebrow. "What was that about, babe?"

"I think you know what that was about." I shook my head. "This is a hot mess."

"You're telling me. My almost-fiancée slept with my cousin yesterday!" He pulled a comically shocked face, but I could see the wicked spark in his eyes. "Oh my gosh. What is the world coming to?"

"Lucas, this is not funny. I don't know why you're trying to make a joke."

"What else can we do?" He shrugged. "I mean, you're just going to have to be some sort of femme fatale who's not really that trustworthy, but I love you so much that I forgive you."

"Lucas. Really? Do I look like a femme fatale?"

"I think you don't understand just how absolutely gorgeous you are." He looked serious for once. "I mean, yes, I'm gay, but I can appreciate your beauty. You are stunning. I don't understand why you don't see that."

"I'm not stunning." I shook my head. "I mean, I'm okay."

"Girl, please. With your long, brunette tresses, and your big, beautiful brown eyes, and your golden skin, which is I know is natural because I know you don't go to the tanning salon."

"You know I don't have money to spend on a tanning salon. Let's thank my Italian ancestors for that one."

"Girl, you're beautiful. You know that, right? And I don't know what happened with my cousin, but you're better off without him. Trust me on that."

"Well, it's not really like I had much of a choice. He was an asshole."

"Isabella, I need all the details. You know that, right?" He was acting like an eager paparazzi interviewing a Z-list celebrity who had information on an A lister. I didn't know whether to laugh or cry at how badly he wanted to know my sordid story.

"Yeah. But this is not the right place."

"I know," he nodded. "Want to go and get some ice cream?"

"Yes, please."

He turned toward his grandmother. "Hey, Nana?"

"Yes, Lucas?"

"Can I borrow one of the cars? I would love to take Isabella into town to get some ice cream."

"Okay, dear. Sure. Take whichever one you want."

"Even the Bentley?"

"Even the Bentley." She smiled indulgently.

"Wow. Thanks, Nana."

"Be careful with it now, son." Edward looked slightly concerned. "Don't be driving all crazy like you used to when you were young."

"Papa, it'll be fine," Lucas assured him. "Come on,

Isabella. I'm about to show you the local sights in style."

"Well, don't I get an invitation?" Jack stepped forward and cleared his throat. Lucas and I paused and glanced at each other.

"You want to come?" Lucas looked at him suspiciously. "Really? Why? You never want to go into town for ice cream. Not even when we were kids."

"Yeah, but I haven't seen you in a while and I'd like to get to know your girlfriend." Jack looked over at Edith and Edward. "Plus, I think that Nana and Papa could do with some time alone whilst they get ready for everyone else to arrive tomorrow."

"Yes. Take your cousin into town. It'll be nice for you guys to catch up," Edith chimed in. "I know that you haven't been spending as much time with each other as we would have liked. And Isabella, do enjoy the village. It's quiet, but you'll like it, I think. Greenwich is such a beautiful town, and so close to New York. Maybe when you and Lucas are married and have kids, you'll think about living there."

"Yeah. Maybe," I said, avoiding Jack's eyes. I could tell that he was laughing at us.

"Okay, it's set," Jack said. "Do you want to take the Bentley or the Rolls? Or would you rather I drive, Lucas?"

"I will drive," Lucas said. "I already said I want

the Bentley. You can take the Rolls if you want to go by yourself. I mean, you don't have to drive into town with us."

"Oh. You're funny, Lucas." Jack ran his hand through his hair, which I could tell he'd cut since I last saw him. Was I so into him that I could tell when he'd had his hair done? I was really a lost cause.

"Okay. I'll meet you in the foyer in five minutes?" Jack turned. "I'm just going to go and freshen up really quick and we'll head off. Yeah?"

"Yes, sir," Lucas said, and then rolled his eyes at me. "Come on, Isabella. Let's wait for him outside."

"But I thought he wanted to meet in the foyer?"

"He can meet us outside," Lucas said. "We need to talk, and we need to talk fast," he whispered.

"Okay. It was nice meeting you, Mr. and Mrs. Windsor."

"Edith and Edward, remember, dear."

"Oh, yeah. Sorry. It was nice meeting you, Edith and Edward. We'll be back later. Bye."

"Bye, bye."

Lucas and I headed out of the room and down the long hallway towards the front door. As he stood outside, Lucas shook his head. "What the hell is Jack playing at?"

"You tell me. He's your cousin. I don't really know him."

"He obviously knows something's up," Lucas growled. "If he tries to stop Papa from giving me this money, that's it. The coffee shop is done. I just don't know what I'm going to do." He sighed. "Man, oh, man. Why?"

"I'm sorry," I said softly. "If I'd known he was your cousin I wouldn't have." Though that was a lie. I would have. I'd been so horny and so into him that night that I wouldn't have said no. But Lucas didn't have to know that. I didn't want him to think I was a bad friend. Because I really wasn't. I was here, after all.

"It's fine," he muttered. "What's the game plan, then?"

"What do you mean, what's the game plan?"

"I mean, my cousin slept with you a couple of days ago. I'm trying to convince my grandparents that we are totally in love and I'm about to propose. My cousin either knows that is not true or thinks that you're a hussy. And you said you don't want to be a hussy in front of him, so then he knows it's not true."

"I mean, isn't there any other way?" I didn't want to hurt Lucas and his chances, but I didn't want Jack to think worse of me. I knew it shouldn't matter. But it did. I couldn't stand him, but I didn't want him to think I was some sort of ho.

"I mean, I guess I could tell him," Jack sighed.

"Yeah. I mean, why not be honest with him?"

"Because he's not my favorite cousin." He rolled his eyes. "And he might tell Nana and Papa, and then I might not get the money."

"But if your company's worth billions, what does he care if you get a couple of million to start your business?"

"You'd think he wouldn't care. Right?" He shrugged. "But you know how it goes with family and money."

"Do you really think he's like that?" I didn't know Jack well, but he didn't seem the sort of person that would be homophobic or stingy or hold it over Lucas' head. I mean, he drove me crazy, but aside from that, he seemed like a pretty level-headed guy. I didn't get vibes that he'd be prejudiced or bigoted in any way.

"I know," Lucas admitted. "I don't think he would be. But he's not the sort of person who will lie for me. You know?" He sighed. "So, even if I trusted him with my secret, I don't think he would actually lie to my grandparents or my parents. Then, what happens then? I'm out."

"But would your grandparents really care? Edith and Edward seem so lovely and—"

"They *are* lovely," he nodded. "But they very much want me to have a traditional family like them. They want me to get married and to give them great-grandkids and ..." he signed. "That's not going to happen."

"I mean, you could do IVF with a surrogate if you met someone."

"Yeah." He rolled his eyes. "I'm not even into kids. So, unlikely."

"You just don't want kids anyway?"

"Not really."

"Lucas, why don't you just then tell them that?"

"I just don't know how, I guess. I've been living this lie for so long."

"Have you, though? When I met you, you were out and proud."

"Yeah. I mean, it was easy in college. There were so many other gay guys and everyone was so open and welcoming. It was a completely different environment. This environment, well ..." He shrugged. "It's just difficult. You know? I didn't know how to tell them. I don't want to disappoint them."

"You wouldn't disappoint them, Lucas. You're a wonderful human being. You're—"

"Am I interrupting something?" Jack said, standing right behind us. I looked up at him and for a few seconds, all my old feelings of lust came back to me. He really was handsome.

"No, you're not interrupting anything," I said quickly. "Lucas and I were just talking."

"About us?" He raised an eyebrow.

"What do you mean about us?" I said quickly.

Jack chuckled. "Look, I don't know what's going on here, if you're trying to pull a long con or something. But whatever. Lucas, I am pretty sure you probably know by now that your girlfriend and I had sexual relations the other night. So, are you going to tell me what's going on, or we're just going to keep playing this game?"

"We're not playing any game," Lucas said. "This is my girlfriend and I love her, and we're going to get married, and we bang every night. In fact, we banged ten minutes ago."

"Really?" Jack looked skeptical.

"Really," Jack smirked.

"You banged *ten* minutes ago. When was this? When we were in the living room with Edith and Edward, or when you were waiting out here? You just have a quick bang in front of everyone?"

"Fine. We didn't bang *ten* minutes ago. It was more like ten hours ago, but—"

"Lucas, seriously?" Jack sighed. "Look, I know we have very different approaches to life. But I'm your cousin. And I love you. And I don't know where you met Isabella, if you met her on the same dating app as me, and presented her with some plan to try and get money. I don't know what's going on. But please believe me. You can't trust her."

"Excuse me?" My voice rose. "*I'm* not to be trusted? I'm—"

Jack started laughing. "Hey, you're the one that completely lied to me on the dating app, then came back to my place to hook up and then—"

"Enough." Lucas interrupted him. "Isabella is one of my best friends. I've known her since college. Do we have to have this conversation here? Can we go into town first?"

"Whatever you want," Jack said. "I'm open."

"Well, let's get the Bentley, and I'll tell you on the drive to ice cream." Lucas sighed.

"You don't have to do this if you're not ready yet, Lucas," I told him.

"No, it's fine." He rolled his eyes. "You're my best friend, and I don't want my jackass cousin thinking you're some sort of hussy or gold digger. Because I don't really know what went down between the two of you, and I don't know if I want to know." He paused and started laughing. "Actually, that's a lie. I want to know all the dirty details. But more about that later."

We got into the Bentley and Lucas started it up. It purred to life, and I just couldn't believe that I was sitting in a Bentley in Greenwich with Jack and Lucas. How surreal was this life?

Lucas put the car in gear and cleared his throat. "Hey, Jack. There's something I have to tell you."

"Yes, Lucas?" Jack said from the back seat.

"I'm gay."

"I know."

"What? You knew?" Lucas hit the brakes, put the car into park, and then looked into the back seat. "You knew?"

"Are you joking me?" Jack said with a laugh. "You thought I didn't know? I've known since we were little kids."

"What do you mean you've known since we were little kids?"

"I've probably known as long as you've known." Jack shrugged. "I mean, right?"

"So why didn't you ever say anything?"

"Because it felt like you were keeping it a secret, and I didn't want to make you tell me if you weren't comfortable telling me."

"Oh." Lucas looked pleasantly surprised. "I didn't realize you'd be so considerate. You always teased me when we were younger, made fun of me, and—"

"I teased you about inconsequential stuff. Your sexuality is not inconsequential." Jack shook his head.

"I would never try to out you or make you tell me something you weren't comfortable with."

"Wow."

"I'm not a jerk. You realize that, right?"

"I guess I do now." Lucas laughed. "Well, kind of. You were a jerk to Isabella."

"No, I wasn't." Jack shook his head. "I definitely wasn't."

"I would say you were," I said. But then I pressed my lips together. "But this is not about me right now. You guys continue."

"So why is Isabella pretending to be your girlfriend if you're not interested in members of the fairer sex?"

"Because I have a business idea, and I want to ask Papa to give me part of my inheritance upfront so that I can get it off the ground."

"That's the coffee shop you were talking about?"

"Yeah." Lucas nodded. "I really want to have a go at it. I really, I've had this idea for a long time and I need the capital." He shot Jack a look. "I know. You probably think it's a stupid idea, and—"

"I didn't say that," Jack responded, and I looked at him in surprise. "Do you have a business plan?"

"I do," Lucas said quickly.

"And where does Isabella fall into all this?"

"Well, she's an artist, and I thought part of the

coffee shop could also be like a bookstore-slash-art center, so she'd have her gallery and she'd teach classes there, and ... I know. It sounds like a lot."

"No, it actually sounds like a pretty good idea." Jack frowned at me. "Hmm, so you really are an artist, then?"

"Yeah. I wouldn't lie about that." I stared at him, my lips pressed together. Who would lie about being an artist?

"Just like you wouldn't lie about how much you love football."

"Look. It's just a long, complicated story. I didn't mean to lie about loving football. I—"

"You wanted to impress me, huh?"

"No, I didn't want to impress you. I just thought that was what you'd heard about me."

"What do you mean? Heard about you from who?" He rolled his eyes.

"Look, I didn't set up my profile on the dating app. When you were talking initially it wasn't with me."

"What?" He stared at me for a few seconds and nodded. "Ohhh. This is actually starting to make sense. So, what exactly—"

"Hey, guys," Lucas interrupted us. "This is about me right now and not you two. You can chat later. So, are you going to help me convince Papa to give me the loan?"

"No." Jack shook his head. "I'm not in on a lie, Lucas. You know I'm not that sort of person."

"Fine." Lucas deflated. "So, I guess it's over. That's it. No money. No coffee shops. No art studio. No—"

"I didn't see that," Jack said, slowly smiling. "I'll give you the money. I'll be an investor in your business."

"What?" Lucas sounded shocked. "You would invest in my business? But I don't need you to invest. I can get my own money. I—"

"You *do* need me, Lucas. Because you're not a businessman. You have no clue how to run a business. And as many great ideas that you have, it's not going to be successful unless you have someone backing you who can help you with the business side of things. I will do that."

"For free?"

"No." Jack laughed. "I'm a businessman. Do I look like I'm going to do it for free?"

"So, what do you want?"

"15% of the profits."

"What?"

"I'll give you a year or two to make it profitable. But after that, I want 15%."

"For how long?"

"Twenty years."

"What?"

"Hey, it's a good deal. Normally I want 50%, and for a lot more than twenty years."

"I don't know." Lucas looked at me. "What do you think?"

I looked from Lucas to Jack and back again. I couldn't stand Jack, but he was right. Lucas has had no idea how to run a business, and neither did I. Lucas would need the help. He had grand, lofty ideas, but he wasn't always good with practical details, and I did want his business to be a success.

"I think you should do it," I said. "I think that was a kind offer for your cousin. He could really help," I told Jack. I turned back to Lucas. "It's up to you, of course. I mean, it's your business. I'm just going to work for you."

"You're not going to work for me. You're going to be a part of it. You're going to be a—"

"We'll have to actually work out a contract for the fine details," Jack interrupted. "This is money I'm lending you, Lucas. I don't really know what contract you have with Isabella here, or how much money she's putting in. But—"

"I'm not putting in any money," I told him. "I barely have any money. And I have even less now after that dinner I paid for the other night."

"Wait. What?" Lucas interrupted. "*You* paid for dinner on your date with my cousin?" He looked at Jack and shook his head. "You are a dog, aren't you?"

"I'm not a dog," Jack grinned. "But she offered. Who was I to say no?"

"You could have said no. You knew that I didn't have much money."

"How was I to know you didn't have much money?" He shrugged. "You offered. When someone offers, why would I say no? Plus on the dating app, you said ..." he paused. "Oh, yeah. I forgot. That wasn't you." He shrugged. "I guess that's what happens. You play with fire, you're going to get burned."

I glared at Jack and then turned to Lucas. "Let's go for that ice cream. I need ice cream before I continue either of these conversations."

"Sounds like a plan," Lucas said.

I could tell that he was happy. Really, really happy. I sat back in the car and looked out of the window. I was glad that Jack had been so nonchalant and understanding about his coming out. Which, of course, was reasonable and should have been expected. But I knew that Lucas had been worried and nervous and scared. And now the answer to his other prayer was coming true. He was going to have his business.

But where did that leave me? I could already tell

from the way that Jack had spoken that he didn't really want me to be a part of this. Was I going to get sidelined? Was I just going to go back to my apartment with my friends and teach art to annoying preschool and elementary school kids? Try and sell my artwork on Etsy and submit multiple submissions to art galleries? Was that going to be my life, living paycheck to paycheck?

I sighed. I'd worry about it later. For now, I'd get my ice cream and just see what the future held later.

Chapter Sixteen

"So, I'm going to get mint chocolate chip. Isabella, you want strawberry, right?" Lucas asked me as we stood at the counter in the ice cream shop.

"Yes, please."

"Jack, what do you want?"

"I'll take the vanilla bean," he said.

"Vanilla bean. Really, Jack?" Lucas shook his head. "Who thought you would be plain vanilla?"

"I guess you don't know me as well as you thought you did, hey, Lucas?"

"What's that supposed to mean, Jack?" Lucas rolled his eyes.

"You're always full of drama. You know that right?"

"I'm full of drama?" Lucas shook his head. "Whatever."

Jack looked at me. "So, you guys have been friends since college, I gather."

"Yeah, that's what I said already." I nodded, as I looked at him, "Really good friends. Lucas used to hang out with me, Abby, Emma, and Chloe all the time."

"Abby, Emma, and Chloe?" Jack looked curious. "And they are?"

"Oh, sorry. They're my roommates and my best friends."

"They're lovely girls. All of them hot." Lucas grinned. "Trust me, if I were straight, I'd have fallen for all of them."

"Very funny." I laughed.

"Lucas, you're an idiot."

"Why? It's true." Okay. Let me pay you for these ice creams." He looked at Jack. "No need to offer, this is on me."

"I didn't hear myself offering," Jack said with a laugh. "I think you can afford some ice cream. You do get a nice allowance each month."

"Oh my gosh. We're not going to talk about my allowance again, are we?" Lucas shook his head and looked at me. "Jack is in charge of the family trust fund, and he doles out money to all of us. You'd think it was his personal money, the way he goes on."

"I don't think it's my personal money. It's our family money," Jack said dryly. "And let's hope it's here for many generations."

"Well, we're the last generation right now. No one else even has kids. And the way things are going, no one else is going to have kids." Lucas laughed. "So why not spend it all now?"

"Lucas." I touched him on the shoulder. I could see that Jack was looking annoyed.

"Why? It's true. We have *millions* of dollars. Billions for all I know. And yet I'm going to get called out for buying a watch last month?"

"You bought a Cartier watch for $20,000," Jack said dryly. "That was no small chunk of change."

"For us it was."

"For *us*?" Jack said, "If you want to be spending money like that, come and work for the family business. There are many different things that I can have you doing. And I can provide training before I put you into any real position of power."

"Uh, that's okay," Lucas said quickly and pulled out his phone. "Actually, I have a call to make, can I come back and talk to you guys in a second?"

"Um, what?" I didn't want to be left alone with Jack.

"It's fine," Jack said. "We'll get our ice creams. Go. We'll be here."

"Great."

"See you in a second Isabella. See you, Jack." And with that, Lucas was out of the ice cream shop.

"Well, how's this for life, huh, Isabella?"

"Hmm?"

"We meet again at another eatery."

"Yep. We meet again." I nodded, wondering where he was going with this.

"And you still look nothing like Pamela Anderson." The smile on his face gave me butterflies.

"Ha-ha very funny."

"What?"

"You keep looking at me like I'm the one that's in the wrong here."

"You're the one that sent the message and said to me that people sometimes mistake you for Pamela Anderson."

"What?" And then I sighed. "Oh my gosh. So, I need to explain something."

"Okay. And that is?"

"You weren't chatting with me in the app."

His face darkened. "You mentioned that. Who was I chatting with?"

"You were chatting with my best friend, Abby. She had this idea that we should all create profiles and chat with different guys to find the right guy for each other. She's the one who created my profile, and she chatted with you to get me the date."

"So, everything that she said was not true."

"I don't know if everything she said was not true because I don't know what she said. We had a deal where we wouldn't look and see what the other person had written."

"Well, that sounds really stupid." He rolled his eyes and then he started laughing. "But it makes a lot of sense now."

"Oh, why?"

"She also wrote that if she was lucky enough to come back to my place, she'd make me dessert after dinner."

I groaned. "So that's why you told me to go to the kitchen."

"Yeah. I thought you were being coy or nervous to go to my kitchen because you were so impressed by my house, but that's the reason I didn't get dessert at the restaurant. And that's the reason I told you to go and make me something because you—or rather, your friend Abby—had told me that was going to be happening when we got back to my place." He shook his head. "She also told me that you liked a little bit of kink."

"What do you mean?"

"She told me ..." he started laughing. "She told me you were into spanking. And ..." He started laughing even harder.

"What?"

"She told me that if things worked out, we could both get our nipples pierced."

"*What*? No, she didn't!"

"Yeah, she did. I was having a problem seeing how her conversation and how the way you were acting at the restaurant went together, but I just figured a lot of people are a lot braver when they're chatting online." He sighed. "But I guess now I know that you weren't being brave. You weren't having the conversation with me at all."

"Oh. So, are you disappointed then?"

"Disappointed? Hmm. I don't know how to answer that."

"Well, it's either yes or no. Right?"

"Well, yeah, but it's more complicated than that. I saw the photo, which was you, of course. And I was attracted to that photo. If I'm honest ..."

"Yeah?"

"If I'm honest, I liked your picture more than I liked your conversation." He shrugged. "So, I guess, no, I wasn't disappointed."

"If you didn't really like my conversation, why did you meet me?"

"Because I thought you were hot, and it turns out it wasn't your conversation I didn't like. It was your friend's."

"But—"

"But nothing. Now we know why we had such a bad first date. Or rather, now we know why we had such a bad first and second and last date." He rolled his eyes "Because we were not on the same page at all. "

"Yeah. But—" I stopped.

"What?"

"That didn't mean you had to treat me the way you did after we slept together."

"I think you read something into what I said or did. I don't really know. You women are so complicated."

"What you mean, 'you women are so complicated?"

"I just mean that …" he paused for a second and brushed something off my cheek. "Sorry, you had a bit of dirt or dust or something."

"It's okay. Thanks."

Even the brief flick of his finger against my skin took me right back to that night where he'd been touching me all over. I could tell he knew what I was thinking about.

There was a wicked glint in his eyes as he leaned

forward and whispered in my ear. "You want me again, don't you?"

I stepped back, shaking my head vehemently. "Of course not. Why would I want you?"

"Because I'm probably the sexiest man you've ever been with."

I snorted. "I wouldn't say the sexiest. Maybe the most cocky and arrogant and—"

"Shh ..." He pressed his finger against my lips. "I'm about to start thinking that you just like to hear yourself talk, Isabella."

"What's that supposed to mean?"

"It means that you're always talking, but you're not doing much of anything else."

"Much of anything else? Like what?"

"I don't know, like kissing me or touching me ..." And then he pressed his lips against mine and I swooned. I fell into his arms and his hands wrapped around my waist to keep me steady. "Well, I didn't expect that reaction," he said as he pulled away from me slightly, there was a chuckle in his voice. "You have quite the reaction to me, don't you, Isabella?"

"No, not really. You just took me by surprise and ..."

"And what? You didn't like it?"

"I didn't say that I didn't like it, but I also didn't say that I did like it."

"So contrary." He shook his head. "So ..."

"So what?"

"You're going to have to keep your eyes and your hands off of me when we get back to the house, you know. My grandparents are going to get suspicious if you keep looking at me like you want to fuck me."

"I do not keep staring at you like I want to fuck you. What are you talking about?"

"Okay. Well, maybe it's me." He laughed. "Maybe it's me that staring at you like I want to fuck you, even though I've already fucked you."

"Wow. So classy."

"Hey, what can I say?" He shrugged, "But that doesn't mean I don't want to fuck you again."

"Stop it. That's absolutely—"

"I know it's crude. Isn't it? I'm not generally a crude man. I don't know something must have just come over me. But, anyway, we need to stop acting like we want to be with each other."

"I've never acted like I want to be with you. I—"

"Uh-huh, you can say whatever you want, but Edith and Edward cannot find out, because if they realize that we're together, then they're going to figure out Lucas's secret. And I don't want that for him. At least not like this."

"You really care about him, don't you?"

"Of course I care about him. He's my younger

cousin. I love him. Yeah, he's an idiot half the time, and yeah, he's a spendthrift, but that doesn't mean I don't admire him and I don't understand where he's coming from. I want the best for him. I don't want anyone taking advantage of him."

"I'm not going to take advantage of Lucas. I've never even thought about it. I didn't even know he was rich up until a couple of hours ago."

"Really?" He raised an eyebrow, "And now that you know that he's rich?"

"Now that I know he's rich, nothing. It doesn't mean anything. And anyway, *he's* not really rich, his family is rich, and you control all the money. So ..." I just shrugged. "What does it matter?"

"Wish you could still try and be with me again, huh?"

"What's that supposed to mean?"

"Now that you know that I'm an ex-NFL player, CEO of a multi-billion-dollar company, chairperson of a multi-billion-dollar trust fund. Yeah, *multibillions*. I don't let Lucas know the exact amount because I don't want him getting greedy." He laughed. "Though he probably already is, but I like the fact that he wants to start a business. I like the fact that he's thinking about the future and not just planning on depending on the family money. It gives me faith in him."

"So, you really are going to fund it?" I said, hoping that he was being truthful. It would mean so much to Lucas to have this support.

"Of course I am. I told him I would, but I'm going to need to know more, including your part in all of this."

"What do you mean, my part in all of this?"

"Like, was it your idea for him to open this coffee shop so that you could have somewhere to showcase your art? Which I haven't even seen yet?"

"What you think I'm lying about being an artist?"

"I don't think you're lying about being an artist, but really what is an artist? Anyone can draw and paint. Are you good? I don't know. I haven't seen your work."

"Oh. So, until you see my work, you won't believe that I might be a good artist."

"I didn't say that," he shrugged, "but you got to understand something. Isabella."

"What's that?"

"My family is the most important thing to me and I will not let anyone take advantage of them for any reason, you hear?"

"Well, that's good. I wouldn't want anyone to take advantage of my family either."

"Because I know nothing about your family. I know nothing about what you actually do for a living. I already know that you're a little bit of a liar."

"Excuse me?"

"I mean, you went on a date with me and you pretended we'd been chatting when we hadn't been. It was your friend."

"I explained why."

"The why's don't matter. Once someone proves themselves to be untrustworthy, it's very, very hard for me to actually trust that they can be a good person."

"Okay." I rolled my eyes. "So, what does that mean?"

"Just let it be known that you're on notice."

"Okay. I'm on notice. Well, let it be known to you, as well, Mr. Jim Morrison— oops, I meant Jack Morrison."

He laughed. "See, you can't even remember my name."

"Of course, I remember your name, I just got caught up. I just ..." I was flustered now, "But whatever. I don't care what you think about me. Lucas is one of my best friends, and I have his best interest at heart as well. And if you're not going to give him the money for the coffee shop, because I'm a part of it, then I'll step back. I don't need to be a part of it. I want this for him."

"Okay." He gave me a look of grudging admiration, "Well, try to keep your hands off of me this weekend, then we might have a deal."

"Whatever, Jack." I grabbed my ice cream and headed outside. "You don't have to worry about anything. I don't want anything to do with you. That should have been made clear when I left your apartment in the middle of the night after mediocre sex."

"Mediocre, my foot," he chuckled as he followed me through the door.

Chapter Seventeen

❦

"So, Isabella, we're in agreement, right?"

"Yes," I replied Lucas. "Edith and Edward are not to know that Jack and I had a fling, even though it wasn't really a fling, it was just a one-night stand, but details don't matter."

"If my grandparents know that you were with my cousin a day ago, it's all over."

"But Jack said he's going to give you the money anyway."

"Well, it doesn't matter in terms of money, but now my grandparents think that you're my girlfriend, and they're really happy that I'm in a relationship and almost married, and—"

"But you're not in a relationship, and you're not almost married, and what does this mean for our future? How many times am I going to have to pretend that we're together?"

"Don't worry, we'll figure something out. I mean, loads of people break up in relationships. I'll say you dumped me or I dumped you or something, but just not this weekend, not with all my cousins and everything. We don't want to make this about me."

"Uh-huh, whatever." We walked into the house and I suddenly realized that Jack was no longer walking behind us. "Where did Jack go?"

"Who knows?" Lucas shook his head. "He's probably walking around the estate to see what needs to be done." He rolled his eyes. "He takes this situation so seriously. Like, okay, you're running the family business. But that doesn't mean you're the boss of everyone, dude." He sighed. "But whatever. Who am I to say anything? I'm just Lucas, the funny one."

"Oh, Lucas. I'm sure your family respects what you have to say as well. If you're interested in seeing what's going on around the estate, why don't you check it out too?"

"I'm not interested." He waved me off. "You know I just like to moan and complain."

"That I do." We walked down the hallway.

"Is that you, Lucas?" Edith's voice came from one of the rooms.

"Yes, Nana."

"Is that beautiful Isabella with you?"

"Yes, Nana."

"I'm in the study, dear. Come join me."

"Okay! Here we go," he whispered at me before pulling me into the study. "Hi, Nana." He hurried over to her and gave her a kiss on both cheeks. "Good to see you. Ice cream was delicious. You enjoyed it, didn't you Isabella?"

"Oh, yes, it was absolutely great. Thank you."

"I suppose you're used to gelato."

"Oh no, this was amazing, and actually, I've never had real gelato from Italy or anything." I shook my head. "You'd think I would, but," I shrugged, "I guess I haven't really gotten around out and about that much."

"Oh, that's okay, one day you'll go to Italy and you'll have gelato." She smiled. "I was wondering ..."

"Yeah?"

"Perhaps we could do some painting in the backyard?"

"Oh sure, I would love to. Do you have paints or shall I bring my own?"

"I'm not really much of a painter, but I figured you could show me what you do and maybe show me a couple of tricks. It's something I've always wanted to do. I've always wished I was good at it, but I never really got around to it."

"Oh, but of course. Would you like to join us, Lucas?"

He shook his head. "No, I'll let you and Nana do it."

"Okay. Well, let me go and get my stuff, and I'll meet you right back here."

"Sounds great. Thank you, dear." She gave me that sweet smile.

I hurried to my room and grabbed my art supplies and went back to the study. Edith was standing by the doorway.

"I'm thinking we should go into the backyard. We have beautiful flowers and garden statues and, well, whatever inspires you."

"Is there something in particular that you would like to paint?" I asked her.

"Well, I do have some beautiful roses and it would be quite nice to see if I could get them on canvas or paper or whatever it is you use."

"I think we could do watercolors, and actually, flowers are quite easy for a beginner."

"Easy? Oh, I don't know about that." She laughed. "But I'd be happy to try if you'll teach."

"Yeah, let's do it. We just need two hard surfaces to put the paper on. I don't suppose you have any boards or anything?"

"Let's see what we can find." We walked down the

hallway to another room and opened it. Inside was a library. "Oh no, not in here." She laughed, "This way." She said and closed the door. We walked a couple more steps and she opened it. Inside what looked to be an art studio. I stared at her in surprise.

"Oh, so you are an artist, or is Edward?"

"No, we always hoped one of the children would be into art, and well, I just like to shop. I think that's where Lucas gets it from." She smiled a little sheepishly. "I created this art studio years ago, and we've filled it out, but no one ever used it. Perhaps you'd like to use some of the supplies?"

"Oh, thank you." I nodded. "That's very sweet of you."

"So, have a look around my dear. See if you see anything that you think could work." I looked around, and immediately I saw two hard drawing boards.

"Okay, this is amazing. We'll use these. I wonder if you have any washi tape or ..." I then saw some masking tape. "Oh, this is perfect. We'll use this."

"Oh?" She looked surprised, "And what's that for?"

"We're going to tape the paper to the board with this tape. It comes off easily, so that way we won't rip any of the paper once we're done."

"Oh, how smart." Edith nodded, "I never would've thought of such a thing."

"Oh, it's a trick of the trade. You'll know so much more once I'm done with you."

"Well, I'm happy to learn. Shall we go to the garden?"

"Of course, that would be great."

"I've told the housekeeper to bring us some drinks and snacks in about half an hour. Just in case you get thirsty or peckish."

"Oh, sounds good. Thank you."

"You're welcome, dear. It's so nice to have a new face in the home. I miss everyone when we're up here by ourselves. I do wish that everyone were closer."

"Is most of your family in the city then?"

She nodded. "Yep. Everyone's in Manhattan, and don't get me wrong, we do have a place in the city and I love it, but it's just not the same. You just don't have the green space. You don't have the tranquility, you know?" She paused, "You hear that?"

"Umm ..." I listened but didn't hear anything but a bird chirping. "No. What am I listening to?"

"The sound of silence, dear, the sound of nature. When you get to my age, you appreciate it all the more."

"I love nature," I nodded. "I really do. I mean, I know I live in the city and there's not much nature to be had, but I love coming to places like this. I really think that I could live in the country one day."

"Really?" She looked surprised. "That surprises me."

"Oh, why?"

"I don't know, I find that most city girls these days don't want to leave the city."

"I don't know that I'm really much of a city girl."

"Oh, where did you grow up?"

"Florida." I laughed. "A very small town called Palm Bay. It's on the east coast."

"Hmm, the east coast. Near Palm Springs? Not Palm Springs," she giggled, "I always get them confused. I meant West Palm Beach. Palm Springs of course is in California," she said as much to herself as to me.

"About five hours north of that. Have you ever heard of Cocoa Beach? Where all the surfers go? It's near there."

"Cocoa Beach? Ah, yes, yes, yes." She nodded, "That's near the space center, isn't it?"

"Yeah. That's in Titusville. The Kennedy Space Center. When I was in high school, I used to go on dates there."

"Oh, very interesting. Space exploration." she said, "Who would have thought we'd have space tourism? I never would have thought I'd see it in my lifetime."

"Yeah, well, me either. Not that I will be going

into space anytime soon." I laughed, "I can't really afford it. So, thank you, Elon Musk and Richard Branson."

"Oh dear, you never know what the years may bring." She patted my hand and pointed to the right, where there was a blooming bush of roses, pinks and yellows and reds.

"Wow. It's beautiful."

"Thank you, my dear. They're English roses, actually. The gardener got them for me specially. Reminds me of my home."

"Oh yeah, you're from England originally, right?"

"Yes." She nodded, "I grew up in the countryside. Nothing exciting. A little place called Aylesbury."

"I can't say that I've heard of it. Sorry."

"Oh, don't be sorry. It's beautiful, though. Buckinghamshire." She sounded wistful. "I miss it dreadfully sometimes."

I was surprised. She seemed to have the perfect light oodles of amounts of money. She had this gorgeous estate and she missed a little town in the English countryside?

"I think as you get older, you think about your childhood a lot more, and the things that you did for fun and the people you knew. My parents, they were humble farmers, but I had a good life, you know. Have you ever been to England?"

"No." I shook my head, "I'd love to go, though, one day. A lot of the artists I studied when I was in school were European, and when I think about their portraits and when I think about the scenery, like when I have lilies and everything ..." I gazed wistfully at the roses. "It'd be really nice to see those places, you know? And well, England is someplace I've actually always wanted to visit. I have a soft spot for the country, actually."

"Oh?" She looked at me. "Are you descended from the English as well?"

"No, my ancestors are Italian, but my grandmother's family, they were in Italy when Mussolini was in power and they fled to England, and she lived there for a couple of years before they immigrated to the United States. She always talked about her time in England and a family that was very loving and kind to her. She said she always wanted to go back and thank them."

"Oh, yes. I can remember those days. The Fascists. The war." She shook her head, "Horrible, horrible thing." She sighed, "And look at the world today. Not really that much better, is it?"

"Well, it's a little better," I said, "I guess we're human beings, so nothing can ever be perfect, right?"

"Too true." She nodded. "We are all human beings born into sin and sinners we are!" She laughed. "So you're going to show me how to paint these roses, my dear?"

"I'd love to. So normally, I like to sketch before I start to paint, but we can do it either way, whatever you prefer."

"Whatever would be easiest, dear, I really have no clue." She grinned. "Teach me. Maybe we can do one of each?"

"Sounds fine to me." I opened my little zip bag full of paints. "Oh you know, we need some water." I said, "Maybe I'll run into the house and get some water so we can wet our brushes."

"Oh, I didn't even think about that."

"It's okay, I got it." A deep voice sounded from the right, and I looked over, surprised.

"Jack!"

What was he doing here? And how long had he been there? I felt self-conscious sitting there with his grandma as if I were doing something I shouldn't be doing.

"Isabella." There was an odd expression on his face.

"Hey, I didn't even see you there!"

"I know." He winked.

"What are you doing there?"

"I was just walking around the gardens. I'm a bit of a botanist, I like to study the plants and the trees."

"Oh." I stared at him in surprise. I never would have guessed he was into flowers. "How long were you standing there? Did you hear our conversation?"

"I ... Just a little bit." He smiled, "Enough to know that you need some water. I'll go and get it for you."

"That is a good boy. Thank you, Jack." Edith said with a big smile. "My favorite grandson." She put a hand over her mouth. "Oops! I love Lucas as well, of course. Don't tell him I said that."

"I won't." I laughed.

"I mean, I love them all equally, of course."

"It's okay, I won't say anything."

She smiled at me. "You are a dear girl, aren't you, Isabella?"

"Um ... Thank you?" I didn't know how to answer.

"Go along, Jack, go and get the water. Is there anything else that we'll need, Isabella?"

"Maybe some paper towels, please." I smiled at Jack, who nodded.

"Your wish is my command." He headed off, down the pathway back towards the house. And I turned to look at Edith, who was staring at me with a curious expression on her face.

"You know, my dear ..."

"Know what?"

"If I were a different sort of woman, I would have been setting you up with Jack instead of Lucas."

"Oh ..." I said, chewing nervously on my lower lip. Had I given something away just now?

"Just something about your chemistry, but I'm just a silly old woman." She laughed. "You and Lucas look very happy together, and I'm just happy to welcome you to the family."

"Thank you, Edith. You're very sweet."

"Now, my dear, I'm just honest. Because what do we have in the world if we don't have our honesty, right?"

She studied my face for a few seconds, and I nodded, reaching down and grabbing some paint brushes, my face turning hot. I didn't know how to answer her. All of a sudden, I felt very, very guilty.

* * *

"Wow. This looks beautiful." Edith beamed with pride as she stared down at her painting. "I can't believe I painted this myself. You're an absolutely wonderful teacher."

"Thank you," I said. "I think you're a natural. It actually has more to do with your skills than my teaching." I was being truthful as I gazed at her painting. She had a natural talent and had figured out how to mix colors quite beautifully.

"I don't know about that," she laughed. "But thank you."

She studied her painting for a few more minutes, admiring her work, and I smiled to myself. This was why I loved teaching classes. I loved seeing people staring at their works of art with pride and delighted surprise. "I'd be happy to paint with you another time," she said firmly. "I'm a convert. I think I might buy myself some watercolor paints. You'll have to tell me which one do you think I should buy."

"Definitely," I promised.

"We should go inside. I think Becky, Cindy, and Jenny are here, my granddaughters. I'm sure Lucas has told you about them. I'm not sure if you've met them yet?"

"No, I haven't met them yet." I shook my head, "Although I've heard about them."

"Yes. I had a feeling you hadn't met them. They call me all the time, so if they knew he was seeing someone, I'm sure they would have told me."

"Oh, of course." I nodded, feeling guilty again. I hated lying to Edith about being in a relationship with Lucas. It just didn't seem right, but it wasn't my secret to tell. If Lucas wanted to go down this road, then that was on him.

"They're having a party tonight," Edith added.

"Who is?"

"My grandkids. Becky, Cindy, and Jenny. They asked me about it earlier."

"Oh, I didn't realize that. Are you sure it's tonight? It might tomorrow."

"Sorry. I'm befuddled these days. Old age. You can forget your own name."

"Oh, I'm sure you wouldn't forget your own name."

"I try not to." She smiled but she looked a little sad. "But at some point, it's not really in your control, is it?"

"No. I guess not." I smiled gently. "Shall we go inside?"

"Let's."

As we got back to the house, I saw Jack standing there.

"So, let's see these masterpieces then." He held out his hand to look at his grandmother's painting, and I could tell from the look on his face, that he was very surprised.

"Wow, Nana, this is absolutely beautiful."

"Why, thank you, Jack." She looked proud. "It's all thanks to my teacher, of course. The wonderful Isabella."

"Not-Rossellini," Jack said.

Edith frowned. "Sorry. What?"

"It's an inside joke."

"Oh, you two have inside jokes already?"

I could tell from the look on Jack's face that he realized he'd messed up. "No, it's just a bad joke, Nana. I guess I came up with it when we went to get ice cream."

"I see." She looked back and forth at us. "But, Isabella, you must show him your paintings. If he's impressed with mine, I can't imagine what he'll think when he sees yours."

"Oh no, it's fine."

"Let me see." He held out his hand. "Let me see this talent that I've heard so much about."

I shot him a dirty look but handed him my painting. He stared at it for a few seconds and nodded.

"It's quite good," he said. "You are a true artist. I believe.

"I'd like to think so. It's how I make my money," I reminded him. "My day job and all that."

"Indeed." He nodded. "One might think that you should have your own gallery in a coffee shop or something."

"One might think that," I agreed.

Edith yawned. "Well, I think that I should go and have myself a little nap before dinner. Jack, are Becky and the other girls here yet?"

"No, Nana. They're arriving tomorrow. Remember?"

"Oh, yes. of course. And the party's tomorrow."

"The party," Jack groaned. "Oh, you didn't say yes, did you?"

"Of course. My granddaughters can have a party whenever they want. I love being around their friends and enjoying what it's like to be young again."

"Nana." He shook his head. "Ah, I thought it was just going to be a family affair."

"It *is* a family affair with some friends. What's better than friends and family?"

"I guess not much." He shook his head. "Would you like me to escort you to your bedroom?"

"No, dear. I'm fine. Thank you, though."

"You're welcome."

We watched Edith walked down the hallway towards her bedroom and then Jack spoke once again. "You're good."

"Thank you. Did you think I was going to be crap?"

"I don't know." He shrugged, "But you're really good. You're talented. I'm surprised that you're not in a gallery somewhere.

"I'm in a couple of random galleries." I shrugged. "But I don't sell enough to pay the bills."

"I'll buy a piece from you."

"You don't have to do that."

"I know I don't have to, but I'd be happy to."

"I'm sure you'd be happy to, but—"

"But what? You don't want to take my money now?"

"What do you mean I don't want to take your money *now*? Did I ever want to take your money?"

"I'm joking."

"I don't feel like that's a joke."

"You're sensitive, aren't you?"

"I'm sensitive?" I shook my head. "No, I'm not.

"Maybe one day you'll give me an art lesson."

"Maybe."

"So, you really do want to go to England?"

"Yeah. Why do you say that?"

"I remember you mentioned it when we were at dinner and then you just mentioned it to my Nana, as well."

"Yeah, I kind of have ties. I mean, not strong ties like you, but some ties."

"I guess they have a lot of great museums and galleries in England, huh?"

"Yeah." I nodded. "The Tate, The Victoria and Albert. The British Museum. They've just got so many. It would just be cool, you know? One day I'll get there."

"I'm sure you will." He nodded. "Well, I will let you go about your business for the evening. I'm sure

Lucas must be looking for you so you can conspire over how the night is going to go."

"We don't conspire. We just—"

"I don't need to know the dirty details." He shook his head. "I'll see you at dinner, Isabella."

"I'll see you at dinner, Jack."

I watched as he walked away then hurried to my room and sat on my bed. It was interesting being here, getting to know Jack better, and meeting his family.

Edith was really nice, much nicer than I would've thought for someone who was so rich, but who was I to judge? It's not like I had any firsthand experience with rich people before, certainly not millionaires and billionaires. These were good people, and I didn't like deceiving them. I needed to speak to Lucas again to see if he wouldn't just tell them the truth. I hated that he was lying to his grandparents, and I hated being part of it. And to be honest, I hated that Jack was a witness to it all. He'd already had negative thoughts about me and now he probably had even more.

Chapter Eighteen

"So, Becky, this is Isabella. Isabella, this is Becky and this is Jenny." Lucas introduced me to his glamorous cousins.

"Hey, don't forget me," a little blond girl squealed.

"And Cindy. No one could ever forget you. This is Cindy."

"Hi. Nice to meet you, Isabella." Cindy ran over to me and gave me a big hug. "So happy to finally meet someone that Lucas is dating."

"Cindy," Lucas frowned, "what is that supposed to mean?

"It means that we've been asking you for years and years and *years* to introduce us to someone you're dating."

"I just think it's funny that you're bisexual," Becky said, and everyone went silent.

Lucas looked exasperated. "Really, Becky?"

"What?"

"Nothing." He shook his head.

I looked around from Lucas to his cousins, and I was pretty sure that every single one of them knew that Lucas was gay. Did they think that he was in the closet, or that he didn't know he was gay, or something else? I didn't even know what to think anymore. I was going to ignore it. Maybe if I ignored it long enough it would sort itself out. I hoped.

"So, what are you going to wear to the party tonight?" Cindy said excitedly. "I hope you brought a fabulous dress. Did you bring a fabulous dress?"

"I didn't bring any dresses, actually." I glared at Lucas. "Someone forgot to tell me there was going to be a party."

"I didn't know!" Lucas rolled his eyes. "Sorry."

"We always have a party," Becky said. "How could you not know? Lucas, that's absolutely ridiculous." She studied me. "But you look like you're close to my size, and I brought ten dresses, so you can definitely borrow one of mine."

"Oh, wow. Thank you so much. I would really appreciate it," I replied. I'd feel a little bit of an idiot wearing jeans to the party.

"Oh, girl, don't worry. I've got you," Becky grinned. "So, have you met John yet?"

"Yeah. So, do you guys call him John or Jack? I'm kind of confused about how this whole thing goes. Or is it interchangeable?"

"Well, he was born John, but he goes by Jack." Becky shrugged. "To be honest, I call him whatever he wants me to call him in order to get my check. I'm just joking," She added with a giggle. "Well, kind of. I mean, I'm sure you've met him. He's like the boss of the family. He treats us like we're his little kids or something, not his cousins."

"See. Didn't I tell you that?" Lucas gave a firm nod.

"Jack likes to act like he's the big boss of the family, and, like, hello, we're equally descended from the same relatives, so actually all of us should have a say."

"Well, he is the CEO now," Cindy said. "And ..."

"And what?" Lucas prompted.

"And you know Papa trusts him the most."

"Whatever." Lucas rolls his eyes.

"I think you're being unfair to him." Cindy pouted.

"I know. Who said I had to be fair?" He laughed. But if he's going to get on my back for buying a Cartier watch when we have millions ..."

"Then I'm going to get on his back as well, for being a bossy-boots and a—"

"Enough, enough," Becky said. "Come on, let's go and get ready. I have invited, like, 100 people. This party is going to be banging."

"Yeah. It's going to be something, all right," Lucas said with a grin. "I hope you invited some hotties."

"We did, but don't you have Isabella here?" Becky raised an eyebrow.

"Well, yeah, I have Isabella here, but you know what I mean."

He cleared his throat and everyone started laughing. I didn't know why everyone was laughing. Maybe there was some sort of hidden joke that I wasn't in on, but I was scared to ask. I didn't want to know any more secrets. I was laden as it was. Whatever was going to happen was going to happen, and hopefully, the party would be fun.

Still, I was ready to leave this gorgeous house. Lucas's family was amazing, but I just felt weird being here. I couldn't be my true, authentic self because I couldn't tell anyone everything about myself.

I was single, and I was poor, and I lived in the city, and Lucas and I were best friends. I couldn't talk about any of that stuff. I just had to play this role that I wasn't really made for playing. Thank God I never decided to try and be an actress, because I suddenly realized that I'd make be a shitty one. I wasn't the sort of person who could pretend well. I always thought that I could, but now I knew that I couldn't. I had much more of a conscience than I had ever realized, which I suppose was a good thing. It meant that I couldn't just lie on command. But that didn't really help me now. I had to remind myself I was doing this for Lucas. I was doing it for Lucas, and that's all that mattered.

I wasn't a bad person; I just had found myself in a bad situation.

* * *

"Wow. You look absolutely gorgeous." Lucas stared at me in awe. I beamed at him. His three cousins had done my hair and my makeup, and I was wearing a Versace gown, something that I'd never be able to afford in my life, but I was so grateful that Becky had lent it to me.

"Thank you."

"I mean, you look really sexy. Really, *really* sexy." Lucas stared me up and down.

"Wow. Um, okay. Thank you."

"I've never seen you showing so much cleavage before."

I looked down at my bosom, which threatened to overflow the dress. "Do you think I'm showing too much? Do you think your grandparents won't approve?"

"It's fine. It's a party. Everyone's going to be exposing leg and showing boob. You're fine." He was sold. "Beautiful."

"Wow. Now you're starting to make me feel a little bit self-conscious," I laughed. "What do I normally look like?"

"I mean, you're definitely a beautiful girl, Isabella. Let's not get it twisted, but you look out of this world tonight."

"Thanks. Shall we head down? It sounds like the party's really happening."

"Yeah, it is really happening," he laughed. "I think there must be two hundred people there already."

"Oh, wow. And your grandparents are okay with that?"

"I'm pretty sure Edith and Edward have gone to bed already. They like to mingle, but not with this many young people."

"They're so cool."

"Yeah. I love them." He smiled fondly

"Lucas." I grabbed ahold of his shoulder.

He peered at me "What? You look really serious right now, Isabella. What's going on?"

"Don't you think you should tell them the truth?"

"Oh, no, not again."

"I mean, I had a wonderful afternoon with Edith, and I know she loves you, and I just feel like maybe you should talk to them. It's making me feel really uncomfortable being here, lying."

"Maybe I will one day, but today's not the day. Can you please just go along with this for the rest of the weekend, please?"

"Fine," I sighed, "but you're going to tell them the truth, right? I really think that they'd understand. And now that you're getting the money, it's almost pointless."

"It's not pointless, it's just ..." He shrugged. "You wouldn't understand. You've never had to keep a secret like this."

"Yeah, but I don't know that you have to keep this secret," I said softly. "Granted, I don't know your family that well, but they all seem really cool, really loving. Your grandma, well, she reminds me of my grandma, and I feel like if I were gay or had something to come out about, she'd understand, you know?"

"Really, your grandma would understand? Your Italian grandma would understand?"

"Yeah, I think she would. She loves me and she just wants the best for me. I mean, I know it's hard, and I'm not lecturing you to do something you don't want to do. Obviously, you've thought about this for a long amount of time, but I guess I just feel weird, you know? I didn't expect to feel this way. I thought it would just be fun and we'd come up here and we'd fool them into thinking we were together and you'd get your money. And we'd open this coffee shop and I'd get to showcase my art, but it feels icky. Not pretending to be your girlfriend," I said quickly, "because you're amazing, but just the lie itself, you know?"

"I know." He nodded. "I feel a little bit bad as well. I'll tell them at some point, and I'll let them know that it's not your fault."

"Thanks."

"But this is really serious for the evening," he said. "Let us go and have some fun."

"Yes, let's dance the night away," I said.

There was a DJ playing music in the great hall and the room was packed. Everyone was dancing and having fun, and Lucas and I were part of the crowd of people moving along to the beat and drinking. I was glad that I was here with these people. They were a completely different class from me, but they didn't make me feel excluded. It was amazing.

As Lucas and I danced, I could see Jack staring at me from the corner of the room. His eyes followed me across the dance floor, and I wondered what he was thinking. He looked handsome in his suit, far more handsome than should be legal, but I was going to ignore him. I was not going to let him know that I thought that he was a hot piece of meat.

"You're staring at my cousin again," Lucas said dryly.

I looked at him guiltily. "What? No, I wasn't."

"Yeah, you were. But it's fine." He shrugged. "He was staring at you, too."

"He was?"

"Really? Come on now, Isabella. You know he was staring at you. You know every man in here was staring at you."

"Well, I don't know about that."

"You want to go outside?"

"Sure," I said. "To do what?"

"There's a group of people outside, I think, playing a game. We can see what's going on."

"Sounds good to me." We grabbed our champagne flutes and headed outside. Out of the corner of my eye, I noticed Jack and another man following behind us.

"Good evening, Lucas, Isabella." Jack nodded at us. "Haven't spoken to you guys all night."

"Hey, cuz." Lucas grinned. "What's going on? Hey, Max."

"Hi, good to see you, Lucas." The guy Max stared at me with dazzling blue eyes. He held his hand out.

"These two are being rude, but I'll introduce myself. I'm Max. Nice to meet you."

"Hi, I'm Isabella."

"Isabella. Beautiful name." He smiled at me.

"Now, now, no flirting," Lucas laughed and then turned to me. "Max works with Jack at the company."

"That I do." Max nodded.

"That sounds like it must be fun," I said, making a face and then looking at Jack.

"Well, you know, it is what it is," Max laughed. "So you know Jack as well as Lucas? How do you know them both?" he asked.

"She's a really good friend," Lucas replied.

I was surprised he didn't lie, but maybe he realized that it was just making me look and feel even worse with every person he told I was his girlfriend.

"Ah, good friends?"

"We're best friends from college." I nodded.

"Well, any friend of Lucas's is a friend of mine."

I smiled back. "Why, thank you."

Jack snarled, and I looked at him in shock. "What's your problem?"

"Do you really think you should be flirting up a storm here, Isabella? Really?"

"Excuse me?" I stared at him. "What are you talking about? I'm being friendly to your friend."

"My coworker."

"Ouch," Max said, looking chagrined. "I'm just a coworker now?"

"You know what I mean," Jack grumbled. "Lucas, what's going on here?"

"Um, what are you talking about?" Lucas responded with a sly smile.

"Nothing," Jack huffed. "Where are you guys going, anyway?"

"We're going outside to hang out. See what's going on. What about you two?"

"We're doing the same," Jack said.

"Well, then I guess we're all going together," Lucas said.

"So, Isabella," Max said, "are you having fun?"

"Yeah, this is really cool. I've never been to a fancy to-do like this."

He looked me up and down. "But you certainly have the right attire."

"Oh, this isn't my dress. Becky lent it to me."

"Oh, well it's beautiful. It fits you like a glove."

"It does, doesn't it?" I laughed and then look down at my cleavage. "It's a bit more revealing than I would normally go for, but—"

"Seems like it suits you," Jack said.

"What's that supposed to mean?"

"What do you think?" he said.

"Ignore him," Lucas laughed. "He's just a grumpy old man. Isn't it past your bedtime, Jack?"

"I don't think so, Lucas. Very funny."

"Very funny," Lucas mocked him. "Come on. Let's go and have some fun."

"Hey, Isabella?" Jack grabbed ahold of my arm.

"Yeah?" I said. "What is it?"

"Um, I think we should have a little chat."

"Now?" I raised an eyebrow. "We're all about to have fun."

"Yeah, now. Lucas and Max, you just go up ahead. Isabella and I will join you in a second," Jack said.

"Okay." Lucas continued on. Max flashed me a nice smile before leaving with Lucas. I couldn't believe that Lucas had just gone. Couldn't he tell that I didn't want to be stuck talking to his cousin? Like, this was ridiculous.

"What do you want, Jack?" I snapped.

"Do you really think it's appropriate for you to be flirting with other men when you're here pretending to be dating my cousin?"

"What other men am I flirting with? What are you talking about?"

"I'm talking about the fact that you ..." He paused. "Fuck it." And then he leaned forward and kissed me. I tried to resist, but I couldn't. I kissed him back passionately, moaning as I felt his hand on the small of my back, bringing my body into his.

"What are you doing?" I said, finally pulling away as his hand squeezed my ass.

"I was just saying hello properly."

"You're the one that told me that we shouldn't even be looking at each other. You can't kiss me like this in front of—"

"In front of who?" He looked around. "There's no one here. There's no one that can see us."

"Yeah, but—"

"But what? Are you telling me you didn't like it?"

"Jack. I don't know what game you're playing at, but—"

"But what? Are you interested in Max now? You're going to go for him? First you had me, then you try to get my cousin, and now you're going for my employee? Really?"

"What are you talking about? How am I going for your employee? I literally just met him. I— You know what? Forget about it. I don't have time for this. You do you and I'll do me."

I pushed him away and stormed off after Lucas and Max. I ran over to them as soon as I saw them.

"What was that about?" Lucas looked curious.

"You don't want to know." I shook my head. "So Max, are you single?" I asked him flirtatiously, not even caring that I was flirting with him in front of Lucas. Lucas, as far as I was concerned, was being a shitty-ass friend. Here I was trying to help him out and he'd left me with his jackass of a cousin when he knew his cousin was being ridiculous.

"I am single, as a matter of fact." He smiled. "Can I get you a drink?"

I finished my champagne and nodded. "Another drink would be great. Thank you."

"Why don't you come with me?" he said. "I think there's a little bar at the back here."

"Okay." I grinned. "Is that okay, Lucas?"

"Of course." He shrugged. "What's it to me?"

"Well, you know what's it to you." I gave him a look.

"Ah, no, one's bothered with us tonight." He shook his head. "The grandparents are in bed. Do what you want to."

"Okay. 'Night, Lucas."

"'Night? This is it?"

"Well, I mean, I don't know if I'll see you again for the rest of the night because I don't know how much longer I'll be out here. You know what I mean."

"I'm not sure if I do," he laughed, "but whatevs. Maybe I'll see you later and maybe I won't, huh?"

"You got it," I laughed. I followed Max over to the bar and he grinned down at me.

"What's going on with you and Lucas? And what's going on with you and Jack?"

"You don't even want to know." I shook my head. "But what's going on with you?" I flirted with him even though I wasn't that interested, but I could see Jack staring at me from across the way. I could feel his eyes on me. And I wasn't going to let him dictate how I could act or who I could flirt with.

"You want to dance after we get our drinks?"

"Sure." I nodded. "Sounds good." Max got me a drink and then we headed to a little area on the back patio where people were dancing. Before I knew what was happening, Jack was also there with a tall, striking woman with long, blonde hair. She was gorgeous. Absolutely beautiful. I tried to make eye contact with him so I could glare at him, but he didn't even look at me. He just held her close to him and danced. She was pressed up against him, beaming up at him. I wondered if they knew each other intimately. Who was this bitch? And why did I care? I shook my head and turned away, dancing closer with Max.

"Well, I'm glad I came to this party after all," he said with a soft smile.

"Oh yeah?" I asked him, staring up at him, loving the fact that I could see Jack staring at us out of the corner of my eyes.

"Yeah. You've made my night. These things are normally so boring. I don't normally meet cool women like you, but, hey, maybe my luck is changing."

"Maybe it is," I said, feeling nervous and out of place. I really didn't want to give him the wrong idea, but I did want to make Jack jealous. I giggled loudly as he pressed his hand into my back. I looked to the side and my eyes finally caught Jack's. He was glaring at me and shaking his head and I just raised an eyebrow and turned back away from him.

Take that, Jack Morrison. You don't control me. You don't own me. And I can do whatever the heck I want.

Chapter Nineteen

The crowd was starting to die down, but there were about eight couples surrounding me and Max on the dance floor. They seemed to be very loved up. One of them, directly next to us, was making out, and I was starting to feel uncomfortable. I wasn't sure if Max thought that something was going to happen between us, but even though I found him attractive, I certainly didn't want to make out with him. I stepped back slightly when the song ended and yawned. "It's been such a pleasure dancing with you, Max, but I think I need to get back inside. I'm feeling quite tired."

"Oh." He looked disappointed. "I can walk you to your room if you'd like."

"Oh no, no, no. Thank you though," I said quickly. "I just need some time by myself."

"I understand. It's been a long night." His blue eyes sparkled. "May I give you a kiss?" He paused, "on the cheek?"

"Sure," I said with a sweet smile. He kissed me on the cheek I saw his eyes looking at my lips. I really hoped he wasn't going to go for a kiss. Before he had time to do it, I quickly took another step back. "Well, it was a pleasure meeting you Max. Maybe we'll see each other again."

"I sure hope so," he said.

I hurried away back towards the house. As I walked through the back door and into the hallway, I slipped my heels off. I wasn't used to wearing high heels for so many hours, especially dancing, and my feet were absolutely killing me. I walked down the hallway barefoot, singing the Nat King Cole song that had just been playing to myself.

It's been a nice evening, even though Jack and I had had words, and even though I felt weird about Lucas, Edith, and Edward. I turned down the corner to head to my bedroom, and then I heard footsteps behind me. I groaned inwardly. I really, really hope that it wasn't going to be Max. I didn't want to have to tell him that I wasn't interested.

"Isabella."

I paused and froze, turning my head around

slightly. It wasn't Max, but it was someone even worse.

"What's going on, Jack?" I said quickly, my heart racing as I saw the look in his eyes. It was undiluted lust. I licked my lips nervously. Why was Jack here? Why was he doing this to me? "I'm headed to bed, so ... good night."

"You're headed to bed?" He frowned, "but where's your new friend?" His eyes looked at me suspiciously.

"He's in the backyard." I rolled my eyes back at him. "Where's your new friend?"

"Which new friend?"

"The girl you were dancing with on the dance floor."

"Oh," he started laughing. "Jealous, are we?"

"Not at all." My voice rose slightly. I knew I sounded a little bit weird and awkward, but I didn't want him to know how pissed off and upset I'd been seeing him holding that beautiful blonde lady so tightly.

"You don't lie very well, Isabella," he grinned.

"I'm not lying," I said.

"Yeah, you are." He grabbed me and pulled me into his arms and then his lips were on mine and he was kissing me passionately. I couldn't help myself. I kissed him back, running my hands through his hair and pulling on his tresses tightly.

"Come," he said. He grabbed my hand and pulled me into a bedroom. He closed the door and then pulled me into his arms again. "You look really hot in that dress," he said.

"Oh yeah? I didn't think you noticed."

"I noticed," he nodded. "All the men noticed. Max noticed," he growled as he looked down at my heaving breasts. His arms encircled my shoulders, then I felt his hand pulling down the zipper of my dress. It fell to the ground in one fell swoop.

He grinned. "No bra, huh?"

"I couldn't wear a bra with this dress," I said, loving the look on his face. He reached down and touched my breasts, tweaking my nipples. I moaned. It felt so good.

"This is how I like to see you," he growled. "In that thong and heels. I could picture you like this all day long."

"You could picture me like this, huh?" My eyes narrowed. "Really? Is that your way of telling me that you have been picturing me like this?"

"Maybe, maybe not."

I shook my head and walked over to him quickly undoing his tie and unbuttoning his shirt. I felt his hot breath on my cheek as my fingers deftly removed his shirt. I pressed my lips against his chest. His skin felt warm and smooth against my mouth.

He was just as gorgeous as I remembered. Just as gorgeous as I'd dreamed about. I didn't care that he was an asshole. I didn't care that he was Lucas' cousin. I didn't care that I'd told myself this was never going to happen again because here I was and here, he was, and it just felt right. My hands fell to his belt buckle and started to undo it, but they were trembling slightly and I was having a hard time. He chuckled, pushed my hands away, and undid his belt quickly before undoing his pants and stepping out of them. He stood there in a pair of black briefs.

They were tight on his skin and I stared at the way that the material clung to his hard cock. I licked my lips again.

"If you keep licking your lips, I'm going to suck on them," he said, leaning towards me, grabbing my ass and pulling me towards him. I felt his hardness pressed up against my stomach. As his tongue entered my mouth, my breasts crushed against his chest and I moaned as his chest hair tickled my nipples. "You're fucking hot. You know that?"

"I know." I laughed as he pulled on my hair. He grabbed me and pulled me towards the bed, positioning me in the middle of his pillows before he straddled me. His lips pressed against my collarbone and he kissed all the way across my chest and down towards my belly button. When his tongue slipped into my belly button, I giggled and he looked up at me with laughing eyes.

"You're ticklish, huh?"

"I guess I am." I ran my hands through his hair, loving the warmth of his body next to mine. His teeth grabbed a hold of my panties and he started to pull them down. I shimmied on the bed so that he could pull them down faster. I wanted to feel his mouth against my wetness, wanted to feel his tongue inside of me. "Hurry," I said to him, urging him on. He grinned up at me and then nipped my inner thigh, and I yelped. He ran his tongue along my wetness, and I closed my eyes, gripping his sheets, getting ready.

Knock knock.

I froze. There was someone at the door. Jack and I looked at each other.

Knock, knock.

"Who is it?" Jack called out.

"Jack, it's me, your grandfather.

"Fuck," Jack muttered under his breath. "Get under the duvet, quick!" He pulled the duvet and the sheet down and I hurried under the bedclothes. He covered me quickly and then he adjusted himself so that he was lying slightly on me. "I was just about to go to bed, but you can come in for a moment," he said.

"Hey, sorry. I didn't think that you would be going to bed so early." I could hear Edward's voice talking, even though it sounded muffled through the duvet.

"It's fine, Papa. Is everything okay?" Jack sounded anxious, but maybe it was because of the duvet. I'd never heard that tone in his voice before.

"It's okay." I heard footsteps coming towards the bed and then they stopped. "Did you have fun at the party tonight?"

"Yeah, it was a good time. You know, Becky and Cindy love to have a good shindig."

"They do, they do," Edward chuckled. "It's good for them. They deserve to have fun."

"Yes, they do."

"So, my boy ..."

"Yes, Papa?"

"My latest prognosis isn't as good as I would have hoped."

I froze as I listened to Edward talking. What was he talking about? What prognosis?

"Oh, no." Jack shifted on the bed. I knew he wanted to get up, but it would become more obvious that there was a lump in the bed if he got off completely. "Oh, Papa. I'm sorry to hear that."

"It's okay. I'm not going to die tomorrow. I've got the best doctors. Thank God for having a lot of money," Edward chuckled. "But I will be gone sooner than I would like. And I want you to promise me that you'll look after Lucas and Becky and Cindy and Jenny, and of course, Edith."

"Of course, Papa."

"You'll be the head of the family, and they will need your guidance. I don't know what happened to my kids," he sighed. "Useless bunch, but my grandkids ... You're all wonders of my life. And you, Jack, you are the one trustworthy, dependable man in the family. I apologize for being so demanding when you were younger. I apologize for thrusting this responsibility onto you at such a young age, but..."

"It's okay, Papa." Jack's voice was choked up and I could tell that this was a very meaningful moment. I felt uncomfortable lying there in bed. I knew I shouldn't be listening to this conversation. I felt like I was completely invading their privacy, and I hated it.

"You're a good boy, Jack," Edward continued. "I hope you find a good woman. Like Lucas' girl. What's her name again?"

"Isabella," Jack said, my name sounding like music on his tongue. I loved the way he said my name. As if it were beautiful and delicate. As if he were protecting and savoring it all in one breath.

"Yes, Isabella. She's a pretty young thing, isn't she?"

"I guess so." I glared as Jack said that. Jerk.

"She's one of those rare beauties. She seems very sweet as well."

"Well, you don't really know her, Papa, and neither do I and we'll just see what happens with her and Lucas."

"I can tell good women when I meet them. I may be an old man, but I am a wise man," Edward chuckled. "Well, I'll let you be. I know you must be tired, but I did want to have this conversation whilst everyone else was engaged and having fun, you know?"

"I understand, Papa."

"I know you do, boy. You're a good boy. Have a good night, son."

"Yes, Papa."

"Good night, Jack."

"'Night, Papa."

It went silent for a few seconds and then the door closed. After that, I felt Jack pulling down the duvet cover. "Hey," he kissed me on the lips.

"Hey," I said softly, staring at his face, looking into his eyes. That was a lot of responsibility to take on. Looking after a whole family. He couldn't have been more than thirty-something. "Do you want to talk?" I said, my voice full of emotion. I so badly wanted us to have this moment together. I so badly wanted us to share something of depth. He stared at me blankly.

"Talk?" His hands moved down between my legs and he rubbed gently.

"Jack," I moaned, as he slipped his fingers inside my panties and rubbed my clit.

"Yes, Isabella?"

"I asked you if you wanted to talk about ..."

"No." He leaned down and took my nipple in his mouth. I closed my eyes, feeling myself growing wetter and wetter. He moved his lips back up to my mouth and he stared at me. "Don't tell Lucas anything, okay?"

"Of course not," I said. "I wouldn't tell him."

"Okay, well just make sure you don't."

I stared at him, wondering what was going on in his head. What were all the feelings and emotions he wasn't telling me about? And if he wasn't telling me, who did he have to tell? Did he have anyone? And was that someone a woman? Jealousy surged through me, and I tried to ignore it. I didn't want to think about Jack with another woman. He wasn't mine. Not by any means. If anything, we were frenemies. And nothing more than that.

Chapter Twenty

❧

Jack's lips pressed against mine and then moved down to my neck and then to my breasts. There seemed to be an increased energy in his kisses and touch, as if he were full of some pent-up emotion that he needed to get out.

"I want you to scream out my name, Isabella."

"I can't do that!" I shook my head, moaning as I felt his fingers slipping in between my legs.

"Spank me, Isabella."

"No! Jack, I ..."

"Beg me," he growled. And I felt a finger slipping inside of me.

"Oh, Jack!" I cried out. I couldn't stop myself.

"I think about that lap dance you gave me every minute. You know that, right?"

"You do?" My eyes fluttered open, and I stared at him. His eyes were dark as he looked down on me.

"I do. It was probably the hottest lap dance I've ever gotten in my life."

"And you've gotten a lot of lap dances?" I ask.

"What do you think?"

"I think we shouldn't be doing this," I mumbled breathlessly. He slipped another finger inside of me, and I cried out, "Jack, please!"

"Please, what, Isabella?" His eyes glittered as he stared down at me, his lips pressed against mine, and he kissed me hard. "What do you want?" he said against my lips.

"I want you."

"Where?" he growled.

"Inside of me. Please."

"Scream my name. Beg me."

"I am!"

"Beg me louder."

"Jack, please!" I cried out. As he slipped his fingers out of me, I felt bereft at the sudden loss of his touch. I stared at him, kissing him back hard, letting him know with my mouth how badly I wanted him.

"What do you want, Isabella?"

"I want you to fuck me now!"

"Now?" he said. "Not later?"

"Stop teasing me!" And then I paused. "Unless you don't want it. Unless this is just a game to you."

"This has never been a game to me, Isabella."

He reached over to the side of his bed and grabbed a condom. He had it on before I could blink, and his cock was thrusting inside of me. I cried out at the immediate feel of him inside of me. It felt even more wonderful than it had before. It felt like he fit me perfectly. I moved my hips back and forth, wanting him to go even deeper.

"Fuck, you're so tight and wet," he growled as he palmed my nipples. He started moving faster, not worrying that we were shaking the bed. I dug my fingers into his back, squeezing his skin, and I bit down on the side of his neck as he thrust into me harder and harder. It felt amazing. I felt like I had died and gone to heaven. I never wanted this feeling to end. I never wanted to be anywhere but in this position with him, which was absolutely ridiculous because this was never going to happen again. I was never going to sleep with him again. But I couldn't even think about that now. He was bringing me to orgasm. I was so close, so close. His fingers started rubbing my clit, and that was all it took for me to reach the edge of the cliff—and fall.

"Oh, yes, Jack! Oh, yes, Jack!" I screamed as he slammed into me one last time, his last thrust more powerful than any others. My orgasm took me over the edge, and what was so perfect was that he started orgasming at the same time, and our bodies trembled and shook together before finally he collapsed on top of me.

"That was good," he panted.

"That was amazing," I agreed.

He kissed me lightly on the lips, and then he pulled away.

"I think ..." he said and then paused. There was a light in his eyes that I hadn't seen before. An inner torment that made me want to pull him into my eyes and hold him tight.

"Jack, what's wrong?"

"I think it's time for you to go to your room, don't you?"

"What?" I blinked, surprised at his words. Was he sending me away?

"The first time we made love, you left. I didn't want you to, but you left. So, the second time, I'll send you away before you can leave me again." He shrugged and turned on his back. "It was fun, though. Let's do it again sometime."

I felt dismissed. I felt horrible. I felt like my heart was breaking into a million different pieces, and once again, I realized how much I hated him, how much I hated myself for sleeping with him again, for giving him my body. He was a jerk, a complete and utter jerk.

I quickly got out of bed and grabbed my clothes and headed for the door.

"Have a good night, Isabella."

The words sounded mocking to my ears. I was furious. I was rejected. I was broken. Jack was a man unlike any I'd ever met before. I hated him and I wanted him and I had no idea what was going on in his head.

So I ignored him. I left the room and went to my own bedroom, thankful that I'd be leaving tomorrow and going back home. I didn't care what Lucas wanted for me after this. I was done. I was never coming back to this place. I was never going to pretend to be his girlfriend again. I didn't care what he needed me to do to get this coffee shop. He could do it by himself. This wasn't worth my dignity and self-respect. This wasn't worth a broken heart.

Chapter Twenty-One

"Thanks so much for coming with me this weekend, Isabella. I know it wasn't exactly what we had planned, but I do hope you had fun," Lucas said as the taxi stopped outside my apartment building.

"It was an okay time." I forced a smile. "I mean, your grandparents are lovely, and they have a beautiful house and well, you know, I had fun, but ..." I made a face.

"I know," he sighed, "Jack. I'm sorry. I know he's a jerk, and I hate that he's treated you like this. I really don't know why he has been such an asshole to you."

"It's fine. I mean, I don't even care about him. Whatever. I'm glad he's going to help you, though, with your business."

"Me too." Lucas looked excited. "It's really happening, Isabella. We're going to do this!"

"Well, who knows if I'm going to be a part of it." I looked away. "It doesn't seem like Jack really wants me to have any part."

"I don't care what Jack has to say. He can't tell me that you can't have your art gallery there, and he saw your artwork. I mean, Nana was going on and on about your skills. There's no way he can tell me no. We all can tell you're so very talented."

"Well, you're sweet, Lucas, but I should get out. The meter's running." I could see the taxi driver watching us through the rearview mirror. He looked pissed, even though he was still getting paid. "I'll see you later?"

"Yeah. Text me later, okay?"

"Okay, bye." I jumped out of the taxi and hurried into my apartment building.

I was happy to be home. Greenwich was beautiful, but I liked my place. Even though it was cramped and small and stuffed with all sorts of knickknacks that my roommates and I had collected, it felt like home. I hurried up to the apartment and opened the door, hoping that someone would be home.

"Hello? It's me," I called out.

"Hey, Isabella, come into the living room!" Abby shouted.

I was glad she was home, even though I was still a little pissed at her.

"How was your trip?" She jumped off the couch and headed towards me, "Don't touch my nails."

"Um, okay," I laughed. "Why would I be touching your nails?"

"Just in case," she grinned, "I'm doing them. Guess what? I got a new job!" She started jumping up and down. "Sorry, I was going to wait to tell you because I want to hear all about your weekend, but I'm so excited! I got a job!"

"Wow, that's amazing. What are you going to be doing?"

"Have you ever heard of Dylan McAllister?"

"Um, no."

"You've never heard of Dylan McAllister? He's like in every who's who of young eligible hot men in the city."

"I don't really read those, Abby."

"Oh, well. Anyway, I'm going to be working for him as his secretary. Can you believe it?"

"What? I can't believe it. You're going to be a secretary? You can't even type well."

"Shh!" She giggled. "I'm going to take one of those classes online to practice my skills. It's just so cool. I'm so excited. I'm slightly nervous, of course, because I heard he doesn't have a great reputation, and his last five secretaries have all left within a couple of weeks, but the money is amazing."

"Oh yeah? How amazing?"

"Like 10K a week amazing."

"Get out!" My jaw dropped. "10K a *week*? Like, 40K a month?"

"Oh, oops." She shook her head, "I got that wrong. I mean 10K a month," she laughed. "I wish 10K a week."

"I was about to say we would be so out of here."

"Yeah, we would," she agreed. "After I paid off my student loans, of course."

"Of course. So how did you get this job? Tell me more."

"I'll tell you more later. I want to hear about your weekend. How was it with Lucas's family and—"

"Girl, guess who Lucas's cousin is?"

"... Um, I don't know? Andrew Rockefeller?"

"Isn't he dead?"

"I don't know." She laughed. "Teddy Roosevelt?"

"Honestly, Abby, you're not even trying."

"Well, how am I supposed to know who his cousin is?" She made a silly face. "I barely know him."

"Jack is his cousin."

Abby looked blank. "Jack and the Beanstalk?"

"Abby? Really?"

"Sorry. Um, Jack and Jill from Jack and Jill Went up the Hill?"

"You're such an idiot."

"I'm sorry. I just really don't know what you're talking about."

"Jack that I went on the date with. That obnoxious guy."

That got her to focus. "No way! Not the guy that you slept with?"

"Yes. Him."

"Oh, this is juicy. Okay, tell me everything. He's Lucas's cousin? Whoa. So, what did he say when he found out you and Lucas were dating?"

"Obviously he knew Lucas and I were not actually dating. I just slept with him last week. I know he doesn't know me from Adam, but I'm not that big a ho."

"Yeah, but he doesn't know that," she pointed out.

"Abby!"

"What?"

"I've got a bone to pick with you, by the way."

"Oh, gosh. What did I do now?"

"He told me some of the things you said to him on the dating app."

"Oops." Her cheeks turned a little pink. "Okay, I might've got a little bit carried away, but I wanted to ensure you got the date. And I mean, he was a hottie in his photos, and I knew I had to push it if he was going to say yes."

"Well, thank you. He totally thought I was going to be someone I wasn't. But anyway, that doesn't matter now."

"Um, so, you had a good time within this weekend or ...?"

"He's a jerk," I sighed, "Just like I thought. And I was stupid again."

"What do you mean you were stupid again? What did you do? Oh my gosh, you did not have a threesome with him and Lucas, did you?"

"Ew, no! I didn't have a threesome with him and Lucas—who's *gay*."

"I know, but maybe Lucas wanted to sample the goods."

"Sample the goods with who?" I shook my head, "Jack is his cousin, and I'm one of his best friends, and I'm a woman with breasts and a vagina. He doesn't like that, remember?"

"Okay, okay. So, you slept with Jack, then?"

"Yes, I slept with him again. Ugh, I'm such an idiot."

"It was bad?"

"No, it wasn't bad. It was amazing. He's got the touch of a Greek god. Oh, I can't stand him!"

"You can't stand him because he's good in bed?"

"No, I can't stand him because he's such an asshole."

"Girl, you knew he was an asshole before you slept with him again."

"I know." I went over to the couch and sat down. "But ... there's one thing."

"What?" She came and sat down next to me, still holding her fingers in the air.

"He seems like he actually has a slightly deeper side."

"Oh? Really? Like he can get into you *deep*." She gyrated her hips a little bit, and I giggled.

"He can get into me deep," I conceded. "But that's not what I'm talking about."

"So then, what are you talking about, if it's not his ginormous cock."

"Abby."

"What?" She laughed. "If he can get into you so deep that you're giggling about it, he has to be pretty big."

"I mean, I wasn't complaining." I winked at her.

"I want *all* the dirty details, girl."

"Nope, I am not kissing and telling."

"What about fucking and telling?"

"No, Abby. I'm not going to tell you any more. Plus, I don't even want to think about it again."

"So, okay, how is he deeper?"

"So, the night that we slept together, I was actually hiding under the duvet because his granddad came into the room."

"Ooh, that sounds so hot and sexy."

"Trust me, it wasn't sexy. I thought I was going to suffocate. I was so scared we'd get caught, and what would his grandfather have thought? I'm dating one grandson, but I'm in bed with the other one? So tawdry. It's like one of those TV shows about royals."

"What's that TV show where that one girl's like hooking up with everyone in the royal family?" Abby mused.

"I have no idea. Is it on Lifetime?"

"No," she giggled, "Does Lifetime have shows about the royal family?"

"I think so. They've got a movie about Meghan Markle and Prince Harry almost every week," I said drily.

"Oh, yeah. That's true. That movie was so shit."

"It was, wasn't it?" I laughed then got serious again. "But anyway, his granddad was there and was talking about how his prognosis isn't good, and he wants Jack to take care of the family and I guess to run the business, and I didn't follow everything he was saying, but I assume that his granddad's going to die soon."

"Whoa." Abby's face looked serious all of a sudden. "That is deep shit. Jack's not that old, is he?"

"No, I think he's in his 30s."

"Wow, and he has to take care of his family. That's a lot."

"Yeah. I feel like that must be a lot of pressure. And I told you, right?"

"Told me what?"

"He's a football star. Or, at least he was. I guess he was in the NFL."

"I know." She nodded.

"How did you know?"

"You said his name was Jack Morrison, right? He was pretty big when he was in the NFL. Everyone knew about him. He was like in the newspapers all the time and on all those entertainment shows."

"He was? How do you know?"

"Because he was dating like every model and actress in Hollywood," she laughed. "But I mean, I doubt he's doing that now," she said quickly.

"I don't care. He could be screwing half the world for all I care," I rolled my eyes. "That's not my problem."

"Okay," she nodded, "So you *don't* like him …?"

"No, of course I don't like him."

"Okay, I'm just checking because the first time

you slept with him, you said you didn't like him, but here you are, and you've slept with him again."

"I didn't even know he was going to be there. It was a lapse of judgment."

"Girl, you've had two lapses of judgment with this guy already," she laughed. "I mean, I hate to say it, but it sounds like he's got you dick-matized."

"He's got me what?"

"You get it, right? Dick-matized. Like hypnotized but with his dick? I just heard that saying recently. I thought it was funny."

"It's so stupid," I laughed, "But I can't lie. He has got me a little bit dick-matized. Oh my gosh, girl. If you could see his body. It's totally amazing."

"I can imagine." She sighed dreamily. "I need to meet me a Jack Morrison and get me some dick too."

I snorted at the crude language. "Really, Abby?"

"What? It's been a while for me as well, girl. Maybe you should go on the dating app and get someone for me now."

"Uh uh. Remember we said that we weren't going to do this anymore?"

"What? That's not fair. I did it for you."

"Uh-huh. And look how that turned out."

"Hey, hey, we all live and learn, right?" She grinned. "And anyway, I'm not going to have time today. I've got to focus on impressing Dylan McAllister."

"Dylan McAllister. Wow," I shook my head, "You're really excited about this job. He must be really good looking for you to care this much."

"I mean, I've never seen him in person, but the photos I have seen of him, he looks mm-mm good!" she sang.

My phone started beeping just then, and I pulled it out of my purse. "Huh, I've got a text from an unknown number."

"So, it's probably spam, girl. Just delete it."

"No, hold on. Let me read it. The person knows my name," I read the text out loud, "Hey, Isabella. It was great meeting you this weekend. This is Max. The guy that works for Jack? The guy you danced with just in case you forgot. I was wondering if you'd like to go for drinks sometime." I raised my eyebrows as I looked at Abby.

She looked back at me in confusion. "Who the hell is Max? What is going on here, girl?"

"He's a guy that I met. We kind of danced on the night that I slept with Jack, but—"

"What? You're such a player! You have one guy and you slept with another one, and all while you're pretending to be someone else's girlfriend. You go, girl," she put her hand up to high-five me, and I started giggling.

"You don't want me to touch the fingers, remember?"

"Oh, yeah," she said, blowing on her fingernails, "I do not want to have to paint my nails again. This is already my second go-around."

I looked back at the text. "I don't know what to do."

"What do you mean you don't know what to do? Go on the date. If you were dancing with him, you must think he's kind of good-looking."

"He's cute, but it would be kind of awkward."

"Why would it be awkward?"

"Because he works with Jack."

"So? You've already said you're not interested in Jack, right?"

"No, I'm not."

"And you're not going to see him again, right?"

"No way."

"So go on this date with Max. Have some drinks. See what it's like. Have some fun. We're young, girl, and we're not going to have these chances when we get older."

"Fine." I quickly texted him back, "Sounds good. When are you thinking?" and then sat back. "Okay, well, we'll see what happens."

"I'm so excited for you, Isabella."

"Excited about what?"

"That you're finally getting some action."

"More like drama."

"So? Drama is exciting."

"No, it's not. I like just eating pizza and watching TV. I don't need this drama in my life. I want a boyfriend, a stable, handsome, loving boyfriend who will sit on the couch with me and kiss me and eat pizza with me and love me. Is that too much to ask for?"

"Yes," she snorted. "That's what we all want, girl. And none of us in this house have it yet."

"Maybe one day," I sighed.

"I hope so." She sat back against the couch. "But you've got me for tonight. Want to grab a pizza and watch a movie?"

"I guess you're off the diet as well?"

"Oh, yeah," she grinned, "I'm off the diet as well. We'll try again next month."

"Sounds like a plan to me."

Chapter Twenty-Two

"So, I have a date with Max tonight," I told Abby as I entered the kitchen. She was taking a box of cereal out of the cupboard.

"Want some?" She held it up.

"Sure."

"So, are you excited for your date?"

"I guess, kind of? I'm not sure. It's weird. I don't really know him, but I guess it will be fun.

"How's Lucas? Have you spoken to him recently? Do you know what's going on with the coffee shop?"

"No, I haven't seen him since last week when we got back. I figure he'll tell me when he knows something. I'm teaching a class tomorrow." I rolled my eyes.

"You don't sound happy about it."

"It's at the senior center in Queens."

"Oh, you really don't like those classes, do you?"

"I mean, they're okay. I just feel like there's so many people in each class, and I don't have enough time to go one-on-one with each of them, you know? If I had my own studio and could teach my own classes, I'd limit the number of students so that I can really provide great feedback and help people. Because everyone wants to paint something that they're proud of, and I just don't feel like I can do that when I'm in a class with 30 different people for two hours, trying to teach them how to paint a plant or something, you know?"

"I understand, girl. So, what are you going to wear for your date tonight?"

"I don't know. A cute dress or something. We're just going to get a drink, so I don't want to overdo it."

"Well, you always look cute, whatever you wear."

"You're so sweet."

"Who's so sweet?" Emma asked as she walked into the kitchen and joined us.

"Abby is. She was just telling me that I always looked good."

"Because you do," Emma yawned and ran her hands through her hair.

"Isabella's going on a date tonight," Abby told Emma.

"Ooh, that guy that you met the other day?"

"Did I tell you about him?" I frowned.

"No, but Abby did." Emma opened the refrigerator door.

"Thanks, Abby."

"What? There are no secrets among best friends. I didn't think you'd mind if I told her what went down."

"I don't mind. So, you got all the details?" I asked Emma.

"Yep. I know all about Jack and Max and Lucas and whichever other guy you have coming up next."

"Ha-ha, very funny. There are no more guys." My phone dinged. "Oh, someone's texting me. Be right back."

I hurried to my bedroom and picked it up. There was another unknown number. Why were so many unknown numbers texting me?

"Hey, Isabella, this is Jack Morrison. Would love to chat with you about the coffee shop and your ideas for the art studio. Call me."

I took the phone with me back into the kitchen. "You will not believe who just texted me."

"Barack Obama?" Abby said with a grin.

"Abby, you're such an idiot."

"I don't know. Brad Pitt?"

"Yeah. Brad Pitt just texted me. He just wanted to say hello."

"I know," Emma said. "Bradley Cooper."

"Why would Bradley Cooper be texting me?"

"I don't know. Maybe he wants you to be in one of his movies."

"Yeah, that sounds very logical, doesn't it?"

"Okay, then tell us who. Your question was just as stupid as our answers," Abby replied.

"Whatever, but it was Jack."

"No way!" Abby handed me the bowl of cereal. "Jack?"

"Yep."

"*Jack* Jack?"

"How many Jacks are there, girlfriend?"

"I mean, I know there aren't many, but I just wanted to make sure. What did he say?"

"He said he needed to talk to me about my ideas about the gallery part of the coffee shop."

"Oh wow. That's positive, right?"

"Why does he need to talk to me? It's none of his business. That's between me and Lucas."

"Okay. So, what are you going to tell him?"

"He asked me to call him and I'm going to tell him no."

"Really?"

"Yep." I pulled out my phone and typed "Sorry, not available for a call."

He responded immediately. "You have no time all day?"

"Nope. No time all day," I sent back quickly.

"Well then, I guess we can just text about it."

"What do you want to know?"

"How much space do you think you'll need for your art supplies and for the classes? How many people do you envision in each class?"

I looked up at my friends after I read the text. "Well, it looks like he's serious about these questions."

"What's he asking?"

"He's asking the sort of space I'm going to need for the art supplies in the classes."

"Do you know?"

"Girl, I have no idea." I responded "The classes will be five people max. So, one big table should work. And I'm hoping that we can fit in two drawers for the art supplies and then wall space for the paintings."

"Can you not meet for lunch today?" he responded.

"No, sorry."

"Dinner?"

"Busy. Got plans."

"Are you going to make this difficult, Isabella?"

"Nope."

"You can't meet me tonight?"

"I honestly can't meet you tonight. I have plans. Sorry."

"Plans with who?"

"As if I'm going to you that," I responded quickly.

"What's he saying? What're you saying? You're typing ferociously," Abby said, sitting next to me at the table.

"He is just trying to convince me to go to dinner with him and I'm telling him no and that I have plans. And he wants to know with who."

"He's nosy, isn't he?" Emma said.

"Yeah, like that's any of his business."

"I wonder how he got your phone number."

"I think it's quite obvious how he got my phone number. He probably got it from Lucas. I'm going to kill Lucas," I grumbled. My phone beeped again as another message came through.

"I've been thinking about you."

I stared at his texts. I wasn't going to tell him I'd been thinking about him as well, though I had been. I didn't respond. He sent another text right away.

"Knock, knock."

I wasn't going to respond, but I couldn't stop myself. "Who's there?"

"Lettuce."

"Lettuce who?"

"Lettuce in, it's only a joke."

"Ha-ha," I responded. "I think I told that joke when I was in first grade."

"Fine. Knock, knock."

"Who's there?"

"Boo."

"Boo who?"

"There's no need to cry, it's only a joke."

"Really, Jack? Don't you have time for anything better? I thought you were a CEO of a billion-dollar company. Why are you wasting your time sending me these ridiculous jokes?"

"Because I wanted to make you smile. And I wanted to make you have dinner with me."

"I already told you I'm busy."

"Tomorrow then."

"Tomorrow nothing."

"You really hate me, huh?"

"I don't hate you; I just don't think we have anything to say to each other."

"Fine," he said, "I'll leave you alone."

"Good," I responded. I put the phone down and I stared at Abby and Emma who were gazing at me with wide eyes.

"What is going on?" Abby asked, breathless. "You looked absolutely fierce as you were sending those text messages back and forth."

"I just don't understand why he's texting me. I don't understand why he wants to see me. He's the one that pretty much dissed me and now he's trying to meet up for dinner to talk about something that I'm really not even that invested in. I'm not putting up money for this. This is between him and Lucas," I said.

"Hey, slow down Isabella," Abby held her hand up. "He's really got you riled up, hasn't he?"

"Yeah, of course he has. He just—" I forced myself to stop as I realized that I was talking a mile a minute. I sighed and closed my eyes. "It's hard, girls. I mean, I don't really know how to feel in this situation. We met on a date. The date was okay. I was really attracted to him. And then he ruined that. And then we met again and I thought, well maybe, just maybe, he's an okay guy. And then he ruined it again. And now I just don't want to deal with it, you know? I'm not looking for someone that's going to hurt my feelings or make me feel bad about myself. If he doesn't know and trust that I'm a good person, and if he doesn't know and trust that I'm someone that he wants in his life, then he can just piss off. I'm not going to play these games with him."

"Good for you, girl," Emma said with a huge smile on her face. "I'm so proud of you for sticking up for yourself and for not settling. Just because he's hot and rich doesn't mean he gets to treat you any which way and then come back for more."

"Exactly," I nodded, "I'm glad you get it."

"Of course we get it." Abby squeezed my arm. "He probably regrets treating you the way he did. It's probably because he's only been around women that accept whatever he has to give. And now that he's with a real woman who he can't just treat like shit, he's in denial and trying to just play mind games."

"He was sending me knock-knock jokes," I said in disbelief.

"Knock-knock jokes?" She looked surprised.

"Yeah. Like 'Knock, knock.' 'Who's there?' 'Lettuce.' 'Lettuce who?' 'Lettuce in. It's only a joke.'"

"No way!" she giggled.

Emma started laughing as well. "You're joking, right? Not Jack Morrison, NFL player, CEO, handsome bachelor. He's sending you knock-knock jokes?"

"Yeah. Crazy, right?"

"I think it's kind of cute," Abby said with a grin. "I know you don't want to hear that because we hate him and he's a jerk, but I think it's kind of cute sending knock-knock jokes."

"I agree," Emma said with a soft smile. "Most guys wouldn't do that—But that doesn't mean we forgive him. Right, Abby?"

"Right," Abby agreed. "Stick to your guns,

Isabella. A few knock-knock jokes aren't enough to make things better. He has established that he's an asshole."

"Yeah, he is," I sigh. "Okay, well, I need to get some stuff ready and then get ready for my date this evening. I'll talk to you guys later."

"Have fun tonight. Can't wait to hear all about it."

I arrived at the bar in the Lower East Side at about seven o'clock. I was apprehensive about seeing Max. Excited, sure. But still slightly apprehensive. I didn't know what he knew about me and Jack, I didn't know what he knew about me and Lucas, and I was hoping not to have to answer any awkward questions. I walked into the bar and saw him standing off to the side of the room. He saw me immediately, came over, and gave me a big hug.

"Isabella. I'm so glad you made it."

"Me too. Thanks for the invite. I'm glad to be here."

"What would you like to drink?" He walked me towards the bar.

"Something stiff," I laughed. "It's been a long day."

"Oh, I bet. It's been a long day for me as well," he said. "I am glad to be off of work finally. Well, kind of."

"Oh, what does that mean?"

"You don't want to know." He chuckled ruefully.

"Okay." I wondered if he had a pager or was constantly getting texts about work or something. I didn't want to ask him any more questions, though, because I didn't want him to bring up Jack.

"Rum and Coke?" he asked.

"Sure, sounds good."

I stood next to him at the bar as he ordered two rum and Cokes, enjoying the fact that I was out with a handsome man and was able to just relax. And then, who should I see but Jack.

I froze as he headed towards us at the bar. What was he doing here?

"Hi, Isabella. Hey, Max."

"Hey, Jack." Max gave him a pleasant smile. "How's it going?"

"What are you doing here?" I said, not bothering to hide my disgust at seeing him.

He looked at me as if I was stupid. "This is my event, so what do you think I'm doing here?"

Max gave me an awkward smile. "Oh, did I forget to tell you that this was a work thing?" He made a face. "I thought I would kill two birds with one stone."

"No. You didn't tell me."

If he had told me, of course I wouldn't have come. And what sort of date was this? Who invited someone to a date at a bar for a work event? Two birds with one stone? I tried to figure out whether I should leave or go. Max squeezed my hand.

"Sorry. I thought ..." he paused. "Actually. I don't know what I thought. This was a bad idea. We can leave after a couple of drinks."

"You can leave when I say you can leave." Jack glared at Max. "We can't go anywhere until the clients are satisfied. Do you hear?"

"Yes, sir. I know," Max nodded and made a face. "Hopefully we can do the deal soon?"

"Hopefully. Come with me, Isabella. I have a quick question for you," Jack said.

I glared at him, but I didn't want to make things awkward for Max with his boss, so I followed him to the other side of the bar.

He turned to me with his arms crossed over his chest. "This is why you couldn't meet me this evening? This was your big plan? Drinks with Max?" He shook his head. "Really? You like Max?"

"Max and I had a date planned for tonight, and I wasn't going to cancel it to meet you at your whim."

"He invited you to a work event at a bar that I'm picking the tab up for," Jack smirked. "But okay. That was too important for you to meet me."

"Well, weren't you going to be here anyway?

Wouldn't you have been inviting me to the same work event?"

"I'm the boss," he laughed. "I wouldn't have been here if you would have agreed to meet me."

"So, you would have blown this off?"

"In a heartbeat," he said and stared at me for a few seconds. I stared back at him, noticing that his green eyes looked golden in the dark light. He was so handsome. I could fall into his eyes.

"So how have you been?" he asked.

"Fine. Busy. Working."

"Been working on dates as well?"

"Jack, I don't really know what you want from me or what you want me to say."

"I don't want anything from you, Isabella. I just want to make sure that my cousin is going into business with someone who's trustworthy, and he doesn't seem to know what's going on with the art gallery side of the coffee shop. So I thought I should speak to you."

"Okay, then. So, we're here now. Let's chat."

"No, I think we should meet tomorrow with Lucas and discuss. The three of us."

"I have a class that I'm teaching tomorrow."

"Send me the hours of the class and we'll meet before or after that."

"Okay, fine. Is that it?"

He brought his fingers down to my chin, and I stared at him obstinately.

"That's it," he said, moving his lips closer and closer to my face. I held my breath as I waited for him to kiss me. I wanted him to kiss me, but he didn't.

Disappointed. I was disappointed when I realized that he wasn't going to kiss me.

"Have a good evening, Isabella. You and Max enjoy the night." He gave me a quick smile and then turned away and left me standing there. I felt annoyed and slightly embarrassed as I walked back over to the bar. Max was standing there with the two drinks in his hands.

"Conversation done?" he asked.

"Yeah," I nodded, waiting for him to ask me what the conversation had been about. But he didn't, he just handed me the drink.

"Come, let's go and join the others. Maybe we can dance tonight," he said with a smile.

"Maybe," I said.

We walked back over to the group of executives that were on the other side. I saw Jack standing there, and I resolved that I wasn't going to make eye contact with him.

Well, first I was going to glare at him. *Then* I was going to ignore him.

I stared him down, but he didn't look at me. Instead, he flirted with some beautiful redhead whose hands were all over him. I could feel myself growing jealous. Who the fuck was this? And why was she touching him? And why was he looking like he enjoyed it so much?

Max followed my gaze and shook his head. "Ah, that's Davina," he laughed. "She's had her hooks into Jack for a long time. Or, rather, I should say she's tried to get her hooks into Jack."

"Oh, so are they sleeping together?" I asked lightly, pretending I didn't care.

"Who knows?" Max shrugged. "Probably. I'm pretty sure Jack's slept with half of Manhattan. Not that he stays with them," he laughed. "Jack doesn't date. He just sleeps around."

"I see," I nodded. I guess I was in that number of women.

I was annoyed and pissed off at myself. And then I felt Jack's eyes on me. I knew that I was acting immature, but I turned to Max and I touched him lightly on the chest.

I stretched out my arms and rolled my hips. "Let's dance."

Max grabbed me around the waist and pulled me to him. "Of course. I love to dance, especially with a beautiful woman like you."

We'd danced for only a minute before I felt the presence of another couple next to us. It was Jack and the redhead. He didn't look at me, but I knew he'd moved there because of me. His hands were moving up and down the redhead's body. And she was pressed into him tightly, laughing, whispering something in his ear. I glanced over at him and for a few seconds, his eyes met mine and he just winked and turned away.

I could feel my face burning, but I wasn't going to let him know he got the better of me. I downed my drink and continued to dance with Max. I wanted to leave, but I'd wait a couple more hours. I'd pretend I was having fun. But then I was going to go home, and I was going to block Jack for my phone. I hated the way that he made me feel. I hated the way that he was trying to make me jealous. I hated the way that he flaunted this woman in front of me. Who did he think he was?

He was just an asshole. Just because he had money and he was hot, he thought he could tell me what to do and when to do it. Well, he had the wrong woman. I was nobody's concubine, and I never would be. As far as I was concerned, Jack Morrison and Davina or whatever other woman he wanted to be with could dance the night away because I did not care.

Chapter Twenty-Three

❦

Jack, Lucas, and I were going to meet outside a coffee shop at four p.m. My class ended a little bit early, so I headed over there. I figured I could get a coffee and some cake and give myself some time to just relax before I had to deal with Jack again.

But apparently, I wasn't the only one with that idea because when I arrived, Jack was already there, sitting at a table in the corner. I debated pretending not to see him, but who could pretend not to see him? He stood out like a sore thumb, with his crisp white shirt and faded blue jeans. He looked like an Adonis. He looked up as soon as I entered, as if he knew I'd be arriving early.

"Hey," he said. He gave me a slight smile, not as self-assured as normal. I nodded in acknowledgment.

"Would you like something to drink?" He stood up and headed over towards me.

"I'll get it. It's fine."

"I don't mind getting it. I did invite you."

"This is a business meeting, it's not a date. I can get my own drink."

"But I owe you. From the time we did go on a date."

I shook my head.

"Please, I'd like to get this for you."

I was a bit perplexed about his sudden change in demeanor. He wasn't the same Jack that I had gotten to know. Shoot, he wasn't the same Jack that I'd seen last night.

"Fine, if you really want to buy me a drink, go ahead. I also was going to get something to eat so ..."

"I'll get whatever you want, Isabella."

"Okay. I just don't want you to think I'm using you for your money."

"I think I can spare $20." He laughed.

"Yeah, I'm pretty sure you can. So, did you have a good day at work?" I figured I could at least be polite.

"Yeah, it was pretty good."

"Great. It must be very intense having to run a multi-billion-dollar business."

"It is." He nodded, not giving me much.

"I guess it's very different to when you were a football player?"

"It's very different. Do you remember me now, then?"

"Ha, ha, very funny."

"How was your class? You said you taught today, right?"

"Yeah, I taught at a senior center in Queens. It was okay."

"I'm sure they must love having you there."

"I think they do, but it's challenging, you know?"

"Oh, why is that?"

"There are so many of them and they all want to create the finest art possible, which is totally understandable, but I just don't have the time or resources to help everyone, you know? So, I always feel like I've let someone down. It's disappointing."

"Oh, I guess I can see how that would be. What would you suggest to fix it?"

"Smaller classes?" I shrugged. "I don't know."

"But smaller classes would mean not everyone would get to partake in the experience, correct?"

"That's correct."

"And do you think for some, just being around others and painting is part of the experience that makes it fun?"

"That's true." I nodded. "I hadn't thought about it like that."

"Do you think that it's better for 20 people to be somewhat happy with their pieces and enjoy the company as opposed to five people being very happy with their pieces and enjoying the company?"

"I mean, I don't know." I shrugged. "I just feel like so many people have so many questions, and want so much help, and I always feel guilty that I'm not able to help each person as much as possible."

"You really love what you do?"

"I do," I said. "I really do."

"Most people, they don't like to teach. They just like to do. As an artist, don't you wish you could just spend most of your time painting as opposed to teaching classes?"

"Why do I feel like this is related to the coffee shop?"

"It's not," he said, sincerity in his voice. "I'm just curious. If you had a million dollars and you didn't have to teach classes, would you focus just on your art or would you also teach classes?"

"I'd teach as well," I replied. "I really like teaching. I thought I'd be a teacher one day, you know?"

"And you don't want to be a teacher?"

"I didn't enjoy teaching in schools as much as I thought I would. Too much bureaucracy, too much that's not about the art, you know? I like to be one-on-one. I like to be creative, and I like to bring out the creativity in other people. Everyone has a creative side to them."

"Not me." he chuckled. "I don't have a creative bone in my body."

"I bet you do."

"I bet I don't."

"We'll see," I said with a small smile.

"So, I will get a mocha, and a ham and cheese croissant. And a red velvet cupcake. Oh, and a bag of chips. Anything else?" he asked.

"Maybe an apple." I rubbed my stomach. "I'm hungry, really hungry. I didn't get to eat lunch, and I rushed here right after class."

"So, is this going to be enough? Would you prefer to go somewhere else? We can get some real food if you want."

"No, this is fine. And Lucas is meeting us here."

"I'm sure Lucas will be late, and he'll be happy to meet us anywhere I say."

"No, it's cool. I like this coffee shop. I've been here once before."

"Okay. Well, a ham and cheese croissant, it is," he said.

I realized that this was maybe the first normal conversations we'd had. There was no bickering or bantering back and forth. There were no cheap digs, there were no flirtatious conversations and comments with sexual undertones and innuendoes. We were just being us. Normal. Talking about our day, talking about our likes and dislikes, a little bit of teasing. It felt nice.

"So, Jack?" I asked after he paid for my drink and food.

"Yes, Isabella?"

"I was thinking about the other night."

"Which night?" he said.

"When we were at your grandparent's house, in the bedroom."

"Yes?" His eyes darkened.

"And I just wanted to say that I can see where you probably have a lot of responsibility on your shoulders—"

"I do."

"If you ever want to talk or anything like that, I mean. I'm sure you have plenty of friends, and probably a therapist, and lots of other women to talk to. But if you ever want to talk, I'm here."

"Thank you." He looked surprised. "I appreciate it."

"Cool." I smiled, happy he hadn't shot me down immediately. "So, do you want to talk?"

"No. I appreciate the offer, though."

"Okay."

I was disappointed as we walked back to the table. I'd really hoped that he'd let me in a little bit more. I wanted to know more about this man. I wished that we could go on our first date again, that we could get to know each other as people got to know each other when they first met. Even though we'd had a first date and it'd been crazy and not fun, I felt like I knew him a little bit better now and would approach the situation better, but there was no point in wishing for another first date. It was never going to happen.

About ten minutes later, Lucas walked into the coffee shop. "Hey, hey, I'm not late or anything, am I?"

"No." I checked the time on my phone. "For once, you're exactly on time."

"Thank God for that. I tried my very hardest to make sure I wasn't late."

Jack looked surprised. "You're usually always late to everything."

"Yeah, but that's not professional. I wanted to show you I'm serious." Lucas sat down, and I noticed he had a pile of folders in his hand. "I created a business plan. It's not that good, but it's the best I could do." He handed it to Lucas and then he handed a folder to me. "Sorry, I haven't been in touch much recently, Isabella, I've been working on this really hard."

"No worries. Good for you."

I was impressed. I'd never seen Lucas so focused. I mean, I knew we talked about the coffee shop, and we talked about how exciting and amazing it would be. But I hadn't been really sure that he genuinely wanted this and would work hard for it. As I opened the folder, I realized that I hadn't given him enough credit. He'd put a lot of work into this. I looked over to study Jack as he read the paperwork and could tell he was also impressed. He looked up and nodded at his cousin.

"You really should come and work for the company, Lucas. You have a fine eye for business."

"You think so?" Lucas seemed happily surprised. "I mean, I did a lot of research, and I wanted to make sure that I got all the information as best as I could, but I wasn't sure I did a great job."

"You did an amazing job, better than some of the executives at the company." Jack nodded. "I'm impressed."

"Wow. I never thought I'd hear that from you." Lucas beamed with pride. "Thank you."

"You're welcome."

"So, I wanted to discuss some options with you guys," Jack said.

"Options?" I asked curiously.

"I found a couple of different buildings." Jack looked excited. "And I figured seeing as you two will be in the space, we need to find the location and the building that will work best for you."

"So, this is going ahead?" Lucas's jaw dropped. He was super excited and I could feel the blood rushing through my veins as well. This was really going ahead.

"Yeah, that's why I wanted both of you here," Jack said. "I know that this is important to both of you guys. And I know that it's going to be a coffee shop as well as an art gallery, so we need to find a space that works for both, correct?"

I looked over at Lucas, who nodded. "Yeah."

"So how do you guys envision the space? Two distinct separate entities or sort of cohesively working together?"

"Well," Lucas said, "I see it as more cohesive. Like, I see you walking in, and directly to the left there being an art wall full of beautiful pieces of art. Centrally located will be Isabella's pieces, but also other local artists and students from the class."

"Oh, that's an amazing idea." I nodded. "The students would really love that."

"Right?" Lucas was excited. "And then we'd have some tables right there, where people can drink and eat. And then to the right, we'd have more tables.

And past those tables, we'd have one large wooden desk where people could do their art classes."

"That sounds doable, so we're definitely looking for a very specific type of space." Jack looked thoughtful.

"Yeah, I think so."

"When are you guys available to go and look at some places?" Jack asked.

"I'm available all week. What about you, Isabella?"

"Yeah, I'm available pretty much all week. I just have to check my schedule." Just then, my phone started beeping. I hesitated.

"You can answer that," Jack said with a grin.

"Oh, I didn't want to be rude." It was a business meeting after all.

"It's okay. We're not in a boardroom or anything. You can answer your phone."

I pulled my phone out of my handbag and saw that it was a bunch of text messages from Max. I chewed on my lower lip as I read them; he was asking me to dinner. I was about to respond when I looked up and I realized that Jack staring at me. There was a weird expression in his eyes.

"Are you going to answer that?" he said. His face had darkened, his mood changing completely.

"Umm, just really quick." I texted back, "Not sure

about tonight, but maybe this weekend." I quickly put my phone back into my bag, Jack still staring at me.

"So, if everyone's done with their personal calls, maybe we continue with the business talk."

I wanted to point out how unfair that was since he was the one who had told me to answer the phone in the first place, but I kept my mouth shut. He'd been pretty nice this entire time, and I didn't want to antagonize him.

"So actually, I had an idea," I said, thinking quickly.

"Oh?" Jack said. "What's the idea?"

"Well, I have some of my supplies because I just came from a class, and I figured, what about I give you both a really quick lesson. Show you one of the classes I would teach in the coffee shop."

"I don't know …" Lucas glanced at Jack.

"Hmm, sounds interesting. I'd be down," he said.

"I really actually have to go," Lucas said. "I have other plans, but maybe another time."

"Okay, sure. We can do it another time."

"No," Jack said. "I'd like to do it today. If Lucas doesn't mind, you can give me the class by myself."

I looked over at Lucas, begging him with my eyes to say no. I didn't want to be stuck with Jack alone.

"Okay, sounds good to me." Lucas grinned. "I

have a pretty important call to take right now. Can I come back to this conversation in half an hour? Or are we done for now?"

"It's fine, Lucas, you can go," Jack assured him. "Thanks for this. I'll look over the paperwork." He held the folder up. "And then I'll start sending you guys some real estate listings."

"Great." Lucas jumped up and gave me a kiss on the cheek. "Lovely seeing you as always, Isabella. I will see you later, okay?"

"Okay." I glared at his back, not believing that he'd left me.

"So, I guess it's just the two of us now," Jack said with a wicked smile. When he smiled like that, I could see the dimple in his right cheek. It was adorable, which was a weird word to describe Jack. With all his hunky sexiness, "adorable" wasn't the first word that came to mind to describe him, but it worked.

"I guess so," I agreed.

"Unless you have to go?"

"No, I don't have to go anywhere."

"Didn't Max ask you out to dinner tonight?"

"Maybe," I said, annoyed that he'd read my messages.

"And are you going?"

"I really don't think that's any of your business."

"Really? Okay."

"I don't understand you, Jack," I finally said.

"What's there to understand?"

"You're so interested in my love life, and in my business, and what I'm doing. And yet you have this wall up. That first night you met, you said I had my defenses up, but so do you. I just don't know where you're coming from. I don't know what you want for me. I see you out and you ignore me, and you flirt and dance with other women—"

"I wasn't flirting and dancing with other women. What do you mean other women? Was there a first woman in the first place?"

"Me. I was there."

"You were there with Max. Seems like you and Max are dating now or whatever."

"We're not dating. I met him for drinks, and he invited me to dinner."

"Have you kissed him?"

"Excuse me?" I couldn't believe he was asking me this question, but even more so I didn't really want to answer him, because no, Max and I hadn't kissed and I didn't want to kiss him, but I didn't want Jack to know that.

He leaned towards me. "Have you guys kissed?"

"What?"

"Has he kissed you like this?" He grabbed the

back of my neck and pulled me towards him, pressing his lips to mine. He kissed me softly, passionately, his fingers playing with my hair as his tongue played with my mouth, ravishing me as he kissed me.

Finally, he let me go, a smug smile on his face. "Has he kissed you like that? Have you felt the way you feel right now with him?" He chuckled and stood up. "I sincerely doubt it."

"What?" I mumbled as I stared up at him, not knowing what to say.

"There's no need to answer me, Isabella. I can already tell I've left you breathless. Now I'm just going to go and get some water and then you can give me that lesson, okay?"

I just nodded dumbly, feeling completely and utterly lost.

That kiss had been the best kiss of my life. And he was right, no one had ever kissed me like that before, no one had ever made me feel the way that he made me feel. And yet he still hadn't let me in, he still hadn't answered any of my questions. He'd completely deflected everything. He had so many walls up that I didn't even know how high I'd have to climb to get over any of them.

As I sat there waiting for him to come back, I realized just how much I liked him. Just how much I wanted him to let his walls down. Just how much I really wanted to see who he was inside.

He was more than a pretty face. He was more than a handsome billionaire. This was a man with depth, with layers. And as an artist, I wanted to peel back every single one of them and see who he truly was inside.

Chapter Twenty-Four

⚜

"So, Isabella, how was it?" Abby greeted me as soon as I walked in the front door.

"It was fine." I eyed her suspiciously. "Why are you waiting for me?"

"I was just curious because I know you were going to see Jack again today."

"Yeah. I actually gave him a lesson."

"Ooh, you gave him a lesson in the bedroom?"

"No, goofy. An art lesson."

"Wow. You gave him an art lesson? How did that go?"

"Surprisingly, it was pretty good. He seemed to enjoy it."

"Awesome! So, you're friends with him now? You like him?"

"It's so complicated. I just don't understand him,

you know. He's like this really tall, really good looking, really rich guy, and he's an asshole on the surface, but underneath it all, he seems like a really sensitive, caring man, and ... I don't know, I just wish he'd open up to me."

"You sound like you really like him."

"I mean, I guess I like him? I think he's..." I sighed, "Girl, I just don't even know what to think anymore. I feel like I'm kind of falling for him, which I mean, makes sense because I've slept with him, but it also doesn't make sense because neither of those two meetings were great."

"They weren't great, but you had a connection with him, right? I mean, obviously, you guys are attracted to each other, or you wouldn't have slept with each other."

"Yeah, but you need more than that in a relationship, you know? Not that he's looking for a relationship or anything. I mean, I know that he's not."

"What do you mean you know that he's not? How do you know that he's not? I mean, you met him on a dating app."

"Yeah, but a lot of people are on dating apps and aren't looking for relationships."

"Have you ever asked him what he's looking for?"

"I guess not. I mean, we pretty much ruled each

other out after the first date." I shrugged. "It wasn't great, remember?"

"It was great enough for you to go back to his apartment."

"Yeah, but that was a sex thing. Men can have sex and have not mean anything. So can women, I guess ..."

"But you're not one of those women, Isabella."

"I guess I'm not." I sighed. "Anyway, you start your job on Monday, right?"

"Yep. I'm excited! But I'm a little bit nervous."

"What do you mean? Why are you nervous?"

"So, my new boss ..."

"Yeah."

"He's already been sending me messages, and I feel like the rumors might be true."

"What do you mean you feel like the rumors might be true?"

"Girl, he's already acting like a bit of an asshole."

"Oh no. Why? What's going on?"

"I'll tell you later. I don't want to get you upset."

"Why would I be upset? He's not my boss."

"I know," she laughed. "I mean, I don't want to get myself upset again reading the emails out loud." She chewed on her lower lip. "I know I was excited the other day, but my excitement is fading. I have a feeling he's going to be a jackass."

"Oh, no. I'm so sorry to hear that."

"Well, I mean, we don't know for sure. And I'm praying that he won't be, but ..." she shrugged. "You know what they say."

"No. What do they say?"

"Prayers don't always work."

"Who says that?" I laugh. "I've never heard that before in my life."

"I don't know. I just made it up." She shrugged. "Do you want to grab some dinner tonight?"

"Yeah. I think that would be really good."

"Do you want to go in or go out?"

"I don't mind. What are you thinking?"

"Maybe we'll stay in?"

"Thank God you said that."

"Why didn't you say you wanted to stay in?"

"I mean, just in case you wanted to go out."

"Oh, Isabella, you're such a good friend, but if you've had a long day, which it seems like you had, we should just chill."

"What about Emma and Chloe, are they going to join us?" I asked her. "I haven't really seen them around much."

"I think they're actually going to something on Coney Island. I'm not really sure what it is, but it didn't sound like they were going to be back tonight."

"Oh, okay. So just you and me then. Yay! It'll be fun. Girls' night in."

"Yay to girls' night." My phone started ringing then. Abby looked at me. "Who's that?"

"Not sure," I said, hoping it wasn't Max. I looked down at the screen and I saw that it was Jack calling me. "Speak of the devil. It's Jack," I said.

"Ooh, what does he want?"

"I don't know."

Abby looked eager. "Well, answer him! Find out."

"Yeah, I guess I should, huh?"

"Yeah, you should." Abby flapped her hands impatiently at me.

I answered the call. "Hello?"

"Hey, Isabella. It's me, Jack."

"I know."

"I just wanted to thank you for today. I had a good time."

"I'm glad."

"What are you up to right now?"

"Not much. I just left you about an hour ago."

"Are you staying in?"

"Why?"

"I was just curious."

"Are you trying to find out if I'm meeting Max?"

"No. Why would I be trying to do that?"

"I don't know why you'd be trying, but—"

"I thought maybe we could hang out?"

"Sorry. I'm actually hanging out with my roommate tonight."

"I see."

"I mean, you can come over if you want." I looked at Abby, hoping she'd understand. Her eyes widened, but she grinned and nodded. "I mean, it's okay with my roommate. We were just going to grab dinner and maybe watch a movie or something. You could join us if you want. Or not."

"I'd love to join if you're sure your roommate wouldn't mind."

"No, she wouldn't mind."

"So ... will you text me your address?"

"Okay. I'll text it to you right now."

"Sounds good. Is there anything I can bring?"

"Maybe a bottle of wine."

"Sounds good. And did you want me to pick up some pizzas and bring them as well?"

"That would be amazing. I definitely wouldn't say no."

"Okay. Well, just text me what you guys want, and I will bring them over."

"Awesome. Thank you."

"You're welcome."

He hung up, and I stared at Abby, not really sure what had just happened.

"Did you just invite *the* Jack Morrison to our house?" she gasped.

"Yeah, I think I did."

"What's going on, Isabella?"

"Honestly, I really don't know. I am in as much shock as you are."

"He likes you, girl."

"No, he doesn't like me. I think he just wants to—"

"He *likes* you," she cut me off. "Why is he coming over to our house if he doesn't like you? Why is he checking up on you?"

"He wanted to see if I was going out with Max."

"Why does he care if you're going out with Max? If he didn't like you, he wouldn't even care, girl. Trust me. I know men."

"Maybe he's just one of those guys that doesn't like when women are with other people or—"

"He likes you. Now you've just got to figure out if he's worth liking back."

"What do you mean?"

"I mean, there are some guys that are obnoxious because they've been hurt or because they don't know how to interact with women. And then there are other guys who are just jerks. You need to figure out which one of the two he is, because ..." she paused.

"Why did you stop?"

"I just wanted to make sure I had your full attention."

"Oh my gosh, Abby, you really are a drama queen."

"No, I'm not. I just wanted to make sure you were paying attention."

"I am paying attention. Now tell me what you were going to say."

"I was going to say that if he's the right sort of guy, then go for it."

"Go for what?"

"Go for him. I have a good feeling about this guy."

"What do you mean you have a good feeling about this guy?"

"I think he could be the one for you."

"What? Are you crazy?"

"No," she said. "I think there was a reason why I matched with him in the first place. I think this could be someone special."

"Abby, really?"

"I know. I know. I might just be saying that and maybe I'm wrong, but I have a good feeling about him, girl."

"Well, I guess we'll see."

"We will see. I can't wait to meet him."

"Yeah," I said, not wanting her to know just how much this meant to me. I wanted Abby to love him. I wanted her to see the side of him that I was falling for. I was scared that she would just think he was a jerk and wouldn't like him. Because if your best friend didn't like the guy you were crushing on, then it was all over. "I'm actually really excited for you to meet him as well."

Jack arrived three hours later carrying two bottles of wine and two big boxes of pizza. He had a dazzling smile on his face, and I knew as soon as Abby said hello to him, that she was smitten. I mean, it was hard to dislike the guy at first glance. He was gorgeous and charming.

"You must be Abby. The woman I was actually speaking to on the dating app."

"Guilty as charged." She blushed, and then looked at me with a wicked smile. "I'm sorry about that. I didn't mean to ruin your first date."

"You didn't ruin our first date," he chuckled, and then he looked at me. "Okay. Maybe a little bit. I have no idea why Isabella said half the things she said. Don't hold it against her. Please?"

"I don't," he said. "So are you girls hungry? Because these pizzas smell amazing and I would love to chow down."

"We've been waiting for these pizzas." Abby

nodded enthusiastically. "I'll go and get some plates. You guys want to head out to the living room?"

"Sounds good," I said. "Follow me, Jack." I led him to our living room and sat down on the couch. "Feel free to sit on the couch. Or you can sit on one of the chairs or wherever you want."

"Thank you," he said.

He sat on the couch right next to me. I could feel the warmth of his thigh on my skin as it rested against mine. "You don't have to sit so closely."

"I know I don't," he grinned and moved even closer to me.

I said, licking my lips nervously. "I am surprised to see you again so soon."

"Why? Wish it was Max?"

"No, I don't wish it was Max. Do you wish you were with Davina?"

"If I wanted to be with Davina, I'd be with Davina," he said. "And you remember her name, huh?"

"Of course, I remember her name." I made a face. "Anyway ..."

"She's not competition for you. You know that, right?"

"What?" I said too loudly.

"I said, she's not competition for you," he grinned. "Just in case you were worried."

"Worried about what?"

"That she was someone I was seeing."

"No, I'm not worried. I mean, it doesn't matter to me. I mean, I—"

"Okay," he grinned.

"So here are the plates," Abby said as she walked into the living room. "What did I miss?"

"Nothing," I said quickly. "I was just thinking about what movie we should watch. Is there anything that you guys really want to see?"

"No," Jack shrugged. "I really don't mind."

Abby shook her head as well. "There was this reality show called *The Circle* that I really wanted to watch, but," she looked at Jack, "I don't know if he'd be interested."

I laugh. "Yeah. Jack doesn't strike me as a reality TV sort of guy."

"Hey, don't judge a book by its cover." Jack laughed. "Maybe I'll love it."

"Okay, then let's watch it," Abby said quickly and grabbed the remote control. "*The Circle,* season one is upon us."

I looked at Jack and laughed. "You have no idea what you just let yourself into, do you?"

"No," he said, "but I don't mind." He bit down on a slice of his pizza and looked at me and settled back into the couch. "Sometimes it's the people that you're with and not what you're doing that counts."

So, did that mean he liked being with me? Did that mean that he was softening towards me? I didn't know, but I was happy that he was here and I was happy that he and Abby seemed to be getting on so well. It felt comfortable. It felt nice. I wondered if he was going to spend the night. If he was, I wondered if I had time to quickly shower and shave because my legs were a little bit prickly. And if we were going to get down and dirty, I wanted to be as smooth as a baby's bottom.

An hour later, Jack got up to leave. "Well, I hope you both have a good night," he said, as he walked to the front door. I was disappointed. He hadn't even tried to spend the night. I didn't know why, and I didn't want to ask him. I didn't want him to think that I expected him to stay. I mean, it was totally up to him. If he didn't want to stay, he didn't have to. "'Night, Abby," he called out.

"Night, Jack!" she called from the living room. It was just him and me standing at the front door.

"I had a good night. Thank you for inviting me."

"Well, I wouldn't say that I invited you. More that you sort of weaseled your way in," I joked.

"Well, perhaps that was so," he said, "but I'm glad you let me weasel my way in. I had a good time. I can see why Lucas enjoys your friendship and loves you so much."

"Wow. I'm surprised that you're saying this to me."

"Why?"

"I don't know, I guess I just didn't expect you to give me any sort of compliments."

"You don't think I'm the sort of man that can give compliments?"

"I mean, I don't know," I shrugged. "I guess I don't know you well enough."

"Well, you're getting to know me."

"I am."

"Can I kiss you?" he asked.

"You've never asked before."

"I've never tried to be a gentleman with you before."

"And you're trying now?"

"I am. Isn't that obvious?"

"But why?" I said, butterflies fluttering in my stomach as I gaze up at him.

"Because you deserve a gentleman."

I wanted to ask what he meant by that. Was he saying that he wanted to date me? Was he saying that I deserved someone like him? I didn't know. And I was too nervous to ask. "Jack?"

"Yes, Isabella?"

"When's the last time you had a girlfriend?"

"A girlfriend?"

"Yeah. You know, someone you see one-on-one monogamously."

"I know what a girlfriend is. Why do you ask?"

"I was just curious, you know? You're on the dating app, after all."

"You want to know why I was on the dating app?"

"Yeah. I mean, I'm curious."

"To meet women to date."

"I see, and do you date a lot of women?"

"A few." He laughed.

"Okay. You're a really hard person to get to know, you know that, right?"

"So are you."

"I don't think I'm that hard of a person to get to know."

"You'd be surprised."

"We're sort of going around in circles here, aren't we?"

"I don't think so," he said. "I think we're getting to know each other quite well. Don't you?"

"Not really, but ..."

"But what? What do you want to know about me that you don't yet know about me, Isabella?"

"There are so many things."

"Maybe you don't know things because it doesn't help for you to know."

"What does that mean?"

"Maybe you wouldn't like who I was if you knew everything about me."

"Is that why you have all these walls up and don't let me in?"

"I've let you in more than I've ever let anyone else in," he said.

I laughed. "Why do I not believe that?"

"Because you don't know me well enough yet." He pulled me into his arms and pressed his lips against mine for a sweet, short kiss. "I really like you, Isabella. Like, I really like you. And ..."

"And what?" I said, gazing at him in adoration. I could hardly believe that this was the same Jack that I had met on my worst date ever.

He shook his head quickly. "And nothing. I'm glad that we've had these moments to get to know each other."

"You are?"

"Yeah, I am. I'm going to go now."

"Okay," I said, disappointed.

"You want me to stay?"

I stared into his eyes and I nodded slightly. "I do."

"You want me to stay, huh?"

"I just told you that I do."

"That makes me happy."

"Really?"

"Yeah. But I'm not going to stay."

"Why not?" I was disappointed yet again.

"Because I don't want you to think that this is the sex thing, because this is so much more than that."

And with that, he was gone.

Chapter Twenty-Five

The next couple of weeks passed without any real contact from Jack. He sent emails about different properties to Lucas and me, but he never called or asked me out again. To say I was disappointed was an understatement.

"Hey, Lucas," I answered my phone as it rang.

"Hey, how's it going, Isabella?" He sounded happy.

"Pretty good. Haven't heard from you in a while."

"I know. I'm sorry. I've been so busy."

"With coffee shop stuff?" I wondered if he had really changed? I mean, I knew he was really into getting the coffee shop going, but I'd never known him to be this diligent and hardworking.

"Um, a little bit. I actually have some really awesome news."

"Oh? What's that?"

"I met someone."

"You met someone? Like a boyfriend?"

"Well, it's still early days. We've only been dating for like a week, but we've spent every single day together."

"What? No way."

"Yeah. His name's Noah. I'd love for you to meet him. He's just the most perfect man I've ever met."

"Oh, wow. Congratulations. I didn't even know you were looking."

"I wasn't looking," he said, "That's the funniest part of all."

"Oh? So how did you meet him?"

"At a coffee shop."

"You met him at a coffee shop?"

"Several coffee shops, actually."

"What? How is that?"

"Well, basically, I found this list in *Timeout* about the 100 best coffee shops in the city, and I wanted to visit each of them to see what they had going for them so that I would know what to put in my coffee shop. And I guess he read the same list, but he was going because he loves coffee. And I saw him like three or four times, and then finally, we started a conversation. He recognized me as well."

"Oh, wow. That sounds so romantic."

"I know." He chuckled, "Could be in a movie or

something. I mean, not a mainstream movie because mainstream movies don't feature homosexual men, but you know, one of those indie movies."

I chuckled. "It could totally be a movie, Lucas."

"Yeah," he laughed, "So how have you been?"

"I've been okay. Just been doing these classes and you know."

"Are you still dating Max?"

"We've texted a couple of times, but we haven't met up again."

"Oh, I'm surprised. He seemed like he was really into you."

"He did invite me to dinner a couple of times, but I've been busy."

"Really? Since when?"

"What's that supposed to mean?"

"I'm just saying. Every time I've ever called you for dinner, you were free."

"Yeah, well, maybe I don't want to go to dinner with Max."

"Oh. Still thinking about Jack, huh?"

"Yeah, Jack. I know he's your cousin and all, but I just don't understand him. I feel like he's so hot and cold, and he's so hard to get to know."

"Yep. That's Jack for you."

"Why is he like that? I mean, a part of me feels like he liked me, but anytime I try to get closer to him or ask him anything about himself, he just freezes me out."

"Jack doesn't trust women," Lucas sighed.

"Why doesn't he trust women? I don't understand."

"So, my cousin, he went to Duke."

"Okay."

"And he was like the hotshot on campus. You know, football star and all that."

"Of course."

"And he had this girlfriend."

"Okay."

"Can't remember her name now. I should because she's such a bitch. I think it was something like Italia."

"Italia?"

"No, Natalia. That was it."

"Okay."

"So, Jack was dating this girl, Natalia, and, of course, she was gorgeous."

"Of course she was," I wasn't happy to hear that, but let's be real. Jack was hot, so I understood.

"He was dating this girl, Natalia. I guess he started dating her like his junior year of college? Anyway, they were dating when he graduated, and they continued dating when he went pro."

"So, it was really serious?"

"Yep. He loved her. I guess they were going to get married and all that. He'd actually proposed to her."

"Oh, okay." Jealousy reared its ugly head.

"*But* ..."

"But what?"

"She was a ho."

"How was she was a ho?"

"So, Jack ended up getting drafted by the Philadelphia Eagles."

"Okay."

"*And* ..."

"And what?" I was getting impatient.

"She fucked like three or four different guys on his team."

"No way!"

"Yeah, and the worst part ..."

"It gets worse?"

"He found her fucking one of the running backs in the locker room like in the showers or something. Of course, he ended it right then and there."

"Of course," I said. "That must've been absolutely horrible."

"Oh my gosh, girl, it gets better. Or worse."

"No, what happened?"

"So then, she ends up pregnant."

"What?"

"And she tries to say it's his baby."

"Wow."

"So, then he says, 'Okay, I'll take care of you. It's my child. Of course, I'm going to do the right thing.' She tries to worm her way back into his life and say she wants them to be together so that they can raise the baby as a family."

"Oh, and what did he say?"

"He said, 'Hell no,' of course. Once you do Jack wrong, there's no coming back."

"Oh wow. Okay."

"So anyway, she has the baby."

"Okay, and?"

"She won't let him see it."

"Oh?"

"Yeah. Next thing you know, he gets letters in the mail demanding $5 million from her."

"What for?"

"She said that she's so heartbroken over how he's treated her, that she just wants the $5 million, and she'll raise the kid by herself. But Jack's not going to do that. So of course, his lawyers tell her no, and he sues for full custody."

"What? No way."

"Well, in response, she sends him some text and she says to him, 'Drop the lawsuit now, or I'm going to release private photos and videos of you from college.'"

"Seriously?" I gasped. "What were the videos?"

"So, I guess they were into some kinky stuff."

"Oh?"

"I'm not sure exactly what it was, but basically, they got some sort of sex toys, maybe a sex swing or something. I think they were into like that choking thing."

"Really?"

"Yeah. I mean, Jack didn't really tell me everything, but Becky was telling me some of the story."

"Yikes. I didn't realize he was into that sort of thing."

"Well, yeah. Anyway, Natalia had some videos where I guess something went wrong, and she was screaming, and she basically was trying to twist it and say that he was beating her."

"No way. That's horrible."

"Yeah. So of course, Jack goes ballistic because he would never hurt a woman."

"Okay."

"I mean, I know you don't like him, but trust me, he's a good guy."

"Oh no, I understand that. I don't believe he would ever hurt a woman. So then what happened?"

"Well, basically she was such a dumbass. She released like a five-second clip of the video, but whatever she did was basically, she had dubbed over the rest of it. But Jack had some video forensic scientists or whatever they're called and they were able to retrieve the whole video. And you could see that actually, she was the one that started choking him first, and then he was showing her what to do. And anyway, it basically cleared his name."

"Oh, well, that's good."

"Yeah, but could you imagine the publicity that would have caused? He would have been a pariah at the NFL."

"Yeah," I said. "That's awful. So, I didn't realize he was a father."

"Oh, girl. He's not a father."

"He's not? But, the baby."

"Let's just say the baby had short, dark, curly hair, and big brown eyes."

"Okay, and?"

"Well, you know what Jack looks like, right?"

"Yeah. He's blonde-haired with green eyes."

"Okay, yeah. And the mom, Natalia, yeah, she had long dark hair, but big blue eyes."

"Okay."

"And let's just say the baby looked more like Drake than Leonardo DiCaprio."

"Ohhh," I said. "Oh, wow."

"Yeah. That's why she hadn't wanted him to see the baby right away because it wasn't even his." Lucas started laughing, "It was absolutely crazy, actually. It was one of the guys she cheated on him with, one of the other football players."

"Oh, man. Poor Jack."

"Yeah, so you can understand why he wasn't that sad to leave the NFL. He felt so betrayed by his teammates, you know?"

"Yeah, that's really horrible. I'm sorry to hear that."

"But you want to hear the craziest part?"

"No, what?"

"The teammate. The one that was actually the father?"

"Yeah?"

"He married her."

"No way. What?"

"Yep. They're married. If you look online and you Google them, Natalia and Don Harare, you'll see pictures of them and the baby. So that's why Jack is the way he is. I mean, it's understandable, but ..."

"He can't be like that forever, you know. Lots of women do shit like that. I mean, I guess it makes sense now why he finds it hard to trust women and let them in," I sighed. "I feel so bad for him."

"It's been so long now. That's over ten years ago." Lucas sounded frustrated, "I mean, I get it. He was betrayed, but he doesn't want to be alone for the rest of his life, does he?"

"I would hope not," I said softly.

"You really like him, huh?"

"No," I said quickly. "I was just curious."

"Don't lie to me, Isabella. I know you. You really like him."

"I mean, maybe," I said, "But it doesn't matter. He's not interested in me like that."

"You never know," he said. "Hey, I have an idea."

"Oh, what's the idea?"

"So, my grandparents are in town."

"Oh, I didn't know that. Tell them I said hi."

"You can tell them you said hi yourself."

"What?"

"I'm having lunch with them. Why don't you come?"

"No, I'm not going. I don't want to pretend anymore."

"It's okay. I'm going to tell them," he said, "I want them to meet Noah while they're here, and obviously, I can't introduce them to Noah if they still think I'm dating you." He sounded nervous, "So maybe I could use your support, you know?"

"... Are you sure you want me to come?"

"Yeah."

"And you know who'll be there."

"Who?"

"Jack."

"I don't know. He hasn't exactly reached out to me. I haven't heard from him."

"He's been hurt, really hurt. And I understand why he's probably hesitant and unsure of everything just based on how you guys met and our situation, but he obviously likes you. Please come, Isabella. Please?"

"... I guess so, if you really want me to."

"I really do. I think it will be something good, you know?"

"If you're sure."

"I'm sure. I'll text you the details later?"

"Sounds good," I said.

"Well, I better go. I'll speak to you later. Bye, Isabella."

"Bye, Lucas."

I sat on the bed staring at the phone. Everything Lucas had told me had given me an insight into Jack that I hadn't had before. How horrific everything must have been. He'd been so in love. He was going to marry this woman, and she'd completely and utterly betrayed him in so many different ways. I understood why he found it hard to open up to another woman. I understood why he was hesitant to get into another relationship, but I wasn't like that, and I wished he could see that.

I wished he could see that I was trustworthy, that I didn't care about his money or his fame or the fact that he used to be a football star. I was a genuinely good person, and I really liked him. I'd even go so far as to say that I was falling for him. When I saw him, my heart beat faster, and I felt something that I'd never felt before in my life, but I didn't even know if he'd believe me.

But I'd go to that lunch, and I'd see him, and hopefully, he'd give me a sign showing me that some part of him did like me, some part of him was willing to give me a chance, some part of him was willing to open up to me because if he couldn't open up to me, there was nothing that could be done. There would be no chance for a relationship between us, and maybe he didn't care. Maybe he didn't want anything different.

I could only hope that a part of him felt something when he was with me as well.

Chapter Twenty-Six

My small leather portfolio felt like it weighed a million pounds as I carried down the busy streets of the city. Neurotic thoughts rambled through my head as I tried to avoid eye contact with the other people walking down the street. The portfolio held three pieces of art. Two for Edith and Edward as an apology for my role in Lucas's deception, and the final, most special piece for Jack.

I'd stayed up all night painting it. An abstract gouache piece of the skyscrapers in the city with a line of taxis and cars speeding through the street. I was nervous he wouldn't like it. Apprehensive that he'd think it was the work of an amateur. I knew that art was subjective, and that was okay. But this was a special piece. It was my most favorite piece I'd created in the last two years, and I was scared he wasn't going to like it.

I was nervous for other reasons, of course. Now that I knew more about his backstory, I understood why he held back. At least I felt like I did, couch psychologist that I was, dissecting and trying to understand all the layers that made Jack up, without him having divulged a single bit of his past to me.

I arrived at the address and was surprised when Edith opened the door.

"Hello, Isabella, darling. It's so good to see you." She gave me a big hug.

"You, too, Edith," I said, hugging her back.

"You look surprised, dear. Did you not expect to see me here?"

"No, no. That's not it. I'm just surprised that someone else didn't open the door."

"Oh?" And then she nodded. "Oh, you mean like a housekeeper or something?"

"Yeah. I mean you had the butler and the housekeeper and all the other stuff in Greenwich. I just assumed that you'd have them here."

"Oh, no." She shook her head. "I like to have my privacy as well, and it's hard to do that when you have servants. Come inside. Lucas isn't here yet, but Jack and Max are in the back having a chat."

"Oh? Really?"

I wasn't sure how to respond. I hadn't known Max was going to be there as well. I didn't really want to see him, but I didn't want to be rude. I hope Jack wasn't going to assume anything by my showing up. I'd wanted to see him, of course, but maybe he'd think I'd come for Max? I sure hoped not.

"I have something for you and Edward," I said, opening up my portfolio and pulling out the first two pictures. "I painted them for you. I hope you like them."

"Why, thank you, dear. These are beautiful. They're of the house and the yard. I didn't see you paint them when you were there."

"I didn't," I said. "I painted them from memory."

"Well, you have a very wonderful memory, indeed."

"Well, helped a little bit by Google. I knew your address so I looked on Google Maps for some additional photos."

"I'm impressed. Thank you. This was very sweet of you."

"You're welcome. I hope you like them."

"I love them, my dear. I absolutely love them. Now, come on. I'll get you a drink and then you can go and say hello to Jack and Max."

"Sounds great," I said. "Thank you."

She handed me a Pimm's with lemonade, something she told me was very British, and then I walked through to the back of the house. Of course, it was at a gorgeous apartment, stately and opulent, but understated. It looked Parisian chic. I'd never been to Paris, but I assumed rich people in France would have living rooms like this with long, wide cream couches with wooden legs and a marble table in the center of the room with little gold statues on it. Of course, the walls were filled with huge abstract art. The overall effect was just beautiful.

"Hi," I said, as we walked into the room and I saw Jack and Max. Max's eyes lit up as he saw me, and Jack—well, I couldn't tell what he was thinking. He smiled, but there was something in the way he was looking at me that made me wonder if I shouldn't have come.

"Isabella, I didn't know you were going to be here." Max walked over to me and gave me a quick hug.

"Hi. I didn't know you were going to be there, either," I said quite loudly so that Jack could hear me. "Hi, Jack," I said walking over to him.

"Hey, Isabella." He looked down at me and there was a warmth in his eyes that made me feel like a million dollars. "I heard that you might be here today."

"Oh, you did?"

"Uh-huh." He nodded. "Lucas told me. I'm glad you could make it."

"Me, too," I said. If only he knew how badly I'd wanted to see him. How I'd dreamed about his touch. How he was constantly in my thoughts. I loved being around him. I felt like I could be completely happy in life as long as he was a part of my world. That was so sad, but so true.

"So, Isabella." Max walked over and joined the conversation again, and I withheld a sigh. Couldn't he just leave me alone for two seconds?

"Hey, Max."

"Remember we were talking the other night about possibly going to Vegas?"

"Um, sure," I said, wanting to die inside. He made it sound much more intimate, as opposed to a late-night text where he'd asked if I liked gambling and I responded, "Sometimes." He then said something like, "Maybe we should go to Vegas sometime," and I said, "Oh, sounds like it would be fun." Not that I really wanted to go with him.

I wasn't sure what Jack was thinking as he stared at the two of us.

"I was checking on flights and it looks like they have some really great deals to stay at the Bellagio," Max continued. "When do you want go? Next weekend or do you need a bit more time?"

"Well, I don't know that I actually can go right now, but—"

"Hey, Max." Jack interrupted smoothly.

"Ah, yes, boss?"

"Why don't you go and send those faxes that I was telling you about? They are of the utmost importance."

"Now?" Max frowned. "I thought I could send them later. I didn't think they—"

"I want you to send them now." Jack nodded. "I think there are some staples on the corner or something. Figure it out."

"Um, okay." Max looked at me and then at Jack and made a face. "I guess I'll be back later?"

"Okay." Jack shrugged and then turned to me as soon as Max had left the room. "So, you're going to Vegas with Max? Really?"

"Um, is it really any of your business? I know you didn't just send him to do work because of a trip that we may or may not be taking."

"A trip that you may or may not be taking? Are you taking the trip or not taking the trip?" His voice rose.

"Why are you getting upset with me?"

"I'm not getting upset with you, but why is it every time I turn around you and Max are either drinking or going somewhere or about to do something."

"That's not even true. What are you talking about?"

"You know what I'm talking about."

"This is ridiculous."

"What is ridiculous?"

My voice was rising now, and I could see Edith standing at the doorway, looking at us, a funny expression on her face.

"Jack, your grandma is watching us right now, and this is not a good look because I don't think she knows yet that Lucas and I are not together. I don't want her wondering why we're arguing."

"Come with me," he said.

"Come with you where?"

"Just follow me. Nana, I'm just going to show Isabella the rest of the apartment, okay?"

"Sure thing, Jack."

He walked past her and I followed behind him, giving Edith a quick small smile. We walked down a hallway and he opened the door and I followed him inside. He slammed the door behind me and locked it. We were in the bathroom.

"Um, what is going on here?" I asked him.

"Sorry. I'm just really in a bad mood today," he said, shaking his head, turning his back to me. "I didn't mean to take it out on you. I didn't mean to take it out on Max. I'll apologize to him when he gets back."

"I don't understand why you're being like this. I haven't even heard from you. I mean, I thought ..."

"You thought that what?" He turned around and stared at me, grabbing me and pulling me into his arms. "What were you thinking, Isabella? Tell me."

"I don't know. I just thought that perhaps we could have had a conversation or, I don't know, gone on a ..." I paused. I didn't want to say another date because I didn't know if that's what he wanted from me. "I just wish I could understand where you're coming from. I just wish ..."

"You wish what, Isabella?"

"I don't know. I wish I could figure you out a bit more."

"What do you want to figure out? What do you want to know? Do you want to know that I like you? Do you want to know that I think I'm falling for you? Do you want to know that my head has been turned upside down since I've met you, and I don't know which way is up, and I'm conflicted and confused?"

My heart raced at his words. "Why are you conflicted, and why are you confused?"

"Because I promised myself that I would never fall in love again. I promised myself that I would never be so head over heels for a woman that I couldn't think straight. I don't want to make the same mistakes I've already made in life."

"But liking me is not a mistake, Jack. At least I hope it's not a mistake. I like you, too." I pressed my hand against his chest. "I really like you, and I've been thinking about you as well. And you have to know there's nothing between me and Max."

"I know," he growled. "I know there's nothing between you and Max. Max was just telling me that he hasn't even seen you. It just annoys me that he thinks he can ask you to Vegas and that there might even be a chance. He shouldn't even be able to do that."

"What do you mean he shouldn't be able to do that?"

"He should know that you're off-limits to him. He should know he has no chance."

"But why would he know that?"

"Because you're mine. You should be mine."

He kissed me hard then and I melted against him, kissing him back, loving the possessiveness of his words and the way that he made me feel. I blinked up at him as he slowly withdrew from me.

"Sorry. I had no right to do that. I'm just out of my mind right now."

"It's okay, Jack. I like you, too, and we can go on a date. We can see if we have something. I mean, I'm open to that, if you are."

"I don't know if I'm open to it." He shook his head. "I just don't know."

"I see." I looked down at the ground. I wasn't going to keep fighting for this. I wasn't going to keep fighting for a man that just didn't want me.

"I had my heart broken once," he said his voice cracking, almost imperceptibly, like he wasn't sure if he wanted me to hear.

"Oh?" I said, bringing my eyes up to look at him again, praying that he would open up to me, praying that I wouldn't have to pry it out of him. It wasn't the same if I had to make him talk to me. He had to be open and honest with me himself. He had to feel like he could trust me.

"She was my college girlfriend," he said, his voice cracking. "I thought she was the world at the time. I thought we'd get married and have kids. I thought I'd have what Edith and Edward have, you know?"

"They have something special," I whispered. "They really do."

"But she wasn't the one. She was not my Edith." He shook his head.

"She hurt you?" I didn't want to tell him that Lucas had already told me the story. Somehow, I wasn't sure he'd appreciate that.

"Typical bad girlfriend behavior." He nodded. "She cheated on me. She got pregnant by my teammate." He shrugged. "She tried to blackmail me. She tried to bilk me out of millions of dollars. You know how it goes."

"Yeah." I nodded. "Happens to me all the time."

He smiled reluctantly at me. "You're funny."

"Do you still love her?" I asked because that was the most important question to me. Had he gotten over her, or was there still a part of him that wished that hadn't had happened?

"No." He shook his head. "Honestly, I don't know if I ever really loved her."

"You're just saying that because she hurt you."

"No," he said. "I was young and I was dumb and I was cocky. The signs were there from the beginning. She was actually dating a teammate of mine at Duke and I stole her from him, so what's that saying? What goes around, comes around, right?"

"You still didn't deserve to have that happen to you."

"I know," he said. "She broke a piece of me, you

know? She broke my heart, and she threw away a piece. She didn't keep a piece because I don't have anything for her. I don't care about her, but she broke me in a way that makes it hard for me to trust women. Everything that I went through with her, everything that I ..." He sighed. "But I don't want to carry that with me anymore, and I've never felt that I was ready to grab a hold of that piece of my heart again until I met you." He reached out and stroked my face. "There's something about you, a light, an energy, a beauty that just radiates from your soul, and I think it scares me in a way because you're so pure."

"I'm not pure." I laughed. "You should know that I'm not pure. I slept with you on our first date, and our first date didn't even go well."

"It's got nothing to do with sex, Isabella. There's a light in your eyes when you talk to me, when you talk to my grandmother, when you talk to Lucas. You're kind, you're sweet, you're caring. You've got a wicked sense of humor, and you can banter with me like the best of them. You're not afraid of me. And you're honest, and you care, and I think I'm just scared that ..." He bit his lip and shook his head, muttering something under his breath.

"What?" I prompted him, needing to know what he was going to say. What was holding him back?

"I think I'm scared that I'm going to let you into my heart and you're not going to want me."

"What?" My eyes widened as I stared at this confident, handsome man. "Of course, I want you. You're funny, too, and you're handsome and you're rich." I laughed. "But you know that's a joke. You know I don't care about your money."

"I know you don't care about my money." He nodded. "I knew that on the first date."

"Oh, yeah? Really?"

"Of course. When you paid for a $500 dinner, which you so obviously didn't really want to pay for, but you did it out of pride, I knew. No gold digger would do that." He laughed. "I mean, maybe someone who was playing a long con, but I could tell that you weren't that sort of person."

"So then why did you make all those comments to me?"

"I think because I wanted you to hate me. I wanted you to dislike me because I didn't want us to get close. Because I knew that if I fell for you, it would be real, and I guess I was just scared to have something real in my life. Really real. I have a lot going on in my life, you know? A lot of responsibility, a lot of people to take care of, and sometimes it can feel overwhelming. I'm under a lot of pressure and public scrutiny." He sighed. "I just want you to have the best."

"You *are* the best, Jack. You're the best for me."

"You're so sexy," he replied. "You know how hard it has been for me to not call you or show up at your apartment? Do you know how hard it was for me the other night when I left?"

"Why did you leave? You made me feel like you didn't want me."

"I wanted you to feel special. I wanted you to know that what we had, what we have, it's not based upon sex. And I wanted to give you space so that you could really think about whether or not you wanted to take the next step with me."

"What's the next step? We've already had sex."

"I know we have," he said, as he pulled me close against him. I could feel his hardness pressing against my stomach. "And I want you more than anything, I fucking want you right now, but it's not about that. This is about something deeper. I know it sounds cliché to say I was scared to let you in, but the truth of the matter is that I was scared, and I just wanted to make sure that you liked me, too."

"I really like you, Jack. I really, really like you. Actually, I painted something for you, something really special, and I hope you like it."

"You're darling, you know that?" He caressed my

hair and kissed me on the forehead. "Of course, I'll love it. Anything that you give me I would love. A scribble on a napkin. It could even be a dirty napkin." He laughed.

"Oh, yeah? Want me to scribble on a dirty napkin for you?"

"Well, not really," he said. "But there is one thing I'd like you to do for me."

"Oh, and what's that?"

"I'd like you to bend over that bathtub and pull your panties down." He winked.

"Jack!"

"What? You're not interested in a quickie?"

"I thought you said this was about more than sex?"

"It is about more than sex, but I'm fucking horny right now and I want you so badly."

"Come on, then," I said and grinned at him wickedly. I bent over the bathtub, pulled my dress up, and stuck my ass in the air.

He growled as he walked over to me, unzipping himself quickly and pulling my panties down. I felt his fingers between my legs rubbing my clit. I was already wet for him. I felt him position himself behind me and with a single stroke, he was fully inside of me. I gasped as he thrust in and out of me.

"Shh." He laughed as I whimpered. "Got to be quiet, Isabella."

"I'm trying," I mumbled, biting my lip. He reached around and covered my mouth with his hand.

"Shh," he whispered in my ear as he slammed into me harder and harder, and I screamed into his hand. He chuckled in my ear. I loved the sound and feel of him. We didn't have long and so he thrust into me hard and fast, and I came hard and fast in response. And then he pulled out quickly and I saw him grab a small towel and come into it.

"Whoops," he said. "I guess this one needs to go directly into the washing machine."

"Oh, my gosh, Jack. You're too much," I said, as I stood up and pulled my panties up. We were both flushed, and he pulled me and kissed my lips passionately.

"We should get out of here before someone wonders where we've gone," he said, and I nodded with a laugh.

I kissed him one last time. "I really like you, you know, Jack, and I think what we have is really special as well," I said softly, wanting him to know that I cared about him deeply and that he could trust me. "I would never cheat on you, and I would never lie to you about anything."

"I know," he said and grabbed my hand. He grinned at me as he opened the bathroom door.

I froze as soon as we stepped out.

Standing right outside were Edith and Lucas, shock on their faces as they looked at me and Jack. The gig was up. I gave Lucas an awkward smile.

He was going to have to tell his grandparents the truth, whether he was ready to or not.

Chapter Twenty-Seven

"Isabella, what is going on?" Lucas sat down in shock. "Please don't tell me history is repeating itself? Please, oh, please."

"Lucas, shut up." Jack glared at his cousin as he squeezed my hand.

"Really, Jack? You're going to do this to me. Your own cousin?" Lucas clutched his heart.

I rolled my eyes. Did he really want his grandmother to hate me? If I were to actually end up with Jack, they'd always have negative feelings about me. They'd always hate me. They'd always think that I was some sort of cheat. I didn't want it to go down this way.

"Oh, Nana!" Lucas moaned. "How could she do this to me? She's broken my heart. I thought she loved me, but maybe it really was all about the money."

"Lucas!" I snapped at him.

"It's okay, dear." Edith smiled. "Lucas, you shouldn't play those pranks on your friends. It's not funny."

I looked from her to Lucas and back again. "Um, what's going on?"

"I already told Nana and Papa last night." Lucas grinned.

"You did?" I stared at him. "You didn't tell me!"

"I know, but I didn't want to make it awkward by coming out at a party where there were other people," he shrugged. "And, actually, it turns out they already knew."

"We knew," Edith said. "And it doesn't change a thing. Your grandfather and I love you. And we just wanted you to be comfortable enough to come out to us. I mean, I thought we showed you how much we loved you and how much we wouldn't care, but I suppose you don't really know until you let people know. I'm glad you finally felt you could tell us."

"Me too," Lucas said. "I guess I've seen so many movies and have so many friends who had awful coming out stories, which I actually hate that term, by the way. But anyway, I guess I was just nervous, and you and Papa are so old-fashioned."

"Really, Lucas." Edith shook her head. "How are we old-fashioned? We're rich. We're not old-fashioned."

"I guess that's true. So, what were you two up to just now in the bathroom?" Lucas gave us a cheeky smile. "I have a feeling you weren't showing her how to use the restroom."

"Lucas," Jack shook his head, but he couldn't help smiling. "So, Nana?"

"Yes, Jack?"

"I want to introduce you to my girlfriend," Jack said proudly.

I looked up at him in amazement. Had he just called me his girlfriend? Did he want me to be his girlfriend? My heart soared at his words. I wanted to freeze this moment so that I could remember it forever.

"What?" Lucas almost screamed. "That happened fast! Like, I need some sort of replay!"

"Well, maybe I'm rushing it a little bit," Jack admitted. "Maybe we're not officially boyfriend and girlfriend yet, but I know that I want Isabella to be my girlfriend, and I know that one day she'll be even more than that. And I'm glad that everyone here loves her and is not going to make her feel bad for what may or may not have just happened in the bathroom."

"Yes, dear." Edith gave me a quick hug. "I just want you to know that I think you're a really good friend to Lucas, and I'm more than happy to welcome you to the family."

"Thank you, Edith. I really appreciate that." I grinned at her, and then I poked Lucas in the shoulder. "Also, by the way, your dramatics just now nearly gave me a heart attack."

"Well, why? You didn't know I told them? And there you were slutting it up in the bathroom."

"Lucas!" I glared at him.

"What?" He laughed. "Maybe I'm jealous? Joke, I'm not. By the way, I totally hope you can meet Noah this weekend."

"I don't think she can," Jack said shaking his head. "She has plans this weekend."

"I do?" I looked at him, confused.

"Aren't you going to Vegas?" He winked at me.

"Seriously, Jack?"

"I don't know. It sounded like you were making plans to go to Vegas?"

"Jack Morrison. Really?"

"Okay. Maybe you're not going to Vegas, but I'd love to take you on a date."

"A date? Hmm."

"Yeah. This time it will be a do-over."

"But we already had a do-over, remember, on our first date? And that didn't go so well."

"Mmmm, but we didn't know then what we know now."

"And what is it that you guys know now?" Lucas asked.

"We know that we're meant to be and that we're compatible. And that we're both very, very attracted to each other," Jack said firmly. "So, what do you say, Isabella, will you go on another date with me? Will you make me the happiest man alive?"

"Now who's being dramatic?" Lucas interjected.

"Lucas! I hissed. "You're ruining my moment."

"Sorry. Come on, Nana. Let's go in and get some food," he said. "And leave these two lovebirds be."

"Okay," Edith agreed. I could tell from the look on her face that she was really happy.

"Well, that was kind of awkward," I whispered to Jack. "Like, *really* awkward."

"Yeah. But I'm glad it happened." Jack said with a smile, "Now she knows that we're together."

"Yeah, I guess so."

"Actually, guys," Edith stopped in the hallway and turned back toward us.

"Yes, Nana?" Jack replied.

"I already knew you two were together." She laughed. "Back in Greenwich. I could tell by the way that you looked at her that you were in love with her, Jack. You can't pull anything over my eyes." She smiled. "And Isabella?"

"Yes, Edith?"

"I could tell you were in love with him too." She winked and then continued on her way.

"So, I guess grandma knows best." I smiled at Jack.

"I think she does." He bent down to kiss me. "So, this weekend, you'll go on the date with me?"

"I will," I said.

"And you know what that means?"

"No. What does it mean?"

"It means that you're about to have your best date ever."

"Oh really?" I laughed, "Are you sure about that?"

"I'm positive." He laughed. "Isn't that funny?"

"What's funny?" I asked him.

"You'll have your worst date and your best date ever with the same person."

"Oh, yeah. I guess that will be funny."

"And you know what else?"

"No. What?"

"You'll have your last first date ever with the same person, too." He winked at me and then kissed me again.

I wrapped my arms around his neck and kissed

him back hard. I love this man. This was one of the most special moments of my life, and I wanted to savor it forever. I was so excited for our new first date and I could only imagine, and hope that it would live up to everything I wanted a last first date to be.

Chapter Twenty-Eight

"Why did I have to bring all my ideas and passport with me?" I sat in the passenger seat of Jack's car with a blindfold around my face. "I don't understand what this date is."

"You'll see," he said as he drove through the streets of the city.

"Where are you taking me? Are you kidnapping me?"

"Is it kidnapping if you're willingly going?"

"Yeah, I don't know. I want to know the date is?" I was dying of curiosity.

"It's a surprise, Isabella. I thought you liked surprises."

"I love surprises, but I also like to know what the surprise is before it happens." I laughed, knowing how ridiculous I sounded.

"Did that even make sense?" he asked.

"Maybe not." I giggled, feeling happier than I had in years. "Do you really love the painting, Jack?" I asked him hopefully. That painting had been created out of love for him and our city, and if he really loved it, it would mean the world to me. It would be like praise from a first-class art critic.

"I loved it. I've got it hanging in my office," he answered. "In fact, two executives that had meetings with me last night ..."

"Last night?"

"Yes, because I had to work late. Remember?"

"Oh, yeah. I didn't realize you would have meetings late at night."

"Yeah. That's the life of a CEO, but they asked me about the painting, and I think I may have gotten you a couple of commissions."

"No way!"

"Yep. And even better is that I told them about the coffee shop slash art gallery studio that you and Lucas are creating and they said they'd be very interested in having executive meetings at the coffee shop and possibly team-building exercises in your art classes."

"Really?"

"Yeah, I guess a recent study said that when teams are creative together, they have stronger bonds, and you're probably the best person I know to help encourage and nurture people's creativity. "

"You're too sweet. You know that right, Jack?"

"Really?" He chuckled. I felt his hand on my leg. "I didn't think I'd ever hear you say that I'm too sweet."

"I didn't think I'd ever use those words either."

He laughed loudly then. "Okay. We're here," he said.

"We are? Can I take off my blindfold?"

"It'll kind of ruin the surprise, but I guess. Hold on." He stopped the car and got out, and I heard him opening my passenger door. He leaned over and unbuckled my seat belt before pulling my blindfold off, he then gave me a quick kiss on the lips and pulled me out of the car.

We were in a parking garage full of what appeared to be thousands of other cars. Where were we? I blinked looking at him in confusion.

"Are you a psychopath and I just didn't realize it? And your cousin also didn't realize it?"

"No," he laughed. "Where do you think we are? See if you can guess. "

I frowned and looked around. I had absolutely no clue. And then I saw a couple getting out of their car and taking out suitcases. Suitcases? My jaw dropped as I suddenly realized where we were?

"Are we at the airport?"

"Yeah, you got it, Sherlock."

"Why are we at the airport?"

"Because we're taking a plane."

"Where are we going?"

"That's the surprise."

"What? I have to know where we're going, right?"

"No, Isabella, you don't."

"I don't even have a suitcase myself. I have no change of clothes."

"It doesn't matter. We'll get everything you need once we get there."

"Oh my gosh. Jack!"

"What? Do you not want to go?"

"Of course, I want to go. I just want to know everything. I need to know the details. Oh, this is amazing!" I jumped up and I wrapped my arms around him. "Thank you. This is probably the coolest thing anyone's ever done for me."

"Well, we haven't even gotten there yet. You don't even know if you're going to like it."

"I mean, I'm pretty sure I'm going to like it. Thank you."

"You're welcome. I guess now's the time that I tell you that I also got us first-class tickets. I hope you're excited because we will be flying in luxury."

"Wow. First-class tickets. That's amazing. I could

never afford that first-class tickets. You shouldn't have. I could never pay you back for this."

"Don't be silly, Isabella. Of course, you don't have to pay me back. I'm a billionaire. In fact, I could have charted a private plane for us, but ..." He grinned at me. "I knew you probably wouldn't be comfortable with me doing that. I figured this was the next best thing."

"Oh my goodness. Please do not ever charter a private plane for me. That would just be too extravagant."

"Maybe for our honeymoon." He smiled at me. I stared at him, my heart beating fast. I couldn't believe he just said that.

"Maybe." I gave him a small smile, not wanting him to realize how excited and happy that made me feel. I mean, I knew he was the one, and I hoped he knew I was the one, but I didn't want to go running away with my thoughts about our future together.

"Come on," he grabbed my hand. "Let's go and check in and then we can eat something in the lounge and get drunk."

"We have tickets to the lounge?"

"Well, of course, we're flying first class!" He took my hand and we walked towards the elevator. "I love this," he added.

"What do you love?" I said.

"I love making memories with you."

"I love making memories with you as well, Jack." I pulled him to me and pressed my lips against his, loving the way he tasted and smelled. I pulled away reluctantly after a few minutes and we both just stared at each other for a few seconds, letting our eyes say how much we meant to each other.

Then he gave my hand a gentle tug, and we made our way to the airport.

* * *

"Well, this is awkward," Jack said as we got onto the plane.

"It's not awkward." I laughed. "Why do you say that?"

"Because I wanted it to be a surprise when we got there, but I guess I didn't think about the fact that the sign above the doorway would say where we were going, and that the gate host would say have a fun trip to London." He chuckled with a rueful expression on his face.

"I think that the fact that you wanted this to be a surprise is amazing, but I think what's even more special is that you're even taking me to England in the first place. I can't believe it. I'm going to London.

Like those are words I never expected to say in my life."

"Really?" He raised an eyebrow. "You never expected to go to London? You told me that you wanted to go."

"Well, I mean, okay, I'm exaggerating Jack. Of course, I would have gone eventually, but I didn't have any plans to go anytime soon, and you're making this a reality for me. Thank you."

"I would do anything to make you happy, to see you smile."

"Well, you have made my day."

He looked smug and happy at my words, and I touched his arm lightly. I loved being able to just touch him when I wanted to.

"When we get to London, what do you want to do?" he asked as we settled into our seats in first class. I knew this would be luxurious, but wow. They were wide and leather and comfortable, and I sat back, looking out the window, feeling even more excited.

"Well, when we get there, we have to go to the Tate."

"Of course." He nodded.

I grinned at him. "That's probably the museum I want to see the most."

"And you said you wanted to go to the Victoria and Albert Museum as well, right?"

"You remember?" I asked him.

"Of course," he grinned. "I remember how special you thought a trip to London would be. Remember, I was in the garden that day when you were telling my grandmother about your grandmother and how she spent that time in London, and how you really wanted to visit. And I knew as soon as I heard you telling her that story that I wanted to be the one that made that happen for you. I wanted to be the one who was there to share those memories with you."

"Oh, Jack." I stroked his cheek and leaned over to kiss him. "You're so romantic and sweet."

"I know," he grinned. "What else do you want to do when you get there?"

"Hmm, let me think. I want to have bangers and mash. And I want to try Scotch eggs. And I wanted to try cheese and onion pasties. And they have this thing called toad in the hole. I don't even know what it is, but I want to try it."

He laughed. "Anything else?"

"Oh, and bubble and squeak."

"What's bubble and squeak?"

"I don't know, but I read about it in a book once, and it just sounded amazing."

"You're amazing."

"Oh Jack, I'm not, I'm really not. I'm just a regular woman but I will never ever take you for granted. And I will never ever use you, and I will—"

"I know." He took my hand and squeezed it. "You know, there was a point in my life when I thought there weren't any women who cared more about friendship than they cared about money. I thought there weren't women who were kind and sweet, only greedy, but I was wrong. I was absolutely wrong. I haven't been able to stop thinking about you since the first day that we met, and I am totally 100% in love with you, Isabella. I love you, and I know that this trip is going to be amazing. And I want to show you all the things and take you to all the places and explore the world with you."

"You're perfect, Jack, and I already know that this will be the best date ever in my life. Ever, ever."

"Remember it will also be your last first date ever." He kissed me on the cheek. "I know that this might sound kind of crazy, but I know I want you to be my wife, Isabella. I want you to be the mother of our children." He bit his lower lip. "I don't want to scare you by rushing things but from the moment I let down my guard and let you in. That was it for me. You're it for me."

"I love you too, Jack." I grinned and squeezed his

hand. "I think that I loved you from the first moment I saw you as well. Crazy as it seems. "

"It's not crazy. You know, you just made my whole day, my whole week, month, year, lifetime. You've made everything that I've had to experience so far in my life worth it. Just to be here in this moment with you. It means everything."

"It means everything to me as well, Jack. We will savor it. Not everyone's as lucky as us."

"I know," he nodded. "We are lucky. We're lucky in love."

"You're so cheesy." I laughed giddily.

"At least I'm not trying to do another knock, knock joke," he said.

"That is true. No more, knock, knock jokes."

"At least not until we have kids."

"Okay," I said, "it's a deal."

And then he leaned over and he kissed me. "You want to join the Mile High Club?" he whispered in my ear.

My eyes widened. "Maybe," I whispered back, "if you're lucky."

"Well, if we do," he sat back grand flashed that wicked grin, "then this might just become the best date ever in the world for anyone."

"I think I can drink to that." I took a glass of

champagne from the flight attendant as she walked by our seats.

We clinked glasses and I stared into his beautiful green eyes. I knew then that I would never, ever enjoy and love a man as much as I loved Jack Morrison. We were on our way to London for the best date in the world. And I knew that I would appreciate every single moment of it because I was with him.

Abby had been right. Maybe she'd gone about it a weird way, but if it hadn't been for her, I never would've met Jack. I never would have fallen in love. And so maybe, just maybe friends really did know what was best for each other. I just had to make sure that she got her Prince Charming as well.

That was the least I could do for the friend who had found me my soulmate.

The End

Thank you for reading Worst Date Ever. I hope you enjoyed it. You can read a bonus epilogue by joining my mailing list here. Please leave a review if you enjoyed the book as that is one of the best ways to help me as an author.

Continue onto the next page for a teaser from Abby's book, Worst Boss Ever.

Excerpt from Worst Boss Ever

Chapter One

Abby

The stack of bills sat on the edge of my bed like a mountain that I had no energy to climb. By my calculations I owed more than a hundred thousand dollars. Thanks for nothing school loans and David Adams. David Adams was my con artist of an ex boyfriend. We'd only gone on three dates before he'd convinced me to buy him materials for his flooring business. "I'll pay you back after I finish the job." He said. I hadn't heard from him since. That was an awful way to lose $5000, but as my best friends said as least it was only $5000 and at least I hadn't slept with him. I would have felt even more betrayed then.

"Hey Abby," Emma knocked on my door before poking her head inside my room. "Isabella is going to come over with a pizza. She wants to know what kind you want?"

"Tell her to surprise us." I grinned and jumped off of the bed. The stack of letters didn't even move. It was solid and going nowhere. I glared at it as I walked across the room. "Is Jack coming with her or is it just her?"

"I'm pretty sure she said she wanted a ladies night." Emma glanced down at her phone. "So it will just be us girls."

"Sounds good to me." I grinned. Jack was Isabella's new boyfriend. He was great, but now that she had moved out of the apartment we shared, I was happy to have some alone time with her; without him. "Will Chloe be joining us?"

"No, I'm actually not sure what she's up to tonight." Emma shook her head as she typed rapidly into her phone. "Okay, I'm going to have a quick shower before she gets here." She wrinkled her nose and sniffed herself. "I went for a run this afternoon and I'm stinky."

"You're not stinky." I laughed. "Next time let me know when you're going on a run and I will join you."

"Sure thing." She grinned and I laughed slightly as we both knew that I had no intentions of running with her. I hated running. I'd tried one through Central Park and had ended up running out of breath after five minutes. I'd collapsed onto the ground after ten minutes and I still hadn't gotten over the shame. My body was not made for running. Not at all.

***

"Hey, Isabella." I jumped up as soon as I saw my best friend entering the living room wearing a summery yellow dress and white wedges. She looked beautiful and happy and I "I feel like I haven't seen you in ages."

"You haven't seen me in two days, Abby," she grinned, walking over to me and giving me a hug. She smelled like peonies and I wondered if her new scent was a gift from her new boyfriend.

"Well, it feels like ages."

"I know. I missed you too." She stepped back and I noticed that she had a glow to her that I'd never seen before. I guess that's what happened when you found love.

"So how's it going with you and Jack?"

"Would you hate me if I said it was going absolutely fantastic?" She grinned at me and I shook my head.

"No," I laughed, though I was slightly envious. Her boyfriend was absolutely gorgeous. He was a famous NFL player. He was a billionaire. He was handsome. He was hot. And he loved her. I mean, what more could you wish for than that? And, to top it off, I was the one that set them up. If it wasn't for me, they wouldn't be together which, if I did have to say, made me very proud of myself. I mean, maybe in another lifetime I could have been a matchmaker or something.

"So, are you excited for the new job?" Isabella asked me and I nodded slightly.

"Yeah, tomorrow's the big day. I can't believe I'm finally starting."

"You must be absolutely excited," Emma said with just a tinge of jealousy in her voice, "You're going to be making so much money."

"I mean, it's good money for sure, but it's going to be a lot of work. I'm almost positive. I mean, I'm working for Dylan McAllister. I've heard he's absolutely crazy to work for."

"Those are most probably just rumors," Isabella said. "I mean, he can't be that horrible, right?"

"I mean, I don't know," I laughed. "I've never been a secretary before and I don't even know if he does or doesn't know this. I don't know how he's going to feel about me learning on the job." I shrugged, trying to play off my nervousness. "I mean, I went through the employment agency. It's not like I lied. I told them that I have been a PA before."

"Weren't you a PA for your uncle?" Isabella said with a small smile. "For like a month?"

"Yeah but..."

"But what?" Emma said. "That's a slight stretch, right?"

"It's not a stretch. I was a PA for one summer, it was like three months."

"And you told the employment company this?"

"Well, maybe I didn't tell them it was for one summer." I laughed. "But I didn't say that I have any skills that I don't have. To be honest, I got the feeling that they were desperate for applicants."

"That's not a good sign," Isabella said, laughing.

"No, it's not. I don't want to think about why they settled for me as the secretary to a billionaire at a multi-billion dollar company, and I don't have that much experience, but hey, beggars can't be choosers. I was just doing my finances and those interest rates are killing me. I'm paying so much money each month on these loans and the balance just doesn't seem to be going down."

"Yup, it's going all to interest," Emma nodded. "You gotta make some huge payments to start getting the principal down."

"I know that now. I loved my time at Columbia, but man." I made a face.

"I feel ya," Chloe said.

"Me too," Isabella nodded. We all looked at her and she shrugged. "What? It's true. I've got loans to repay as well."

"But you're also dating a billionaire."

"It's not like I'm going to ask him to pay off my loans."

"Girl, I bet you don't even have to ask him. I bet he'd do it as a six-months anniversary gift or something."

"Maybe," she grinned.

"Oh my gosh, he hasn't done it already has he?"

"We haven't been together for six months yet." She laughed. "So no, I won't let him pay it off."

"So he's already brought it up?"

"Yeah, he's generous, but you know I'm not going to just have him paying off my stuff. I'm not in the relationship because he's rich."

"I know," I sighed, "and that's why he loves you. Because you truly aren't with him because of what we can do for you."

"I'm truly not. I love him for who he is and he just so happens to be rich as well."

"I know." I laughed. "So I have a couple of different outfits that I'm thinking about wearing tomorrow. You guys will have to tell me which one you think looks the best."

"Ooh, I can't wait. And where's the pizza, Isabella. I'm hungry."

"I ordered it. It should be here any minute now."

"What did you get?" I said, excitedly.

"I got anchovies and pineapple."

"Anchovies and pineapple?" Emma made a face. "That sounds absolutely disgusting."

"Well, I heard it's meant to be really good. And you know how much Abby loves trying new pizzas."

"Yes we do," Emma said, and grinned.

It was well known among my friends that I was an adventurous eater. I always liked to try new things, especially on pizza. I love to try different topping combinations, even if they sound gross. I guess I was just adventurous like that.

"Okay. So I'm excited. I guess I'll try on the first outfit and you guys can tell me what you think."

"Sounds good," Isabella said. "And I have a bottle of wine. Actually, Jack sent it over. He sends his regards."

"He is too sweet." I grinned at her. "Ugh, maybe I should have set him up with myself."

"Maybe you should have." She laughed. "I bet you regret it huh?"

"No way." I laughed. "He was made for you. We all can see that."

"Yeah. You guys are perfect together," Emma said.

"Chloe and I were talking about it and you've actually made us believe in love again."

"No way." Isabella blushed, but I could tell she was happy.

None of us had ever expected to really and truly meet the loves of our lives. Yeah we'd always talked about it, but I think at some point we'd always figured we'd just date around and continue living with each other and complaining about men. But when Isabella had met Jack and it worked out, it had given all of us hope and even I was secretly hoping that I'd meet someone. The one good thing about Isabella moving out was that we all had our own bedrooms now. We'd been four girls in a three bedroom apartment, but now we each had a bedroom. So now we could invite people over to hang out without it being awkward.

"So," I jumped up, "Hold on, guys. Let me go and try on my first outfit." I ran to my bedroom excitedly. I like to look good. I like to wear clothes that flatter me. At five foot five, I wasn't very tall, and at 160 pounds, I was a little bit, shall we say, curvy? I loved my body, but I knew I couldn't get away with this sort of outfits that really skinny girls could get away with. I had boobs and I had a waist and I had hips for days and I had long legs and thicker thighs. So I wasn't really comfortable wearing really tight clothes because they emphasize my large butt too much and I wasn't really comfortable wearing short skirts because, well, I didn't want to show too much leg. And I was going to be working at a Fortune 500 corporation and I was pretty sure that HR would frown upon me looking too sexy. I grabbed the first suit that I'd gotten at Nordstrom's and grinned at myself. I looked sexy, hot, yet very, very intelligent.

I heard my phone beeping as I put on the outfit and I grabbed it as I walked back into the living room. "So what do you guys think about this?"

Isabella whistled as I walked into the living room. "Girl, are you going to the catwalk or what?"

"You're not going to an office, are you?" Emma said with a laugh. "Just wait till Chloe sees you. You look amazing."

"You don't think I look too amazing?"

"I mean, it's sexy, but it's not overly sexy. It's not something you'd wear to the club." Isabella shrugged. "I think it's fine."

"Me too, girl. You look hot."

"Hold on," I said, as I looked at my phone. "I've got a text message from the HR department. They said to check my email."

"Uh oh," Isabella said and frowned. "I hope that's not something bad."

"Me too. I hope they haven't delayed my start date again. It's so annoying."

"Why did they delay it the first time again?" Emma said.

"I don't know, something about him being on a business trip and he didn't like his new secretary to start while he wasn't in the office. I'm not really sure. It didn't really make sense to me, but I'm gathering by the way everything is run, that he's super OCD and type A."

"Oh, I can't stand type A bosses," Emma said.

"Me neither, but for this amount of money, I guess I can put up with it."

"True that," Isabella laughed.

I opened the email and read it quickly. "Okay, so they sent me an attachment of files. There's some tips and pointers from the previous secretaries that worked for him, I guess to help me."

"Oh, that's weird," Emma said. "I've never heard of that."

"I think it's pretty standard," Isabella said. "So that she knows what projects they were working on and that sort of thing."

"True. True," Emma said. "So what do they have to say?"

I opened it and frowned. "Okay guys, this is a little bit weird."

"Why?" Isabella said, and they all came and huddled around me.

"So the first attachment is things to be wary of working for Dylan McAllister."

"Huh?" Isabella's eyebrows rose. "Okay, so maybe that doesn't sound so good. What does it say?"

"First thing first it says, **dress like a mousy librarian. Trust me, you do not want him to be on you about your attire.**" What the hell does that mean?"

"I think it means you're not going to be able to wear that outfit," Emma said, shaking her head. "Because you don't look anything like a mousy librarian in that sexy get up."

"What else does it say?" Isabella said.

"Okay. It says," I read quickly, "Never be late. Make sure to do everything that he asks of you the first time. Always take his calls, even if it's the middle of the night. Why would he be calling me in the middle of the night? I thought this was a nine to five."

"Uh oh," Emma said.

"What?"

"He sounds like he might be one of those bosses that expects you to be on the clock all the time."

"Yeah," Isabella said. "I bet you that's why he's paying you so much."

"I mean, it's not like he's paying me a hundred grand a month."

"Yeah, girl, but aren't you making like over 10 grand a month or something?"

"Yeah." I nodded. Dang, I could feel myself starting to feel deflated. This already was starting to sound a little bit nerve wracking. I was starting to lose my excitement.

"What else does it say?"

"It says the names of some coffee shops where he likes to get his coffee. A bakery where to pick up his croissants. To pick up his croissants? What?" I stared at my two friends. "Is this a joke?"

"It doesn't sound like it, girl. You have heard he's difficult to work for, right?"

"Yeah, but I'm a secretary, not his girl Friday."

"I don't know about that." Isabella shook her head. "But just think, you'll be able to pay off your student loans faster, right?"

"Yeah. And I mean, I guess I can live with these rules as long as he's nice and he's friendly and we get on well, plus I've seen photos of him online and he looks gorgeous. So he can't be that bad, right?"

"Hopefully," Isabella said with a shrug. "Good luck girl."

"Thanks." I nodded. "I think I'm going to need it." I quickly closed my email and then looked down at my sexy attire. "Okay, back to the drawing board," I said. "I need to figure out an outfit that is going to fit the mousy librarian description because this sure isn't it."

"You can do it, girl. And why don't you wear your glasses as well?" Emma interjected. "I mean, I know you prefer to wear your contacts, but nothing says mousy librarian like glasses."

"Yeah." Isabella nodded. "And maybe put your hair up in a bun."

"Glasses and a bun? And I guess no heels, huh? I'll wear my sandals."

"You can't wear sandals to work."

"True. I guess I'll wear flats."

"Yeah, wear those ugly ones that you got the other day."

"What ugly ones?" I glared at her.

"You know, the ones that your mom gave you."

"Oh yeah. The Doctor Scholl's?"

"Yeah, them."

"I guess so." I made a face. "All of a sudden, I'm not feeling that excited about this job guys."

"It'll be okay, Abby," they said in chorus, but I could tell from the expression on their faces that they didn't believe what they were saying.

Chapter Two

Abby

"Ugh...who the hell is calling me?" I groaned as I reached for my ringing phone. I glanced at the time. It was 6:02AM. What the hell? "Hello?" I said, yawning, about to go off on my random caller.

"Is this Abby Waldron?" A deep voice asked me with a slight attitude.

"Yeah, who is this?" I leaned back in my pillow wondering if I would be able to fall back asleep. I'd set my alarm for 7am, so it didn't really leave me much time to get some more beauty sleep in.

"This is your worst nightmare, Ms. Waldron."

"What?" I said up then, my eyes flying open. "Is this some sort of prank? Who is this?"

"This is your boss, Mr. Mccalister and your first day is already off to a bad start."

"Uhm what?" I rubbed my eyes in confusion. "Isabella, are you on the call? Is this a prank? Are you using one of those weird voice changers."

"I don't know who Isabella is and no, Ms. Waldron, this is not a prank. This is your boss."

"Uhm, it's 6am. I'm not sure why you're calling me." I was flustered now. I didn't think it was a prank.

"It's actually 6:05 now." He sounded pissed. "You were supposed to call to wake me up at 6."

"What?" I blinked. What the hell was he talking about?

"Your first duty of the work day is to wake me up at 6am. And you've failed."

"I didn't even know."

"Didn't you receive your first day packet?" He sounded angry and I wondered what his problem was. He should have been congratulating me on taking the job. Instead of berating me, he should have been sending me roses or sunflowers or a first day muffin basket ot something.

"Uhm, no...wait, maybe." I sighed. "I did receive an email last night." I hadn't read past the first attachment as I'd been so focused on my first day outfit. Shit! "But I mean, what's the issue? You obviously already woke up without me."

"Excuse me?"

"I mean you're obviously already up. You woke me up. And I didn't ask for a wake up call."

"You're supposed to call me to wake me up and fill me in on all my appointments for the day."

"Every day?" I muffled a groan. Okay, it was official. This job was going to suck.

"What part of your job description and schedule did you not understand?"

"Uhm, I don't believe I received an accurate schedule or I would have been on top of it, Dylan."

"What did you just say?"

"I said, I don't believe..."

"It's Mr. Mccalister," He cut me off. "Make sure you're in the office by 7 with my coffee and croissant."

"But it's 6:10 now, I don't even..." I paused as I realized he'd already hung up. Jerk! Dylan Mccalister was a jerk. I hated him and I hated even met him yet. This was not going to be the job of my dreams. I should poison his coffee, but then he'd most probably make me taste test it first and then I'd just kill myself. I let out a small scream into my pillow before rolling out of bed. I grabbed my phone and searched for the email I'd received the night before. If I was going to get his coffee and croissant I had to know exactly what he wanted. I frowned as I looked at the addresses of the two stores. They were at least 45 minutes apart. The croissant place was in the Upper West Side and the coffee shop was close to Wall Street, which was close to the office, but how the hell was I supposed to have a shower, put on my makeup, go uptown and then back downtown and then to the office, all within 45 minutes? It wasn't going to happen. There was no way that it was possible. Even if I had a helicopter. I headed towards the bathroom and jumped into the shower. Not that I would be able to enjoy it, I literally had time for a lick and a scrub before I had to get out.

By the time I made it out of the apartment in my long navy skirt and loose white blouse, I had 20 minutes left to get to the office and get my new bosses coffee and croissant. I couldn't believe this was part of my job description. Couldn't he get his own coffee? As I walked down the street to the subway, I observed my reflection in one of the store windows. I looked frumpy and dowdy. My hair was piled on the top of my head in a tight bun, my glasses were thick, and I had on minimal makeup. My outfit looked almost Victorian and there was no fashion runway anywhere in the world that would allow me to strut my stuff in my outfit. I sighed as I looked at my phone. I had no time to get the coffee or the croissant. I was about to cross the street when I saw a halal food cart open on the corner. I hurried over and pulled out my wallet. I frowned as I took out a $20 note. How was I going to be getting paid back for all these coffees and croissants. He wasn't paying me enough to buy all of his meals.

Preorder Worst Boss Ever now!

Acknowledgments

To all of the readers that purchased and read this book, thank you. I know there are so many authors out there and the fact that you took the time to read my book means the world to me.

I have been reading and writing stories since I was a little girl. I have loved falling into a story, becoming one with a world that isn't mine and the fact that I can create worlds for readers to escape into for a few hours means everything to me.

Romance books allow us as readers to escape into an alternate reality. One where men almost always realize when they've messed up. And ask for forgiveness. And pledge their eternal and undying love. And yes, maybe this doesn't always happy in real life, but it's a lovely thought.

I want to thank the members of my ARC team

for reading and reviewing my books. The fact that you take the time out of your day to help me is amazing. I want to thank my street team and those that share my books online and tell their friends about them. Word of mouth is everything and helps me more than you will ever know. I want to thank my editor Sarah Barbour, for always doing an amazing job editing my books. I want to thank all the readers that follow me on Facebook and Instagram and comment on my posts and send me messages or emails.

You would not believe how much you make an authors year when you send a message about how much you enjoyed a book. It literally makes my entire week. So, if you're feeling up to it and you enjoyed this book or any others, feel free to email me at jscooperauthor@gmail.com.

And as always thanks be to God for all his blessings. I am so thankful that I get to write and share my work with everyone.

Love,
Jaimie
XOXO

Also by J. S. Cooper

To The Rude Guy in Apartment Five

Accidental Mail Order Bride

The Billionaire's Fake Fiancee

Printed in Great Britain
by Amazon